Path of Totality

KN Gould

**Published by Crystal Lake Publishing
Where Stories Come Alive!**

**Crystal Lake Publishing
www.CrystalLakePub.com**

WELCOME
TO ANOTHER

CRYSTAL LAKE PUBLISHING
CREATION

Join today at www.crystallakepub.com & www.patreon.com/CLP

For Mindy,

'til the end of the world

Prologue

From the outside, the McGarrett house, nestled in its cul-de-sac on Springtime Way, needed a little work. There were sections of fence that should have been replaced a year or two ago, weeds and moss grew along the cracks in the driveway, and the entire house was due a repainting. It was a house that belonged to a busy family.

On the inside, the McGarrett house slept soundly. Faint moonlight shone through the parted curtains of the otherwise dark living room. The room was cluttered, but not dirty. A few toys, left out after bed time, were pushed to the side out of the way. Books and magazines set on the coffee table looked like they would remain there, read or otherwise, until company was expected and a quick cleanup was in order.

The woman walking through the house at this dark hour did not belong to the house; did not belong in the house. Charlotte's graceful, trespassing steps took her closer to the photographs on the walls. Framed pictures, all of them family photos, were abundant. Candid shots of a happy family at the lake along with professional, posed pictures in their Sunday best started in one corner. The kids, two boys as well as their loving parents, got older as the pictures moved down the wall.

This wasn't just a house; this was a home.

Charlotte made her way into the kitchen. Dishes from that evening's dinner were stacked neatly in the sink. Crayon artwork covered the refrigerator. Lunch boxes with cartoon characters on them were lined up on the counter; ready to be packed for school in the morning. The soft glow from the stove top's digital clock partially illuminated Charlotte's long blonde hair, so blonde it was almost white, as she ran her hands along the countertop. Her short, simple, black dress stood out against her pale skin. Her bare feet barely made a sound on the wood floor. On the inside of her forearm, her tattoo, an eight-pointed star as black as her dress, seemed to move with a will of its own in the shadows. Serpents wound around each point; two sets of glinting red eyes piercing the dark.

Backtracking first through the living room, she made her way down the hall towards the bedrooms. She was in no hurry. Nobody in the house would wake unless she became very unruly. Her well-practiced rituals, honed over many years, assured her of that. She was nothing if not careful. An ounce of preparation was always worth a pound of cure.

The first door on the left stood wide open and a child's nightlight softly lit the room. Toys littered the floor, but a space had been cleared to make a walkway from the door to the bed. The young boy in the bed slept soundly with his mouth wide open. He'd kicked his blankets off during the night and was now uncovered and sprawled out, arms and legs splayed in every direction.

She bent down and gently pulled the blanket back over the boy. He rolled over and smacked his lips together a few times, but did not wake. Smiling, she ran her fingers through his hair.

The next door was closed tight. Hinges squealed as Charlotte opened the door. The silence of the sleeping house enhanced the sound tenfold. Without so much as a pause, she entered the room. This bedroom belonged to an older boy. He had outgrown his fear of the dark and needed no nightlight. He didn't even need to keep the door open at night. The boy in the bed was still a child though; still a few years away from needing to shave. He had the same blonde hair as his brother in the other room. Trophies, mostly baseball, lined his shelves. Posters of athletes, again mostly baseball, plastered his walls.

Charlotte picked up one of the trophies, a small statue of an adult baseball player. The statue was ready and cocked back to swing at an unseen fastball. The small wood base bore an inscription.

NOLAN MCGARRETT
7th GRADE
GREEN DRAGONS

She set the keepsake back carefully on the shelf with the others of its kind.

For some odd reason, Nolan slept with his head down at the foot of the bed. She knelt and studied his face. His sleep was sound. He never stirred as she caressed his cheek with the back of her hand.

She saved the master bedroom for last. Stopping at the open door, Charlotte took in the scene. Husband and wife slept back to back on the queen-sized bed. The wife lay closest to the door. Both of them slept with pillows over their head, presumably to block out sound, light, or maybe both.

She approached the lady of the house first. Gently removing the pillow from her head, Charlotte looked over Mrs. McGarrett. Even in her current state of slumber, she was pretty enough in her own way. Dirty blonde hair pulled back into a ponytail and a shirt three sizes too big for her completed her bedtime look. Perhaps the shirt had once belonged to her husband.

Charlotte slowly crawled over Mrs. McGarrett and into the bed. She didn't worry about waking the sleeping couple, even when she was close enough to smell the woman's moisturizer or the man's dried sweat. Sitting between the two, her back against the headboard, Charlotte savored the moment. This was her favorite part; the moment before. When all is right in their little world and they have no idea how soon it will change. Today, their biggest worry was whether they could wait until the next paycheck before getting the brakes fixed in their ten-year-old minivan. Perhaps, when it had all crumbled around them, they would think back on better, happier times. Maybe they would remember this day and how they had all gone to bed thinking how lucky and blessed they were. What was more likely was that the McGarrett Family would have no inkling of the exact point in time it all went so horribly wrong. They wouldn't even know there had been such a moment as it happened.

She turned her attention to Mr. McGarrett. As she removed the pillow from his head, she was struck by how much he reminded her of his youngest son in the other room. Not so much in appearance, the children clearly took after their mother, but in the way they slept. His mouth was wide open and the blankets only partially covered his limbs. To her, he looked like a large child.

She leaned down and whispered into his ear. Her fingertips lightly brushed against his neck and the tattoo on her arm undulated in response. His brow furrowed and his head twitched slightly, but his sleep remained deep. In the morning, he might remember this encounter, but only vaguely; like a bad dream.

After she was done, she leaned down a little closer and bit down on his ear lobe. It wasn't hard enough to draw blood or to cause any pain, but hard enough to leave a small mark behind when she finally let go. Charlotte kissed him on his cheek and smiled to herself.

On her hands and knees, she slithered backwards out of the bed. Adjusting her dress, she spotted the item she sought. The laptop, closed and powered down for the night, sat on a dresser next to where Mr. McGarrett once again slept peacefully.

Three steps took her to the dresser. Opening and turning on the computer took only a matter of seconds. The picture on the screen was of the happy family at the beach. Dad held the camera high while kissing Mom. The kids made faces at the camera over their shoulders. Charlotte closed her eyes, took one deep breath and then another. Running her fingers over the computer screen, she could feel her heartbeat slowing down. As her pulse slowed, she began to whisper. The words she whispered were indecipherable and rapid. A thin sheet of sweat appeared on her forehead. Charlotte tipped her head back and opened her eyes. Her hand moved back and forth over the screen. The picture distorted and deformed with her movements as if the subjects were made of clay. A tinge of red touched the image, darkening until it completely shrouded the memory. She pulled her hand away and the photo snapped back to normal.

"There," Charlotte exhaled, "all done."

She turned back to the marital bed, taking one last look before leaving the room. Charlotte didn't spare a glance at the children's rooms as she walked by. She had done what she came to do and now it was time to leave.

She let herself out the same way she came in, through the front door. She was careful to lock the door before easing it shut behind her. You could never be too careful these days.

Outside, the streetlights were on and sporadically illuminating the neighborhood. Charlotte strolled back into the darkness, pausing every so often to gracefully spin; dancing to a tune only she could hear.

CHAPTER ONE

"Good morning, Tucker."

"Hello, Allison. How are you today?"

The woman behind the reception desk took his ID and gave it a cursory glance. She did this as a formality, mostly, in case someone ever reviewed the camera footage. Tucker visited the Campbell County Jail at least four times a month for the last two years, so she knew him by face.

"I'm doing okay," she replied. "Trying to keep my head above water. It's Monday, so I'm still trying to get back into the swing of things."

It was actually Tuesday, but Tucker knew what she meant. Jail employees worked odd schedules; one of the drawbacks of working in a building that ran twenty-four hours a day, seven days a week.

"You have half the weekend off now? That's a step up from the last time I saw you," he said.

"Yep, moving on up in the world." She rolled her eyes. "Still not as good as you have it working lawyer's hours."

"I'm no lawyer. Just a legal assistant."

"I know you're no lawyer, Tucker. That's why I like you," she said with a smile. "You haven't gone completely over to the dark side yet."

The receptionist might have been flirting with him. His blue-green eyes and well-groomed, dark brown hair, along with looks he considered 'good enough' were known to bring out such behavior from time to time. Tucker was dressed in khaki slacks and a blue dress shirt with matching tie; his normal work attire. He saved the jacket for court proceedings. His clothes were all off-the-rack from

Penney's, purchased the last time the store had a sale. Finding his size was easy. Being five foot ten with an average build meant he never had to special order anything.

Allison finished entering his information into the computer. Tucker already had his belt and shoes off to walk through the metal detector. Today it only took him one time through. No beeps meant he didn't have to go back and do it again. The last step was waiting for Allison to inspect his satchel. No weapons, cell phones, or other nefarious contraband items were allowed inside the jail. They were especially careful when you were going to have face to face contact with their inmates.

"You can head on back," she said after clearing him. "They're ready for you."

"Thanks."

She buzzed him through the first door. Fluorescent light covered the narrow hallway so thoroughly there wasn't a single shadow. The door at the end rattled from the other side with the unmistakable sound of keys turning in a lock. As it opened, Tucker was greeted by the deputy.

"Hello, Mr. Gibsen."

"Hey there, Deputy Bloom."

"You're the first visitor we've had so far. Was beginning to think I might be all by my lonesome today." The gray haired, slightly overweight, deputy took the sheet of paper with a list of names Tucker offered him.

Tucker laughed. "Sorry if I spoiled your magazine reading time."

"It's all the same to me, Mr. Gibsen. Just one day closer to retirement. Besides, Field and Stream will still be there when I get back."

"I don't like to think about how much longer I have until I retire," said Tucker. The truth was at twenty-seven, the thought of not working anymore seemed such a far off and remote prospect, he hardly thought about it at all.

"Trust me when I say it'll get here sooner than you think." Deputy Bloom pointed down the hall. "Anyways, I got you over here in Room 1."

Tucker followed the deputy to the first of four open rooms. They were small, ten-feet by ten-feet, with nothing in them except two chairs and a table hardly big enough for a single legal pad.

"Thank you, sir." Tucker knew the older deputy's first name but never used it. Somehow it seemed inappropriate to do so in this environment. Working in a defense attorney's office meant the people who wore badges didn't exactly view him as an equal or as an ally. They were always friendly enough, but there was always a wall up.

The deputy stepped around the corner to call for the names from Tucker's list. The legal assistant knew from experience there would be a few minutes to kill while he waited for his first client. He removed the folders from his satchel, one for each of the accused criminals he was to speak with this morning and dropped them onto the table with a dull thud.

This was the part of the job he really didn't like. Normally, an attorney would come see the client personally, especially if that client was in jail. It made them feel better about their case. Tucker's boss, the widely-disparaged Delbert Mahoney, disagreed. He felt that actually meeting with the accused and looking them in the eye wasn't worth his time. Not when he could just send his subordinate in his place and bill the clients just the same.

These meetings were just a quick, *how is the case going, we haven't forgotten about you*, kind of affair. No cases were ever broken wide open in one of these little interview rooms. At least, there hadn't been any since Tucker had started coming here. Mostly, the clients went away afterwards thinking that someone was burning the midnight oil on their behalf. If that made them sleep better at night, then maybe it was at least a little bit worth it. To Tucker, it sure seemed like a waste of everyone's time.

Deputy Bloom brought him his first client in a very timely manner. Business must be slow today, thought Tucker. He had the file belonging to Anthony Gates open on the table when the man himself entered the room.

"Hi, Tony. How are you doing?"

After the usual pleasantries, they got down to business. Gates, a twenty-five-year-old who had already been booked in and out of this very jail more than thirty times, was locked up yet again. This time, it was for breaking into several empty homes that had been put up for sale. He, along with a few associates, would pull into the driveway in a van and get into the house through the path of least resistance. This usually meant breaking a back window or two. They would hop in and take anything that wasn't bolted down. Sometimes, they even took things that were literally bolted down. Copper wire, bathroom fixtures, or anything else left behind by the previous occupants was quickly loaded up and into the van before anyone in the neighborhood noticed anything was wrong.

"How's it lookin'?" asked Tony.

"Not real good, man."

"What do you mean, not good? They ain't got nothing on me. This shit's all trumped up."

Tucker had to make a conscious effort not to roll his eyes. Here was another guy who thought he was some sort of jailhouse lawyer.

"Well, it looks like one of the houses had surveillance cameras set up. Seems this has happened there before," said Tucker, trying to keep the sarcasm out of his voice. "One of the guys on the video looks a lot like you. Even has the lizard tattoo on his elbow."

"It's a dragon."

"Sorry," he said and paused to collect himself. "Anyways, we'll do our best, but we're going to have to explain how you ended up in the video but weren't involved in the crime itself."

"But, man, they didn't even read me my rights." Tony suddenly sounded less confident and more desperate.

And so the morning went. Tucker tried not to sound condescending or judgmental while the clients told him how a better lawyer would be able to beat these charges easily. Tucker believed in what he was doing; providing the best defense for people accused of crimes, no matter how heinous those crimes might be. The right to due process was in the Constitution, after all. Sometimes, though, he just wanted to yell at them that the best lawyer can't help you when they have you dead to rights.

Tucker's next visitor was a man on probation which was about to be revoked for using drugs and not checking in with his probation officer. He was full of excuses, mostly blaming his PO for being an asshole. The next two went quickly, which Tucker was grateful for. A handful of easy questions, an update on the next court date, and they were on their way.

It was almost lunch time in the jail as Deputy Bloom ushered in the last name from Tucker's list. Greg McGarrett, thirty-four years old, a ten-year employee of CPOR, the local utility company, and married father of two according to his file. As best as Tucker could tell, this was McGarrett's first meeting with anyone from his attorney's office.

McGarrett entered the room and sat down at the table across from Tucker. A curt nod was his only greeting. He wore the light-brown shirt and elastic pants that signified a jail inmate. Bloodshot eyes and a few days' worth of facial hair gave him that dejected look Tucker had seen many times before. This wasn't a man used to being locked up. This was a man who was used to being respected. Maybe he wasn't a doctor or a lawyer, but he was someone who provided for his family and coached his kid's sports teams. Unlike the rest of Tucker's morning visitors, this man was ashamed to be here.

"Mr. McGarrett, my name is Tucker Gibsen. I work in Delbert Mahoney's office." He paused after his introduction out of habit. This was where the person he was talking to usually complained that his or her attorney wasn't there in person. McGarrett sat in silence; listening but apathetic.

"Um," he continued, "your next court date is in a little more than three weeks. We'll need to find out from the DA about what kind of sentence they'll be pushing for. See if they might offer some sort of deal."

McGarrett nodded as he absorbed the words from Tucker. "What kind of deal do you think they'll offer?" he finally asked.

Tucker hesitated. This was the tough part.

"Well, that's hard to say. Your case has already gone before a grand jury and they indicted you. So, if the DA thinks he has a strong case, which he does, the offer might not be very good. If there even is an offer, that is."

McGarrett shook his head slowly and ran a hand through his hair. "I'm still not sure how I got here. All this has happened so fast."

The two men sat in silence. Tucker fought the urge to look at his watch. Despite Greg McGarrett's charges, he didn't want to appear disinterested or uncaring. He prided himself on being professional, even when he was dealing with people who had no idea what the word meant.

Tucker spoke first. "The search warrant came as a result of a report from a website admin. His site had images offered for sharing, allegedly from you." He paged through the file as if he didn't already know the information within. In truth, he was trying to find the words to give the defendant a proper briefing without being as blunt as he normally would.

"That's not what I mean," interrupted McGarrett. "I know what I'm charged with. I know how bad it looks and I know what you must think of me. I just mean..."

He looked up at the ceiling, searching for the right way to say what he wanted to say.

"Mr. McGarrett-"

"My wife left me. Or, I guess, she is leaving me. She came and saw me here once. Didn't bring the kids. That was okay, I didn't want them to see me like this. Didn't want them to see me in here." He didn't look at Tucker as he spoke, but down at the table. "She said she wanted to tell me in person. Her and the kids are going to stay with her parents in Irvington until she can figure things out, whatever that means. Next week, maybe the week after. This is all too much for her. She said she won't be back."

He covered his face with his hands.

Tucker listened but was unfazed. He'd heard it all before; from a hundred different criminals with a hundred different excuses. It used to affect him. He used to believe them. Not always, he'd never been that naïve, but more than he did now. In a shorter time than he would have expected, he had gone from a motivated crusader to a disillusioned journeyman.

If there was one person who Tucker held responsible for this distrust, it was Jake Lester. Jake had sat across from him in a room just like this one and, with tears in his eyes, told him how his mother had died while he was in custody. Tucker's heart had gone out to him. Being locked up had to be hard enough but to not be there for the ones you love, especially for something so traumatic, was a special kind of hell.

His boss, at Tucker's urging, had gone to bat for their client. The judge turned them down every time they asked for an early release. Eventually, the criminal justice system caught up with Jake and he was sentenced to three years upstate. Tucker felt they had done a good job keeping the sentence that short. It was at that sentencing Tucker met Jake's mother, Carol, alive and well. She read a prepared letter on her son's behalf, asking for leniency.

Tucker thought of Jake as Greg McGarrett agonized over all he had lost. When McGarrett spoke again, Tucker found he couldn't hold his tongue any longer.

"I asked her to trust me. I asked her to remember how she knows me better than anyone." He brought his hands down from his face. There were no tears, just a look of resignation in his bloodshot eyes. "She doesn't believe me when I tell her I didn't do it."

"Mr. McGarrett, investigators traced those photos back to your IP address, back to your personal computer. When they had experts search through your laptop, they found those same pictures along with hundreds of others. There were videos, too." Tucker's index finger hit the folder in front of him. "They even have screenshots from your webcam of you trying to acquire more materials for your collection. Can you explain how all of this came to be stored on your particular computer?"

Tucker tensed. He wasn't sure how this client would react to such a straightforward assessment of his case. McGarrett looked down at the floor.

"You wouldn't believe me if I told you. She didn't."

"No. I probably wouldn't."

There it was. Now they both knew where they stood.

Tucker cleared his throat and continued. "Regardless of how I feel about the case, you should know that child sex abuse charges are felonies. You're looking at a dozen counts. Honestly, we're lucky the DA didn't throw more of them at you. I'm not sure why they didn't. If we're not offered a really good plea bargain, we're probably looking at prison time. A lot of prison time if they run the sentences consecutively."

"You keep saying 'we' like we're going to go to prison together." McGarrett looked up at Tucker.

"No, sir, I'm not. I say 'we' to illustrate that we are on the same team here and I will do my best to help my boss provide you with a defense for the charges you are facing."

"I'm sure you will." Tucker couldn't tell if that was sarcasm or not, but he didn't care.

A knock on the door interrupted the meeting. Deputy Bloom poked his head into the room. "Sorry, Mr. Gibsen, but time is up. I need to get him back to his housing area for lunch."

"Okay," said Tucker. "Thank you, deputy."

The deputy left the door open and walked a few feet away, giving the two men time to wrap up their conversation.

"I'll be back later this week so we can go over the case better. Maybe we can figure something out."

Greg McGarrett stood up and started to say something. He paused with it on the tip of his tongue.

"Did you have a question?" Tucker asked.

"No, just something that's been going through my head a lot since I've been in here." McGarrett looked at Tucker. "This world is a cruel and arbitrary place. Hope cannot last when it turns its gaze upon you."

Tucker stared at the man, wide eyed with his mouth hanging open, speechless.

"Something someone said to me recently. Someone I thought was my friend. Now I know better. Seems fitting right now."

McGarrett turned and left the room, leaving Tucker by himself.

"What did you just say?" Tucker asked the empty room, his voice barely above a whisper.

Chapter Two

Before

The sun was still rising somewhere off to their left as the boat made its way south along the coast. A bleary-eyed ten-year old, wrapped in a bright orange lifejacket a little too big for him, sat up front while his father sat in the back and steered. David Gibsen wore no flotation device; he'd always been more of a "Do As I Say Not As I Do" kind of parent.

His choice of safety gear consisted solely of his lucky ball cap, perfect for keeping his head warm as well as hiding his thinning hair.

The sound of the outboard motor cut through the early morning fog that had already begun to burn off. The boy stared off to his right, out to the open ocean. It was calm this morning, making for a smooth trip in the small motorboat.

"Tucker!" he yelled to his son so he could make himself heard over the motor. David Gibsen pointed ahead at the small cove that was their destination. Tucker nodded and gave a thumbs up. This was the first time his dad had let him come along with him to his super-secret clam digging spot. Tucker was excited and nervous despite the early hour.

David reduced the throttle as the boat got closer to the beach. Tucker could hear the cawing of the seagulls. Those gulls always seemed to be everywhere along the Oregon coast, usually picking at dead crabs in the surf or flying away from overzealous tourists.

There were no tourists on this stretch of beach. The area was isolated and blocked off by large rocks to the north and south. Thick trees kept anyone out to the east and there were no hiking trails in. The ocean was the only way to get here.

When they got to shallow enough water, David dropped the anchor and hopped out of the boat. Tucker followed shortly behind. Hip waders kept the two of them from feeling the chill of the cold water.

It only took one trip for the two of them to carry the supplies from the boat to the beach.

David took the waterproof backpack containing their lunch and bottled water while Tucker carried the five-gallon bucket with the digging tools. The boat, secured and tethered to its anchor, bobbed lazily in the water as they unpacked.

"Dad, why do they call it a clam gun?" asked Tucker, gesturing to the object on the ground as he struggled to unclasp his lifejacket. "It doesn't shoot anything." The metal cylinder was more than two and a half feet long with a handlebar on top that formed a T shape.

"I don't know, bud, that's just what it's called." David was only half listening. He was already focused on looking for good spots to start digging.

Tucker successfully wriggled out of the lifejacket, snatched up the clam gun, and ran over to where his dad stood studying the sand. A huge grin covered his face.

"Tucker," said David. He pointed at the ground near his feet. "Look here. See the hole? The little one? That's an air hole, it's how you know one's there."

Tucker bent down and looked closely. There was a hole there but it wasn't even big enough to fit his finger into, much less a clam.

David gently took the clam gun from his son. "You gotta be quick or the clam will dig down deeper where you can't get to it."

He carefully placed the tool over the dime-sized hole in the sand; slightly off-centered but covering it completely.

"Okay, ready? One, two, three." On three, he pushed the cylinder down into the wet sand. It went in easily for more than a foot. Reversing his grip, David grunted and pulled the tool up and out of the small hole. With a shake, the sand dumped out in a small pile at his feet. He bent down and sifted through the muck with his fingers.

"Damn," said David. "Nothing but sand." Tucker cast a surprised look at his dad for cursing. Mom would have smacked his arm and scolded him if she had been there.

"Don't worry, kiddo. What kind of fun would it be if we caught one every time?"

Tucker thought that actually sounded like a lot of fun, but kept his opinion to himself. He followed his dad farther down the beach, both of them looking for more tell-tale air holes. The Gibsen men didn't give up easily.

"So, you should always wait for low tide if you can. Low tide is best for clam digging," explained David. "High tide goes way up there." He pointed up the beach to where the wet sand touched up against the grass. "We wait until low tide and the whole beach is open for us to get all those unsuspecting clams."

Tucker took in as much of what his dad had to say as he could. He didn't have to feign interest, it was genuine.

"What about this one?" Tucker pointed to a spot in the sand his father had passed by.

"Good eye, kid. How did I miss that?" David looked down at another dime-sized hole in the beach. "Let's give it a shot. Why don't you try this one?" He handed Tucker the clam gun.

"Okay," said Tucker, taking it by the handle with both hands. He fumbled a bit with it before he managed to find what he figured was the right spot. David reached down and helped him move it over just a little bit.

Like before, David counted to three. Tucker moved his lips in unison, count-ing along silently. On three, he pushed down as hard as he could, rotating the handle right and left to cut through the sand.

"There you go. Now lift up. Use your legs." Tucker gripped the handle tighter and used his legs to lift up, just like his dad said. David helped, but only slightly. The clam gun slowly but surely rose from the beach, bringing a tube of sand with it. Tucker dumped the sand out and immediately dropped to his knees, feverishly digging through the pile.

"Here's one! Here's one!" he yelled, grabbing the razor clam and holding it up over his head triumphantly.

David clapped his hands together. "Nice! Good job, kiddo. That's a great first catch."

Tucker examined the hard shell, turning it over again and again in his hands. It was larger than he thought it would be. This one covered his entire palm. He looked up at his dad and showed him his prize catch.

"That's a really good one. They're not all that big, you know." David tousled his son's dark hair.

Tucker nodded, clearly proud of himself and ecstatic with his dad's praise.

"I'm really glad you're here with me, Tucker. I've been wanting to come here with you for a long time. My dad first brought me here when I was just a little older than you. He always told me I needed to keep this place to myself - keep it a secret. Your grandpa didn't really like most people and he sure never wanted anyone stomping all over and ruining it. I think he'd be fine with me telling you, though."

The boy hung on every word. His father never really talked to him; not like this. Most of their conversations were short and to the point. "How was school?" "Learn anything today?" "Pick up your room." Tucker never minded, he liked to keep to himself too, but he knew this trip to the cove was special.

"Anyways," David said, "we're off to a good start." He picked the clam gun up and handed it back to Tucker. "You take this one, I'll take the other one. We'll catch our limit in no time."

Tucker nodded and took the gun from his dad. He carefully placed the clam in the five-gallon bucket. It didn't look quite as big all by itself in there.

They walked slowly, parallel to each other, over the short stretch of beach. David moved along closer to the water's edge while Tucker took the path higher up. They'd stop occasionally and examine the sand a bit. If there was a sign of their prey, they'd dig and try to catch it. Sometimes they were successful and another clam was added to the bucket.

If they weren't, they would simply shrug and move on to the next one.

It was David who spotted the boat first. Maybe it had been there the whole time; unseen through the fog or simply ignored by the two of them on the shore.

"Hey, Tucker, look at that."

Tucker followed his father's gaze to the open ocean. The familiar red stripe marked it as a Coast Guard boat. Living on the coast his entire life, Tucker had seen them plenty of times. Usually, they were on their way somewhere. This one was different. This one wasn't under power. It was sitting stationary; as stationary as a boat could be with the wind and ocean currents slowly moving it.

"Wonder what they're doing out there. Doesn't look like anyone's out on the deck." The boat was close to a quarter-mile out and David wished he'd brought his binoculars with him. It was too far away to make out the identifying numbers painted on the hull, but close enough to see there was nobody moving around on it. It just bobbed slowly on the calm water.

"It's weird that they're just sitting there. Maybe they're fishing," said Tucker.

"Yeah, maybe."

The digging went on and the bucket continued to fill up. Tucker found himself looking back at the boat frequently; expecting it to start up and head off any minute. It just kept drifting.

"It's closer now," Tucker said.

"Yeah, the current's pushing it this way."

David pulled another clam from the sand. It made a clacking sound as he tossed it into the bucket with the others.

"Dad, how many do we have?"

With his mind on the drifting boat, he realized he'd forgotten to keep track of how many they'd caught. A quick check of the bucket told them they had twenty-three. The limit was twenty.

"Crap, we have too many."

"Uh oh, are we in trouble? Is that what the boat is doing here? Making sure we stay under the limit?"

David knew the Coast Guard had better things to do than stake out remote beaches so they could bust people who had three too many razor clams. The boat had almost reached the rocky outcropping that formed one border of the cove. It was only about a hundred yards away now and he could make out the numbers on the hull. The painted 52402 marked the bow while U.S. COAST GUARD stood out along the port side facing the beach. It was one of the fifty-two-foot motor lifeboats stationed in the Pacific Northwest. David wasn't exactly sure, but he was pretty sure there were only four or five of them in existence. One of them was right here in front of him.

"We're fine, Tucker. Don't worry about the limit."

Tucker reluctantly accepted his father's assurance. He sat down and began pawing through the food they'd brought with them. He found the pack of fruit snacks he'd been looking for and opened them up. The pile of clams in the bucket caught his eye.

"Dad?"

"Yeah, bud?" answered David, forcing himself to turn his attention away from the boat.

"How many clams do you think are on this beach? I mean if we dug and caught them all, how many would that be?"

"I don't know, Tucker. Dozens, I guess. Maybe a hundred. Why do you ask?"

"I dunno. Just wondering. Like, if there's so many here, how come we only caught these ones?"

"Hey, we did good today, kiddo."

"I know, I know. That's not what I mean." Tucker bit his lip, searching for the right words. "How come we caught the ones we did? We walked right past other ones without even noticing them. We snatched up some but left the ones next to them alone. Some even got away when we did go after them. Why did these ones end up in the bucket?"

"I don't know, Tucker. Sometimes it just comes down to luck I guess."

"That doesn't seem fair."

"No, no it doesn't."

A distinct crunch and scraping sound interrupted the conversation. The boat, now only seventy-five yards away, was no longer drifting. It had gone into the rocks and got hung up; still bobbing up and down but loudly scraping its hull as it did so.

That uneasy feeling he had before was confirmed. David knew something was wrong. The boat had pretty much run aground and nobody came onto the deck to investigate. Even at such a slow speed, there was no way that anyone on board would be unaware they had collided with something.

"Tucker, pack up your gear." He didn't know what he was going to do yet, he knew he wasn't going to just stand on the beach watching the boat.

Tucker didn't question his father. There was a tone in his voice that he had heard before. It was a tone you never argued with. Their plans had changed and that was that. He quickly gathered up the backpack and his clam gun. He waited for his father's next instructions.

David stood there, knowing he should do something but not knowing what he needed to do. His first thought was to take his own boat over and make sure there was nobody on board. In his mind, there couldn't be anyone on board. What could have incapacitated the entire crew but leave the boat virtually unscathed? Still, he had to know for sure. After he did, he could head back and let the Coast Guard know where they could find their boat.

Having Tucker with him complicated things. The responsible parent in him thought the best course was to get the two of them out of there and call for help as soon as they got back to shore.

But what if someone on the boat needed help?

"C'mon, Tucker. Let's go."

They waded into the water and over to the anchored motorboat. David lifted Tucker up and into the boat. Tucker was scared but did his best not to show it. He could tell his dad was worried and his dad wasn't someone who let his worry show often. To Tucker, this seemed like something the police or fire department should take care of and his father was neither of those things.

The side of the small boat dipped to the water line as David heaved himself in. The old motor puttered to life and he pulled up the anchor. Self-doubt made him hesitate, but only for a second. He pointed the bow at the Coast Guard vessel and hit the throttle.

They covered the distance quickly. Even though the smaller, two-person motorboat had a shallower draft than the larger one he was heading toward, David was cautious as he approached. The last thing he wanted was to hear the squealing of his own hull rubbing against the submerged rocks. The water was deeper out here and he wasn't sure how he would get help if they truly got stuck.

He realized he was holding his breath as he got within a few feet of the seemingly abandoned vessel. There was still no sign of life; no sign of any movement at all. He forced himself to take deep breaths, but he wasn't sure it made much of a difference.

David pulled up along the stern on the port side. A rail, almost like a fence, ran along the outside of the deck of the larger boat. There was a gap in the rail, probably where the crew got on and off when it was properly docked. The sun had risen above the trees to the east, but the father and son were still cold in the shadows of the rocky protrusions around them. He removed the rope from his anchor and looked for the best place to tie the two boats together. In under a minute, he was able to loop the rope around one of the posts, securing them as tightly as he could. There were only a few inches separating the vessels and they bumped against each other with every swell of the tide.

"All right," said David. He had come this far without a plan, so why start now? "Come here, Tucker. I'll help you up." The Coast Guard boat, even in its current state, was still seaworthy and stable. David figured it was safer going together rather than leaving him alone in the smaller boat.

With a grunt, he picked Tucker up and lifted him through the gap in the rail. The boy's weight surprised him. Lifting him out of the water like he had done just a few minutes before had been a lot easier than picking him up on the unstable platform he currently found himself. The boat rocked with the sudden shift in weight and David had to fight to keep his footing.

Father followed shortly behind son, boosting himself up the couple of feet necessary to make the transfer. Getting to his feet, David took in his surroundings.

The flagpole rose from the roof of the topside cabin in front of him. The flag hung limp in the almost windless morning. Various antennae stuck out from the roof around the flagpole. A small door leading into the cabin faced them. David guessed this was the entrance to the control room. A place where they probably kept a radio.

"Stay here, Tucker. I'm going to look inside, maybe find something we can use to call for help."

What he left out was that he was worried about what he might find in there.

A latched, rectangular box that was bolted to the deck formed a short bench on the starboard side across from them. "You sit right here, okay?" said David as he put his hand on the boy's shoulder and ushered him over. "Don't move from right here, understand?"

"Uh-huh." Tucker sat down. He tried to listen to his father but he had become distracted. The small glimpse of orange on the beach caught his eye. His lifejacket lay just out of reach of the gentle waves. In his hurry to get going he had forgotten it. So had his dad. He kept his mouth shut, though. Nothing could be done about it now and he didn't want to stress his dad out any more than he already was.

"Tucker, what did I just say?" David waved his hand in front of his son's face.

"You said to sit right here."

"You weren't listening. I said I was going to go inside and find the radio. They must have one on here. But I don't want you wandering around out here without me, okay?"

David gave his son's shoulder a little squeeze and turned to the cabin door. He saw the body lying there a split second before Tucker did. There wasn't enough time to even think about shielding the boy from it.

"Dad, what's that?" Tucker's voice quavered. He already knew what it was, but he desperately hoped he was wrong.

The dead man was on his back, his limbs splayed out haphazardly. They hadn't seen him at first because the cabin had hidden him from view as they came in from the port side. He blocked the entire walkway along the ocean-facing side of the boat. A crimson wetness pooled around the body and poured off the side into the water below.

The worst part, the part that Tucker would remember for the rest of his life, was the seagull. A smattering of white spots marked the dark gray bird. It picked at the dead man's face and neck with its beak. From the looks of it, the bird had been at it for a long time. Tucker, mesmerized by the sight and sound, couldn't look away from the awful scene.

Suddenly, the bird looked up at them. It looked surprised, like it just realized it wasn't alone with its morbid meal. A strip of bloody flesh hung from its mouth. With one quick motion, the bird flipped it into its mouth and swallowed.

Tucker screamed the piercing scream of a terrified ten-year-old boy.

David took his son into his arms, holding the boy's face against his chest. He hurried through the cabin door and into the enclosed bridge. Tears quickly followed the now muffled screams. David sat his son down on the floor. His eyes scanned the room, searching for danger; dead bodies, birds, or other horrors he could spare his son from seeing.

Too late for that, he thought.

The cramped room contained only one seat and the controls for the boat; a small panel with two parallel levers and a large steering wheel next to a dark computer screen and a group of colored buttons. The levers had orange knobs on the ends and could be moved forward or backward. They currently sat at neutral, right in the middle. To the right of the panel, a narrow staircase went down further into the boat. Surrounding windows gave him a view of the south, east, and west.

Tucker's screams gave way to sobbing and hyperventilating.

"It's okay, kiddo. It's okay," said David. "Daddy's got you."

"Th-th-th-the bird's gonna eat me." Tucker could barely get the words out between rapid breaths.

"No, he's not. You're safe in here."

Tucker whimpered, unconvinced.

"I need you to stay right here. I'm going to go back outside-"

"No! Stay here, stay in here." The boy grabbed his dad's shirt by the sleeves.

"I have to go out and...." He paused. David realized he wasn't sure what he was going to do outside. The man out there was obviously beyond help. He just had to make sure, for his own conscience.

"Tucker, just stay here and you'll be fine. Trust me."

Tucker slowly let go of his dad's shirt. He didn't want him to go but he didn't want to go back out on the deck either.

"I'll be right back." David turned away and went out the door, leaving Tucker alone in the cabin.

Tucker listened to his father's footsteps outside. They went, slow and steady, from the cabin door, turning left, then left again.

"Oh, Jesus, oh, Jesus," Tucker heard his dad say through the thin wall. He closed his eyes and imagined what was happening out there. Approaching the body, shooing away the bird, and trying not to throw up. Tucker knew he would throw up if he had to see the dead man again.

He hugged his knees to his chest and tried to think about anything besides the body and the bird. Tucker thought of his mom. She'd kissed the top of his head and told him to be careful before they left this morning. She'd be so worried. She always worried. He wished he was with her right now. He wished he was anywhere but here.

"Oh my god!" his father yelled, much louder than before. "How did...what the hell happened here?" Disgust, bewilderment, but most of all fear radiated through every word.

Tucker covered his ears, trying to block out the sounds from outside. Every yell, thump, or scrape made him cringe.

The stairway to his left beckoned the traumatized boy. Maybe those stairs would lead him far enough away that he couldn't hear his father sound so scared anymore.

He bolted from his spot in the corner, across the room, and down the stairs. There were only a half dozen steps, but the combination of fear and adrenaline made Tucker take them too fast and stumble. He knew he was going to fall as soon as he hit that first step. His arms flailed and he lost his balance.

Tucker completely missed the last step and went sprawling onto the floor. He heard a pop in his ankle just before his knees and face hit the hard floor below. Holding his arms out helped to partially break his fall, but the impact knocked one of his front teeth cleanly out of his mouth.

Tasting blood immediately, Tucker grabbed at his mouth and grunted. The tears that now flowed were tears of pain instead of tears of fear. All thoughts of man-eating birds or dead bodies fled clean out of his mind on impact. He pulled his hands away to examine them, expecting to see blood from his mouth. His eyes widened when he saw they were thickly coated in crimson all the way down to his elbow.

That's too much, he thought. *Too much blood. I'm gonna die.*

Tucker looked down at his shirt. It, too, was smeared with blood. Lifting himself up to his knees, he realized it wasn't his. He was hurt and bleeding, but not nearly bad enough to cause this much bleeding. Blood covered the floor all around him like a sticky blanket.

It had been there when he fell.

Fresh horror washed over the boy. This was someone else's blood he had all over him. The metallic stench overwhelmed him and he started to dry heave. His mind was only beginning to process the scene before him when a voice called out from the other side of the room.

"That looked like it hurt, Champ. Gotta be careful, that last step is a doozy."

The man sat on the floor, fifteen feet from Tucker. His back rested against the side of a small bunk. Fluorescent lights on two of the walls illuminated the low-ceilinged room. Two other unoccupied beds were lined up against the walls to the right and left, but Tucker's attention was on the one directly in front of him. Sweat plastered the man's hair to his head and he sat limply, like an unattended marionette. He had on a tank top that used to be white, but was now spattered and stained. His arms, like Tucker's, were covered with blood up to his elbows. Lying on the bunk behind him was a second man. This one stared at Tucker with an unblinking gaze. His throat showed a ragged gash that stretched from ear to ear and was deep enough to have almost decapitated him.

Blood no longer poured from the wound; it had all already run down the side of the bed and onto the floor.

Tucker grimaced. "No, no, no, no, no," he whined. *Not again, please not again.*

The sitting man regarded Tucker with glassy eyes. "Don't cry, Champ. There's nothing to worry about. Not anymore." His smile did nothing to comfort Tucker. The man reached behind him and brought out a hunting knife. Rubbing the serrated edge back and forth along his arm, he said, "No, nothing at all. You see, Champ? Do you?"

Tucker pushed himself away using his arms and his one good leg. The stairs behind him seemed hopelessly far and impossibly high. The man with the huge knife could cover the distance between them faster than Tucker could get back up and outside.

The gleam of the knife captured his focus the same way the seagull had. Tucker imagined the blade piercing his own skin, adding his own fresh blood to the tacky pool they were both sitting in.

"Please, no. Please." Tucker's plea was quiet but desperate.

"Shhhhh," said the man with the knife. He pointed the blade at Tucker. "Listen to me, Champ. Listen real good."

With one quick motion, he altered his grip on the knife, flipping the blade so it pointed down. There was no hesitation as he plunged the knife into his forearm. He gritted his teeth and pushed the blade up his arm, towards his wrist and upturned palm. Blood flowed freely from the expanding wound. The sickening sound of tearing, wet meat was sporadically interrupted by the equally sickening sound of metal scraping on bone.

"This world is a cruel and arbitrary place. Hope cannot last when it turns its gaze upon you." He spoke through clenched teeth, never taking his eyes off of Tucker.

Slowly, like he was being lightly pushed over, the man fell onto his side. With his good hand, he reached out to Tucker. The hilt of the knife still stuck out from his other arm. He'd carved himself up to the heel of his palm before stopping.

"C'mere, Champ." His body was practically dead weight but still he used his one working arm to slide himself across the bloody floor.

Fear had rooted Tucker to one spot as the man in front of him mutilated himself. That same fear now compelled him to flee. He turned and scrambled up the stairs. His injured foot was no more useful than a club so he went up as fast as he could on his hands and knees. The stairway and control room stretched out before him.

Too slow, I'm too slow. Bloody spittle shot from his mouth with every shallow breath. Tucker shut his eyes tightly as he crawled, each second he had expected a hand to grab his ankle or a knife to slice into his leg. He didn't dare look back.

He reached the door and collapsed onto his belly. "Help me," Tucker said. His voice was an exhausted whisper. He reached up to the door's latch but his arms were too short. "Help me." He struck his open hand against the door and spoke again. "Help me." This time he was louder. He hit the door again, and again. "Helpmehelpmehelpmehelpme." He was yelling now. Panic took over and all Tucker could do was hit and scratch at the door like a trapped animal.

The door swung open, cool air hit Tucker in the face, and sunlight flooded the room.

"Tucker!" It was his dad. David collected his son in his arms and held him, rocking back and forth like he did when he was a toddler.

"I'm sorry. Dad, I'm sorry."

The last thing he heard before he lost consciousness was his father sobbing. He had never heard his dad cry before. Not even once.

Chapter Three

With a population of just over ten thousand, the city of Pine Harbor was one of the larger cities on the Oregon Coast. Historically, that number would rise sharply during the summer tourist season. Pacific sunsets and clam chowder drew in people from all over the country.

Nowadays, the tourist season stretched from spring until well into the fall.

The jail was only three blocks from the office. It hadn't been raining when Tucker walked over earlier that morning, but it was now as he made his way back. He hardly noticed - rain was common here, after all - but that wasn't the only reason. He navigated on auto-pilot, his memories taking him back to a time and place he had done his best to forget.

Waiting for the crosswalk light to change, Tucker replayed Greg McGarrett's parting words in his head.

This world is a cruel and arbitrary place

This random man who Tucker had never seen or heard of before today had somehow repeated back the same words that had haunted him for the past seventeen years. This same guy was probably going to spend years in prison for his computer full of kiddie porn.

The light changed and Tucker crossed the road. The nicer spring weather, even with the rain, had already began to attract the tourists who couldn't handle the harshness of a coastal winter.

The rain and crisp air helped to clear Tucker's head. The shock faded a little with each step he took. After Deputy Bloom escorted McGarrett out of Visiting, he returned to let Tucker back out to the freedom of the real world.

"You okay, Mr. Gibsen? You're looking kind of pale."

Tucker's only response was a curt nod as he packed up his files. He hustled out of the interview room while his mind raced. Pausing only long enough for the deputy to unlock the outer door, he exited quickly, ignoring the polite goodbyes from both Deputy Bloom and Allison.

Tucker's destination, his place of employment for the past two years, was located a short distance away up a gradually sloping hill just off the highway. Formerly a three-bedroom residential home, it had been remodeled and converted for business use. Other than the tastefully done sign proclaiming it to be the Office of Delbert J. Mahoney, Attorney at Law, it still looked like a family home from the outside. On the inside, hardwood floors covered the entire house. The short entryway opened into the living room where Cheryl Green sat at her low wooden desk.

"Hey, how did it go?" she asked as Tucker came in, brushing the beads of water off of his coat.

"Fine, I guess," he answered. "Is he in?" Tucker gestured toward the second floor of the house, the former master bedroom and current office of the boss.

"No, he had to step out for a minute," she said with a scoff. Their employer had a habit of leaving the office without telling anyone where he was going. He usually returned in a good mood and smelling of whiskey. "Did you need him for something?"

"Maybe...I'm not sure."

"You ok, hon?" Except for Mr. Mahoney, Cheryl called most everyone hon. She was the first person he'd hired when he started his own practice all those years ago and now she was the one who really ran the place. Through all of the temps, legal assistants, part-timers, and secretaries who had passed through, Cheryl was the only constant. She called all of the other attorneys, and even some of the judges, by their first names. If there was ever an issue with a client needing fixed, she was the one who - day or night - knew the right number to call and get it done. Now in her mid-fifties, she often joked she was old enough to be Tucker's mother. With her long, straight, dark hair, smooth skin, and sense of style, she could have passed for at least five years younger. Maybe even ten.

One thing you could count on was her protectiveness towards her co-workers, especially the young man standing in front of her.

"Yeah, Cheryl, I'm ok. It's just something that a defendant said to me over at the jail."

"Which one?"

"Greg McGarrett."

"That's the child pornography guy, right?" She always had her finger on the pulse of the current caseload. Give her a name and she could tell you their pending charges, who the prosecutor was, and even her own personal take on the likelihood of their conviction. "They pretty much have him dead to rights."

"Yes, they do. He says he didn't do it but...." Tucker shrugged. Cheryl rolled her eyes. It was cliché because it really was true; they all say they didn't do it.

"What did he say to you?"

Only a handful of people had heard the story of what happened to him on that Coast Guard boat seventeen years ago and Cheryl was not one of them. He thought of her like a second mother but he still hesitated. How was he supposed to explain what happened today when he didn't understand it himself?

"It's probably nothing. The guy just doesn't seem the type, you know? Usually these guys are weirdos. Like, you can tell something's off. McGarrett seemed like someone you'd grab a beer with after work."

"People like that, the ones with those kinds of charges, are good at manipulating how other people see them. That's how they get as far as they do. They're smart so they know how to cover it up and act normal so nobody suspects. Or, at least, if anyone gets a weird vibe from them, they never have any idea just how much of a low-life waste of space the guy really is."

That was her way of chastising him for not seeing though the facade. Cheryl sometimes sounded more like a prosecutor than the right-hand woman of a defense attorney.

"I know, Cheryl. This isn't my first rodeo. McGarrett just got under my skin, I guess."

"Mm-hm. Well, I'll let you know if I hear from Del." Only Cheryl could get away with calling the boss that to his face. "You better get back to work. Your little brother back there needs adult supervision." She nodded in the direction of the hallway where he shared an office with the only other legal assistant on the payroll.

Tucker tipped an imaginary hat at her and made his way down the hall. Donovan Sandlin, Donnie to his friends, wasn't Tucker's brother no matter what Cheryl said. He was Tucker's slightly older, way more juvenile, co-worker. His tie was undone and his sleeves were rolled up.

"What's up, loser?" Donnie didn't look up from his keyboard as he greeted Tucker.

With his head down, the thinning of the neatly parted, dirty blonde hair on the top of his head was distinct. There were places bare scalp could be seen. He was taller than Tucker, so the minor embarrassment was easier to keep hidden when they were standing. Their two desks were pushed together and facing each other with Donnie's also facing the open door.

When the house was converted from a residence, the doors to the two bedrooms were taken off and the wall separating the rooms had been torn down, creating a single, larger workspace with two entryways. File cabinets and shelves filled with books lined the walls.

"Hey," said Tucker, sitting down in his own chair. "Anything exciting happen while I was gone?"

"Nothing exciting ever happens around here. How was the jail?" Donnie knew exactly how Tucker felt about doing jail duty. His wicked grin showed how proud of himself he was that he was able to get out of doing it himself.

"Same old shit. If we were better at our job, they wouldn't be in jail." Donnie was not someone he confided in or even trusted that much. They got along well enough to keep sharing a workspace, but Tucker never thought they would ever be anything more than workplace acquaintances.

"Speak for yourself; I'm awesome at my job. You're the one that could benefit from a little remedial training." He snickered at his own joke. "But don't let them get to you, little buddy. Loser criminals will always blame others for their failures at life."

Somehow, when Donnie talked like that about their clients, it came across as pettier and even more judgmental than Cheryl was. She saved her vitriol for a select few, but he seemed to lump them all together in a way that was borderline inappropriate considering their job was to defend those very people. Tucker thought about the people he had met with at the jail that morning and wondered how far away he was from permanently acquiring Donovan's grim outlook. The thought depressed him.

Tucker took the files from his bag and set them on his desk. McGarrett's was still on top. He picked it up off the pile and absent-mindedly leafed through it. Like he told Cheryl, this guy just didn't seem like the type. He had been faithfully married for more than twelve years with two kids, stable employment, and no arrest record prior to this. Of course, Tucker was not naive enough to believe that these things meant that McGarrett was innocent. Plenty of people committed crimes and never got caught. Everyone has secrets; some of them so secret even those closest to them were kept in the dark. How many family members or close friends swore to whoever would listen that their loved one could not possibly have done the heinous things they were accused of? They have to believe it. Otherwise, they would have to admit they never really knew the person behind the mask.

Greg McGarrett's guilt was a foregone conclusion. The best Mr. Mahoney could do for him was to try and get him the best plea deal possible. His personal laptop had been used to upload and download the disgusting images. Besides him, the only people who had access to the computer were his wife and young children. No jury would ever believe one of them was responsible. The search warrants all looked to be in order so any chance of getting the evidence thrown out was remote. They would make the motion anyway, that was their job, but Tucker couldn't imagine it being granted.

Tucker realized he was looking for a legal loophole and was avoiding the bigger issue.

Regardless of McGarrett's guilt or innocence, the fact remained that he had managed to quote, word for word, the same ravings of a madman Tucker heard all those years ago.

Hope cannot last when it turns its gaze upon you

Since that day on the boat, Tucker had searched for meaning in the ominous message.

Those words had been burned into Tucker's brain. He'd searched through everything from Shakespeare to the Bible for anything close to a match. He found nothing. There was no explanation or closure for Tucker as he looked for a reason why a man would kill his fellow sailors before killing himself. McGarrett had dredged all of that up again.

"Hello? Dude, what are you reading? You haven't heard a word I've said." Donnie was waving his hands to get Tucker's attention.

"Oh, sorry. It's just a case file. What were you saying?"

"I was telling you about the great time I was showing your mom the other night. You know, nothing important."

Tucker responded with a prominent display of his middle finger.

"That's hurtful, Gibsen." Donnie held his hand to his heart with a mock grimace. "Actually, I was asking if you had talked to Lyric."

"No, still haven't talked to her." Tucker sighed heavily. Lyric was another subject he didn't feel like talking about with Donnie. For the first time in a week, he'd been able to forget about her completely, even if only for a short time. That was the only silver lining from the events of the morning.

"Man, that's too bad. I miss seeing her around here in those yoga pants. Is she, like a gymnast or a swimmer or something? She sure could be."

"Dude, you never saw her in yoga pants."

"Sure, I did," said Donnie. "Right here in my imagination." He tapped his forehead as his grin widened.

Tucker regretted engaging with him at all, especially on a sensitive subject. Donovan could sense when he got under someone's skin and it only encouraged him more.

"She finally realize she's way out of your league? Sorry, Gibsen, it was only a matter of time. I could give her a call and smooth things out for you. Just give me her number and I'll hook you up."

Tucker ignored him this time.

Cheryl's raised voice interrupted Donnie's wit. "Tucker, Del's on the phone. Did you need to talk to him? He said he won't be in for the rest of the day."

"No, thanks. I'm good," he yelled back down the hall. Tucker turned back to Donnie. "Do you think you could cover the office for me? I gotta go take care of something and if the boss man isn't going to be back, I'll take off early."

"Uhhh, sure. Everything ok?" He actually looked concerned.

"Honestly, I'm not sure." Tucker stood with his car keys in hand. "I have to go see my dad."

CHAPTER FOUR

Seemingly overnight, another gray hair showed up. She could see it in the mirror even from five feet away. There were several now, spread through her wavy russet hair. In and of itself, the gray didn't bother her. Rebekah Goodwright didn't put much stock in appearances. What did bother her was being reminded of the unalterable passage of time.

Too much had already passed her by and she had nothing to show for it. She was fine with growing old, all of her hair could fall out for all she cared, but not before she had done what she set out to do.

Rebekah was close, maybe closer than ever before, and had to be careful. Her hopes had been dashed too many times when she thought the finish line was in sight and she couldn't afford any mistakes that would set her back.

The motel room was basic. Brown water stains covered one corner where the wall met the ceiling and the carpet was worn away in several places. A smell like wet dog permeated the room even though she hadn't seen or heard a single dog in the twenty-four hours since she checked in.

What brought her to this particular fleabag motel instead of one of the dozens of others that dotted the coast was the low nightly rate and good location. Tucked away at the end of a poorly maintained road, the U-Rest Motel was close to the geographical center of town but far enough from the water to keep it from being a popular vacation destination. The clientele here wasn't the normal family on a road trip or pretty people getting away from their stressful jobs. Rebekah's neighbors in the fourteen-room, one-floor, motel were the kind of people who avoided the police, didn't ask too many questions of strangers, and liked to pay in cash.

Karen, the daytime manager/housekeeper, had already been by to drop off fresh towels.

The curtains were pulled and the Do Not Disturb sign was out. The sigil Rebekah had hand drawn on the inside of the door would temporarily keep people away from her room.

It wouldn't keep out someone determined to get in, but anyone passing by or thinking about knocking would feel uncomfortable for a reason they couldn't put their finger on.

Those people would unconsciously feel the need to get away. Rebekah didn't need much privacy for what she was about to do, but an ill-timed distraction could throw her off enough to ruin the effort.

Sitting cross-legged at the foot of the bed, open book in her lap, and staring into the mirror, Rebekah focused on her breathing. The book, her precious therimoire, represented the sum of her arcane knowledge, acquired one page at a time over years of toil and frustration. She relaxed her eyes and cleared her mind, focusing on nothing but the depths behind the mirror.

It took some time to get herself to her desired meditative level. She could feel when she was ready; a sort of metaphysical puzzle piece slid into place and assured her.

Rebekah leapt up from the bed and dove straight through the reflective glass in front of her. It parted around her like water and she came out unscathed on the other side. The room she emerged into was an exact reproduction of the one she just left, right down to her blue duffle bag and white sneakers resting on the room's second bed.

She turned to look at the mirror behind her. Instead of seeing her own image reflected back, Rebekah saw *through* the glass. On the other side she saw her physical body just as she left it; sitting on the bed in her room. Her body's eyes stared ahead without emotion.

Her chest rose and fell at regular intervals.

Her book was not necessary for this ritual, but out of habit, she'd brought it out and opened it to the proper page even though she could recite every word from memory.

Projecting was one of the first skills Rebekah learned from her teacher all those years ago when she was practically a child. It only required concentration and the ability to reach a state of inner peace. She never got used to the feeling of looking at her own body from somewhere else. The fascination could be endless, if she let it.

But she had work to do.

In the blink of an eye, Rebekah was outside her motel room. Karen sat two doors down from her in the tiny manager's office, smoking and chewing gum while reading a magazine.

Her stringy blonde hair was tucked behind her ears and the office door was propped open. She looked up for a moment, sure that someone had just walked by, but no one was there. Rebekah was invisible when she was in this state. Every so often, a person might sense her presence, but when they look around there's nothing.

Karen put her cigarette out in the ashtray. She absently scratched at the back of her head before walking over to the door and shutting it. Looking out the window at the gravel parking lot made her shiver.

"Don't make yourself crazy, Karen," she said to herself and shook her head. The lot was empty. "It's only your imagination."

By the time Karen sat back down at the check-in desk and found her place in her magazine, Rebekah was down the street and heading to the highway.

Her pace never slowed as she turned south. The road dipped a bit, and she passed a sign that read "Entering Tsunami Hazard Zone." A few seconds and a mile later, she saw another one informing her she was leaving the zone. How much of Pine Harbor was in this zone? How many of the people she moved past would be stranded in the deadly path of a tidal wave if the time came? Would her dirty little motel be submerged or was it built in their imaginary safe area? It didn't matter where you were, she thought. If it was your time then it was your time and scrambling for higher ground wasn't going to be much help.

With a slight shift of concentration, Rebekah found herself rising above the roadway, then the trees. Soon, all of Pine Harbor spread out below her. From this height, she could take in the expanse of the Pacific Ocean to the west. Waves crashed into rocks nearly two miles beneath her. Beyond that was the endless sheet of blue-green that stretched to the edge of the world. The water was calm and nearly flat, belying the turmoil and destructive potential it possessed.

All this time, all the miles traveled and sacrifices made, and this was the first time she had laid eyes on the Pacific. In another life, the Atlantic Ocean had been a familiar friend.

But that was near home and home was far away, both in distance and years gone by.

Rebekah dared not go any further. This was as high as she had ever been. Each time she could feel the tether to her physical body give a little bit more than the time before. If she pushed too far or too fast, it could break, and she would be lost forever.

Rebekah forced her attention away from the stunning view. Pine Harbor, the town that called itself a city, was below her. Cars moved along the ground like a trail of metal ants.

She shifted again, slowly descending until she could make out individual people. Here and there, Rebekah could make out the mark she was looking for. A purple faint glow surrounded a couple walking down a street near the waterfront. Further down from them, sipping a coffee on a bench, was a man with the same aura. This one was fainter and felt older than the others.

Skimming over the rooftops of Pine Harbor, she couldn't help but be surprised at the number of people in the immediate area with the same aura. She'd been hoping for a significant showing, something to confirm she was on the right track, but she wasn't expecting anything like this.

The purple glow popped up every other block like weeds in a garden. This was more than anywhere else she had been before. Some were bright and new; she could see those from far away. Others were dull and powdery and she had to look closer to detect them.

This didn't make sense. The auras were normally uniform with only small deviations.

Not only was the sheer number of them off the charts, but the sizes and brightness varied greatly. They were all affected, but at different times and with different intensities. How was this possible?

But she was in the right place. She was sure of it.

Not far from the waterfront, an imposing brick building caught her attention. The simple, rectangular building was dotted with barred windows and the fence surrounding it was lined with razor wire. She covered the distance within seconds, moving at ground level until she was at the front doors. The Campbell County Jail. Somewhere inside was a person with the brightest aura in the entire town. Rebekah could only sense the edges of it from where she was. This was a fresh one, most likely the one who brought her here in the first place. It was a solid lead, one step closer.

With a thought, Rebekah was through the doors, past the front reception desk, and down the hall. She weaved around uniformed deputies and brown-clad inmates. The jail was brighter and cleaner inside than she would have thought. She had mentally pictured a darker and gloomier setting instead of the well-lit concrete corridors she flew over. There weren't even any bars; just thick wooden doors with heavy duty locks.

It didn't take her long to find him. With her speed and the finite population of the jail, it was only a matter of time. The cell at the end of one particular tier shone brilliantly, like a beacon. Purple and pulsing, the aura poured from the cell into the hallway.

She went straight through the door and finally laid eyes on the man she was looking for. He sat alone. Unshaven with slightly dirty hair, wearing a brown jumpsuit too big for him, the man absently picked at the tray of food in front of him. Even without the help of her spell, Rebekah thought she might have been able to recognize this was her man. The defeated, helpless look in his eyes - the same look she had seen too many times before - would have been a dead giveaway.

Leaving the building was easier than entering. The only thing separating her from the outside was a singular brick wall. She left the incarcerated man behind and moved through the wall into the daylight.

Then she was in the air again, soaring away from the jail. Splashes of purple shot by as she looked for the other side of the coin. Finding the man in the jail made this part easier. Rebekah could feel the influence that surrounded him, and she followed the invisible tendrils to the other end like she was tuning into a radio station. Trees and sand blurred together with the streets and people as Rebekah flew over the town. As soon as she saw it, she knew. To her, it stuck out almost as much as the man in the jail cell.

The house sat in a nondescript cul-de-sac on the north side of town. A woman in a baseball cap worked in the front yard, pausing occasionally to wipe sweat from her brow.

A pile of weeds rested next to her on the ground. The woman looked up as Rebekah approached and, for a moment, she had the impossible thought that the woman was looking right at her. Surely she couldn't see Rebekah, not the way she was now. She was looking *through* her and at the rain clouds heading their way. Rain clouds that would bring her yard work to a premature end.

The woman in the garden was bathed in a purple light; not as bright as the man in the jail but just as large. Inside the house, Rebekah could sense it even more. Was this his family? Wife and children? That made the most sense but she would need to verify. It never paid to assume anything. The influence affected so many people throughout the town, but the ones who lived in this house had been affected tremendously.

A mailbox stood at the end of the driveway. The name, artfully stenciled on the side, told her who lived here.

McGarrett. She had a name.

Rebekah let her focus wane. Returning to her physical body was only a matter of relaxing her mind and letting her essence return to its natural state. She was able to snap back to her motel room in seconds. Her body was just as she left it, eyes blankly staring ahead, her breathing deep and consistent.

She dove through the glass and back into herself. The transition, though instantaneous, left her dizzy and nauseous. Bile rose in her throat, but she fought it back with some effort. A pinprick of a headache started right behind her eyes. Soon it would grow into a debilitating migraine. This was how it was every time she Projected. The price Rebekah paid for her otherworldly hunting trip was being put out of commission for the rest of the day and most of the night.

Tonight, she would be miserable. Tomorrow, she would get back on the trail; starting with that woman in the garden.

The pinprick was already turning into a sledgehammer.

Rebekah dry-swallowed three Tylenol and rubbed her eyes with the heels of her hands.

This will all be worth it, she told herself. Someday soon, every sacrifice, every night spent in a shitty motel, every minute of pain, would be justified.

Chapter Five

The gray Prius made good time on the highway from Pine Harbor to Nelander Bay.

Twenty-five miles of scenic coastal driving did nothing to diminish Tucker's anxiety.

His father, David, lived in Nelander Bay ever since he and his mom split up. While the two of them got along well enough, they were hardly considered close. The truth was Tucker really didn't want to have to talk to his dad; not about this. It had been at least two months since Tucker had called his dad and more than eight months since he last visited.

He pulled up in front of the house. There was no sidewalk here, the yard blended into street without the need for a curb. The house itself was a single-story with one large front window. It was still painted the same ugly pea-green with yellow trim his dad's girlfriend, Brandy Lynn, had insisted was "cute."

This house held almost no memories for Tucker. His childhood home was back in Pine Harbor. A different family lived there now, he assumed. That old house was a real house. It had character. It also had crawlspaces that could take Tucker from his bedroom on the second floor into the attic, easy access to the roof, and a big backyard full of good places to play hide-and-seek. His parents would have freaked out if they'd known how often he took advantage of that and sneaked out onto the roof to watch the stars. That house was filled with memories; mostly good ones. This was a pale imitation.

Coming to Dad's house was a bitter reminder of the changes his family had gone through. What the green and yellow house dredged up within him was the biggest reason he avoided coming to Nelander Bay.

Nobody answered when he rang the doorbell. No surprise, there. In the early afternoon on a weekday, Dad and Brandy were probably at work. Tucker was in such a hurry to leave the office and get here he hadn't bothered calling ahead to make sure someone was home.

Dad never gave him a key, but he wouldn't have just let himself in even if he had one.

This wasn't his home.

Tucker thought about calling his father. If he knew his son was waiting for him at home, he might cut his work day short. Tucker wouldn't do that, though. He would rather wait a couple of hours than impose any more than he had to.

Settling back into the front seat of his car, Tucker checked his phone. No new messages, just the voicemail from Lyric. That one had been there for the last three days, but Tucker hadn't yet returned her call. Neither of them handled their last meeting very well and he knew there was at least one more conversation they'd need to have. Maybe it would be more than one. Maybe they could patch things up, mend fences and move on, but he doubted it. He'd said things he couldn't take back and she'd done the same.

Any love life problems, though, took a quick back seat after hearing Greg McGarrett's words that morning.

So, there he waited in his car outside the house his father shared with a woman who wasn't Tucker's mother.

Brandy Lynn got home first. Tucker reluctantly got out to greet her as she pulled into the driveway in her blue Mustang.

"Hey, Tucker. Is your dad expecting you?"

"Hi, Brandy." She frowned a little at his greeting. Her mother named her Brandy Lynn and that's the full name she wanted people to call her. Tucker knew this but kept purposefully referring to her by the shortened version. It wasn't that he disliked Brandy, he just didn't like her very much. "No, I didn't tell him I was coming. It was sort of a last-minute decision."

She shrugged and picked up the bag of groceries from the back seat of the car.

"Let me help you with that," said Tucker.

They walked into the house in silence. If things were a little awkward with his dad, they were downright uncomfortable with Brandy Lynn. The two of them could never click in all of the four years since she and Tucker's father started dating. The most they could pull off, it seemed, was to fake civility with each other. Offering to help with the groceries was the furthest Tucker was willing to go to extend an olive branch.

"Your dad should be home soon. We were planning to barbecue tonight."

Brandy Lynn set her own schedule at the liquor store where she worked. David Gibsen had more responsibility than she did, working as a Project Manager for Willis Construction.

David worked his way up from the bottom there, putting in close to twenty-five years with the same company. His hours tended to be longer than most people's. The work wasn't as grueling as it was before his promotion, but it was still challenging in its own way.

He sat the bag down on the counter in the kitchen. Dishes were piled in the sink. Unless company had been by recently, it looked like a few days' worth for just the two of them.

"So, what brings you by?" she asked.

Tucker shrugged and lied. "Just figured it's been too long. Thought it would be nice to visit...you guys."

They both knew he was only there to see his dad. Without him, the two of them would have nothing at all in common. Tucker and Brandy Lynn sat and made small talk while they waited. Yes, the weather was unpredictable this time of year. If you didn't like it, just wait ten minutes and it will change. Yeah, I'm still working at the same job.

Tucker never could understand why his dad was with her. Brandy Lynn Thomas was in her mid-thirties but looked older. Dad was close to twenty years older. She was thin; not petite, but an unhealthy-looking level of skinny. She'd been that way since Tucker first met her. Brandy's teeth had a slight yellow tint to them from coffee and smoking. Most of all, she seemed to be content to drift through life, never setting goals for herself or trying for something better.

Brandy Lynn was nothing like Mom.

The conversation slowly turned to annoying silence. Brandy excused herself and went outside to set up for the barbecue. Tucker wandered through the kitchen and living room.

The house was decorated with a hunting and fishing theme. She might have picked the color to paint the house, but he must have been in charge of what went up on the inside.

The main attraction, out of place amidst the outdoor décor, was the basketball on the fireplace mantle.

In Pine Harbor, the nearest big city with a sports team was Portland and David Gibsen embraced the Trail Blazers with a devotion bordering on fanaticism. He was old enough to remember the championship season of 1977 and would regale his young son with stories of shaggy-haired Bill Walton and Maurice Lucas flying down the court and scoring at will. The following decades of almost-winning-but-not-quite frustration didn't dissuade his passion.

The basketball on the mantle, protected like the Crown Jewels in a glass case, was autographed by the entire 1988 team. When Tucker was little, his father won it in a raffle at some work conference. As far back as he could remember, it occupied a place of honor in the Gibsen household. Tucker never really became a fan. The sounds of squeaky shoes on the court annoyed him and there were so many games in a season he didn't understand how Dad could get so worked up over each one. Even now, with the signatures right in front of him, he couldn't recall more than one or two of the names scrawled on the ball.

Only a few photographs occupied the wall and shelves in the living room. Mostly they were of Dad and Brandy, the happy couple. Vacations, parties, and hiking trips were all immortalized and framed. In the midst of those, almost hidden away, Tucker found one of himself. In the photo, his gap-toothed grin was wide as he held up a fish he'd caught. His dad posed next to him in sunglasses and no shirt. Dad's excited smile was as big as his own.

Tucker remembered that day. It was summer and he was eight. That was the first time he ever caught a fish on his own. Even now, he smiled remembering the sense of accomplishment that came with finally pulling the fish out of the water.

A car door slammed outside, pulling Tucker back into the present. Brandy Lynn appeared out the front window, walking across the yard. She was intercepting Dad to let him know his son had stopped by unexpectedly. He could hear their voices outside, speaking in hushed tones, but couldn't make out what they were saying.

The door swung open and David Gibsen walked in. His work attire had changed in the years since his promotion. A white polo and khakis replaced the Carhartt and work gloves.

His paunch was more pronounced than it was before he became a paper pusher and his hair was moving away from his forehead a little more every day. He smiled when he saw Tucker.

"Hey, kid. Long time no see."

"Hi, Dad."

The two men shook hands. David clapped his son on the shoulder. Neither of them were huggers.

"Well, you picked a good day," said David, holding up a plastic bag full of hamburger buns. "I was gonna fire up the barbecue. You want a burger or a dog?"

"Isn't it raining?"

"Rain doesn't stop us anymore. We put a cover over the back patio. It really has been a long time since you've been here."

"I guess I'll have a burger then."

David went to the fridge and pulled out two cans of beer. He cracked one open with one hand and held the other out to his son. Tucker accepted it with a nod of his head.

The elder Gibsen thought highly of his barbecue prowess. He flat-out refused to use propane, opting instead for the higher quality wood pellet grills. Tucker pretended to listen as his father waxed philosophic about pellet hoppers and auger tubes. He rolled up his sleeves and untucked his shirt, wishing he had thought to change clothes before this spontaneous trip.

"If I'd known you were coming, I would've got something better than this," said David, referring to the ground beef he placed strategically on the grill in front of him. "I could've done up some ribs or something."

"It's all good, Dad." Tucker waited for an opening to speak to his father about his morning meeting but wasn't sure how to broach the subject. On top of that, Brandy Lynn constantly hovered around them and there was no way he was going to bring up such a sensitive subject in front of her.

"You talk to your mom lately?"

"A couple weeks ago. She called me to let me know she moved again. Wyoming this time."

"Wyoming? What the hell is in Wyoming?"

"A job, I guess. She couldn't talk long. Had to run."

Tucker didn't mention the new boyfriend Mom briefly told him about. Some guy named Pete who owned a cattle ranch. "It's so beautiful out here," she said. Rachel Gibsen stopped short of inviting her son to visit, but he was sure it had been on the tip of her tongue. They both knew it would be a hollow invitation. He loved his mother but the chances of him visiting her in Wyoming were next to zero.

Brandy chimed in, "Well, you all don't need to hear my opinions on that subject. I'm gonna go get the rest of the food ready."

She disappeared into the house, closing the sliding glass door behind her and finally leaving the two of them alone.

Tucker watched her go as his father flipped the burgers.

"She's not that bad, you know. One of these years maybe you can give her a chance," David said, not taking his eyes off the grill.

"I never said she was," Tucker countered.

"Sure, you didn't. Thing is, though, you're not that subtle and she's not that stupid."

"Sorry, Dad. I'll try."

"So why did you come up? I mean, I'm glad you're here. You're always welcome. But this isn't like you, just dropping in without it being a holiday or something. Something's up?"

The meat sizzled and smoke rose from the cooking surface. Tucker hesitated, unsure of what to say or how to say it.

"I talked to this guy today at the jail. He's got some serious charges. Everything points to him being guilty, you know how that goes."

"Yeah."

"He didn't say much other than he didn't do it. But what he did say kind of messed me up a little."

"What's that?"

"Right before he had to go, he told me the same thing Ray King did that day on the boat."

David exhaled and closed the lid of the barbecue. Ray King. The Coast Guard sailor they crossed paths with that one morning seventeen years ago.

"Word for word, Dad."

"You're sure? That was a long time ago. You were little. Little and traumatized."

"Yes, I'm sure. It's the kind of thing that stays with you."

David nodded and cocked his head to one side. "How can that be? You think they know each other? Maybe they read the same kind of books or something?"

"I don't think so. This guy was in high school when King killed those people."

"King wasn't very far from being a teenager himself, to be fair."

Tucker paced, covering the patio from one end to the other. "That's what's killing me. There's no easy explanation for this. McGarrett, the guy in jail, couldn't have known about me being on the boat. The papers kept my name out of it because I was so young. Even if he put it all together, why would he sit on it all this time? Just in case he got arrested and I came to talk to him about his charges? Besides that, how did he know what King said to me before he died? That never got reported anywhere. I only ever told you, Mom, and the therapist."

The Coast Guard Murders is what it became known as in the headlines. To a small community like Pine Harbor, it was a tragedy that touched them all. The victims weren't native Oregonians, they hailed from all over the country. They were all considered hometown heroes in the wake of their deaths.

Each of them except for Ray King.

The photo of Raymond King, red-headed and smiling in his dress uniform, was placed right next to the murderous headline following the killings. There was little doubt the young man in the photo had murdered the four other crew members on the boat before killing himself. Two of the victims, Alexander Johnsgard and Winston Schmidt, the ones first discovered by Tucker and his father, were killed with the same knife found near King's body. Stephen Mulasky was hanged from his neck off the starboard side of the boat, near the bow. He was waist-deep in the ocean, swaying lifelessly with the current, when David Gibsen found him. The body of William Gutierrez washed up on the beach three days later.

A blunt object had fractured his skull before he was thrown overboard. The medical examiner concluded he was most likely unconscious when he drowned. All of the crew was accounted for.

The question that plagued the Coast Guard, investigators, and the residents of Pine Harbor wasn't who, it was why? Why did an All-American boy like Raymond King snap and take four other sailors with him? Or maybe the crime wasn't committed in the heat of the moment. Maybe this was a premeditated act; something he planned and waited until the time was right. These were questions nobody could satisfactorily answer.

Given the witness' young age and the sheer brutality of the crime, the name Tucker Gibsen never appeared in any news report. David Gibsen was only mentioned early on and then quickly forgotten. The men who questioned them eased the boy through his story of the encounter with the mass murderer in the bottom of the boat. They were fathers themselves and their sympathy for Tucker's trauma showed. Instead, they had David walk them through the gruesome morning until he felt like he could recite it in his sleep.

With their main suspect dead, the Gibsen's role in the investigation was over pretty quick. There would be no prosecution, no court proceedings, and no testimony. That was some comfort to the family, but the scars from that day stayed with them long after the headlines faded.

"That therapist, what was his name?" David asked.

"Phil. He always told me to call him Phil. Like being on a first name basis made us friends or something."

"You didn't like him?"

"He was okay. Just felt like he was faking his interest. Like it was his job. Just doing his job."

"We hoped he would help you. We, your mom and me, didn't know how to help you, or if you needed help, or how much help you needed. Everyone told us how seeing that, like you did, could really mess you up for the rest of your life."

"You could have talked to me yourselves, you know." Tucker cringed a little. He sounded harsher than he meant to.

"I know. We...I didn't know what to say. What was I supposed to tell you that could make any of that shit better for you? I mean, I had nightmares about it so I could only imagine what you were going through."

"So, you avoided the subject? Let someone else handle it for you?"

"I was afraid of making things worse. The book of fatherhood doesn't exactly have a chapter that covers what to do if you put your own kid in harm's way like I did. I blamed myself, so did your mom, and I did the best I could to make up for it."

Now it was David's turn to sound harsh. As hard as it was to believe, this might have been the first time the two of them had talked about that morning. Tucker couldn't remember another. This was always a subject they avoided.

Maybe there's a good reason we always avoided it, thought Tucker.

"I know you did."

Tucker didn't have any kids of his own, not yet anyways, but the older he got the more he understood how his parents must have felt. He couldn't process his own feelings back then. Couldn't find the words to describe how he felt or what the nightmares did to him.

Even now, almost a decade into adulthood, he was still feeling the effects.

"Have you been out on a boat at all since then?" David said.

"Nope. Not once."

"I didn't think so. I...thought I'd ask."

"Any time I tried I would freeze up, start sweating, heart pounding. One time I hyperventilated and almost passed out. I haven't even attempted to get on a boat in a few years now and I'm okay with that."

"You never told me that."

"I was embarrassed. Felt somehow like less of a man."

"Fuck." David put his hands on his hips and lowered his head. His eyes were closed. "You shouldn't be afraid or embarrassed to talk to your own dad. I don't know what I did to make you feel that way, but I wish I could take it back."

Tucker took a long pull of his beer. He was normally a lightweight when it came to drinking and his empty stomach only hastened the intoxicating effects before he was even done with this second one.

"You never really believed my story, did you? None of you did." Tucker had wanted to ask the question for a long time. Liquid courage made for honest communication.

David squinted and frowned. He hesitated, searching for the right words to fill the silence.

Tucker filled the void first. "I remember you being there, going through the motions, when I told you and Mom about me and Ray King. What he said to me, how he came after me. It wasn't until I was older that I figured it out. You guys didn't believe me."

"That's not it," David said. "We believed you. We believed that you believed what you were saying."

"Not the same thing."

"Your therapist told us you were inserting fabrications and exaggerating specifics. He called it a coping mechanism. He was the expert. He read all the reports and talked with you and came to the conclusion that you finding those bodies and all that blood made you shut down. Like your mind was so overwhelmed it invented a scenario that didn't happen."

"So, you think I made it all up?"

"No, of course not. What-"

"You believed that guy and his bullshit theory instead of me?"

"It made sense...at the time. This murderer, talking to you like that while he bleeds out? Like I said, he was the expert. He worked with traumatized kids. That was his specialty."

"He was wrong. They found King's body at the bottom of the stairs, right? He died coming after me. Just like I said."

The sizzle from the grill was louder now. David opened the lid and flipped the meat again, cursing under his breath at the sight of the burnt meat.

"For the record," David said in between flips, "since apparently we are opening up about this, your mother believed you. All the way. She resented me, kinda like you do now, for taking the other guy's side. It's one of the things we fought about. I think she felt like I was betraying you somehow."

Tucker thought back to that time of his life. His childhood from the age of ten was a blur of his parents fighting, therapy sessions, night terrors, and desperately trying to fit in.

Those all became easier to deal with as the years passed. People adapt, children especially. Thinking about his time on the boat, not talking about it but pushing it down and not dwelling on it, was the way he adapted.

"Mom believed me," said Tucker. What he left unsaid was, *but you didn't.* That might not be fair, but it was accurate.

"Tucker." David looked his son right in the eye. "Why did you come here today? No bullshit. What did you expect to get from me? I've tried my best to forget. Was all this just to bust my balls over my mistakes? Maybe I deserve that. Tell me what you want me to say and I'll say it."

"I...I don't know, Dad. You were there with me, the only one who was. I thought maybe you could help take me through it where no one else could."

"Yeah, I was there. But being there hasn't gifted me with any additional wisdom."

"I guess not."

"If this guy in the jail, the one you talked to today, is the one who sent you into this tailspin, then you should go talk to him again. You can do that, right?"

"Yeah." It wasn't illegal but it would be outside his scope of work. It could even get him in some trouble with his boss. But Greg McGarrett was the one who turned his world upside down. He was the one Tucker should be talking to. "I can't make him answer any of my questions, but it can't hurt to try. Worst thing that happens is he shuts me down and I'm right back here."

"Ask him. There's probably a reasonable explanation."

"Maybe. If I take off now, I can get back in time-"

"You're gonna see him now? But the burgers are done. A little overdone but still good. Can't it wait?"

"Dad, this is going to eat at me until I get it done."

"Is he going somewhere any time soon? He'll still be in the same place tomorrow as he is right now." David Gibsen's disapproving stare made Tucker look away. "Besides, it's been too long since you had a drink with your old man."

That old-fashioned Dad Guilt Trip didn't always work on Tucker, but this particular time it did. Knowing what his father was doing didn't alter the effectiveness.

"Okay, okay. Take the charred meat off the grill. I think they might be stuck on there by now."

"Brandy Lynn brought home some whiskey. You want a shot?"

"Sure, Dad. But only one. I have work tomorrow."

CHAPTER SIX

Morning came too early for Tucker. Sunlight bled through the thin curtains as well as his eyelids.

"Oh, shit. What time is it?" He shot up from the couch in his father's living room. The pounding in his head, a mild ache when he was lying down, flared to a full throb. A reminder of the previous night's poor choices.

The shower was running down the hall. Was it his dad or Brandy Lynn? Glancing at his watch through squinted eyes and mentally calculating how long it would take him to get to work, he realized he was already going to be late.

The drive back to Pine Harbor was more difficult than the one he took the day before.

His stomach was churning, threatening to heave its contents all over the dashboard.

Tucker drove with one eye squeezed shut against the blinding sun.

"Fuck," he groaned. The one shot of whiskey he promised his dad last night was followed by another, then another. He remembered the point in the evening when he knew he wasn't going to be driving himself home, but was a little foggy about what time he stopped drinking and finally crashed out on the couch.

Tucker fumbled with his phone and dialed the office. It was early enough that Cheryl shouldn't be in yet. He crossed his fingers and hoped it would go straight to voicemail.

"You have reached the office of Delbert J. Mahoney, attorney at law. Our normal business hours are..." Cheryl's recorded voice came through clearly.

Tucker did his best to sound like he wasn't dying. "Hey, Cheryl. It's Tucker. Um, I'm running late, I have to take care of a couple things this morning, but I'll be there. I'll bring coffee for you but not Donnie, okay? See you in a little bit."

He had to go home first. His clothes were horribly wrinkled and smelled from twenty-four hours of wear. Maybe he could get in a quick a shower if he skipped shaving. Tucker considered just calling in sick for the entire day, but that would delay his second interview with Greg McGarrett until at least tomorrow. He wouldn't risk skipping work and heading over to the jail anyway. There were too many people who might see him and mention it to Donovan or Mr. Mahoney.

Fighting traffic, nausea, and winding roads took all of his concentration. Luckily, he knew the route home like the back of his hand. Beer before liquor, never been sicker. Tucker knew that rhyme, lived by it, but had set it aside along with his good sense. Now he was paying for it.

He managed to keep his stomach under control all the way back to his place. Pulling into his parking spot never made him feel more relieved than it did this time. The apartment building was five stories tall. The top four were apartments that were stacked on top of Fiore Appassito, the Italian restaurant on the bottom floor. Tucker avoided the restaurant entrance to the left and went in through the door to the right. In the lobby, past the tenant's mailboxes, was the elevator. Tucker got in and pushed the button to take him to the third floor.

"Okay, you got this," he said to himself. The elevator doors opened without a sound. He turned left and hustled down the hall. The woman sitting on the carpeted floor in front of the door to his apartment made him stop short.

She wore her familiar shorts and tank top along with the bright green running shoes he had bought her for her birthday. Her black hair hung loosely down to her shoulders and her hair tie was wrapped around her wrist. She took out her earbuds and looked up.

"Hey, Tucker."

"Lyric. Hi. Sorry, I, uh, wasn't expecting you."

"Yeah, I'm not sure this is going to work out," was what she said to him on their first date.

She said it with a smile and laugh. It was the kind of smile that made her eyes shine and made Tucker forget what he was going to say next. The weekend before, his friend Robbie had insisted on dragging him to a party at a friend's house.

"Jen's friend Veronica will be there. The one I told you about? I'm telling you, she's hot."

So, Tucker went to the party.

Robbie, Jen, and a couple of Jen's friends, Veronica included, chatted around the fire pit as country music played and the other partygoers danced.

Veronica was attractive, Robbie certainly hadn't lied about that. She was almost as tall as Tucker with red hair that came down to just past her earlobes. Maybe she was nervous or maybe she had nothing to say, but the conversation from her end was decidedly lacking.

Veronica laughed awkwardly and wore too much makeup.

Tucker was bored.

"Hey, Veronica," Robbie said. "What kind of music do you like?" He was gracelessly trying to nudge the two of them in the right direction. "Tucker here likes old stuff, like from before he was born."

"I don't know," Veronica said with a giggle. "Little bit of everything, I guess."

"You should be flattered. Tucker here doesn't get out very often. Getting him to a party like this is like pulling teeth. He's what you call 'anti-social'." Air quotes accompanied Robbie's words.

Jen smacked Robbie's arm with the back of her hand. "Don't be so obvious," she whispered.

"What? I'm just sayin'. Tucker, you're my friend but it's not exactly a well-kept secret that you prefer to hang out with not quite as many people as we have at this fiesta this evening."

Tucker played along. "No, you're right. I'm the weird friend. I set fires to feel joy."

Jen's other friend, the one standing next to Veronica for most of the night, perked up and tilted her head at Tucker.

"Wait, was that a line from *Pitch Perfect*?" she said.

"Is it? I guess it is." He held his hand out to her. "I'm Tucker. What was your name again?"

"Lyric. Lyric Howard."

"Nice to meet you."

That was how it began. The rest of the party faded into the background as the night went on.

To say the two of them clicked immediately would be an understatement. Lyric told Tucker about growing up in Centralia, Washington before moving to Oregon to go to college. Tucker told Lyric how his parents divorced after he turned eighteen and how he hated pineapple on his pizza. In between stories, he told jokes. She laughed and they made plans to see each other again.

They met up at a coffee shop a few days later, picking up right where they left off. Lyric wore a sleeveless peach dress, long enough to be respectable but short enough so Tucker's eyes lingered longer than normal. He felt like a slob in jeans and a t-shirt.

Coffee turned into dinner and Tucker covered Lyric's shoulders with his jacket as they walked the two blocks to the restaurant,

"I should have dressed for cooler weather," she said, pulling his jacket tighter around herself.

They split a medium pizza. Sitting across from her in the booth, he couldn't help but be smitten. Conversation flowed effortlessly with her. Not once did he worry about saying or doing the wrong thing. She was beautiful. Her eyes lit up when she laughed; whether it was when Tucker dribbled soda down his shirt or when she told an embarrassing story from high school. Lyric Howard was the type of girl who made you want to write poetry even if you weren't a poet. This was a girl who would be easy to fall for. Tucker couldn't tell her any of this on the first date without it sounding insane, so he kept it to himself.

"I like your necklace," he said.

"Thank you." She plucked the miniature silver cross from her chest and held it up between two fingers. "It was my mother's. She gave it to me when I moved out." Lyric glanced over at Tucker. "You should know that I'm a good Christian girl," she said as she let the necklace fall back into place. There was a twinkle in her eye and a mischievous grin on her face when she said it.

Tucker gave her an exaggerated frown. "Uh-oh, this could be trouble. I'm a bad atheist boy."

Lyric pursed her lips and slowly nodded. She tapped the straw sticking out of her soda, smiled, and said, "Yeah, I'm not sure this is going to work out."

She hopped up while Tucker struggled to find the right key to open the door.

"I didn't see your car, so I thought I'd wait for a bit. I was just about to leave, actually."

"You could have let yourself in," said Tucker. "You still have a key."

"I know. I just thought I should wait for you to get home."

The right key finally made the lock turn. Tucker burped and tasted whiskey as he held the door open for her. He winced, hoping she wouldn't smell it as she glided past him into the apartment.

His two-bedroom apartment was spartan. The walls were mostly bare; his only furniture was an old thrift store couch and a small, round dining room table with two mismatched wooden chairs. On the entertainment center, next to the television, was a framed photo of Tucker and Lyric. Taken last month at a friend's wedding, the happy couple were both wearing sunglasses and smiling at the camera.

"Were you out running?" he asked. Her skin smelled a little of stale sweat but her hair somehow still smelled like flowers.

"Yeah. I don't have to work until later and your place is only a little off my usual route."

Lyric's usual route, he knew, was a five-mile loop around town. It was a run she did at least three times a week without fail. If she was training for a race, that number would increase to five times a week and the distances would get longer.

Tucker could feel her eyes on him. He had to look like hell and smell even worse. Not being home when she got here, when he would normally be getting ready for work, would make her worried and suspicious.

"I went to my dad's last night."

Her eyebrows went up. "Really?"

"Yeah, um, I had a really weird day and I thought he might be able to talk me through it."

Telling her the whole truth might have made her even more suspicious. In the eight months they'd been dating, Tucker never introduced Lyric to his father. There was always some reason, some scheduling conflict that prevented it from happening.

"Uh-huh. Did he? Talk you through it?"

"Not really."

"And you didn't call me? Maybe I could have."

"Honestly, I wasn't sure you wanted to hear from me yet."

"You know that's BS. I called you, left messages, and texted. You never called back."

Tucker sighed. She was right, of course. There were plenty of opportunities the past few days to talk and he'd avoided every single one.

"Now might not be a good time for this. I'm running way behind and I really need to get to work."

Lyric clenched her jaw. "All right. Can I get my sweatshirt then? I left it here last time I stayed over."

Tucker glanced around the nearly empty room. "Yeah. I don't know where it is though."

"Don't put yourself out. I'll find it." She stormed down the hall, leaving Tucker alone.

"Such an asshole," he muttered to himself. He waited until she disappeared into the bedroom at the end of the hall before trudging into the bathroom.

Steam quickly filled the room as he ran the water as hot as he could stand. The scalding water ran down his head and face. Not for the first time, Tucker wondered how he'd let things with Lyric go so wrong, so quickly.

They did see each other again after that first date. Tucker tried to play it cool as long as he could but couldn't resist texting her the next day. Luckily for him, Lyric was just as taken with him as he was with her. They both realized right away they didn't seem to have much in common on the surface. She was a vegetarian and he liked triple-meat toppings on his pizza. She ran for fun, which was something that Tucker couldn't wrap his mind around.

They both liked, but not loved, their jobs. She was a real estate agent, working for a small, local firm. Like Tucker with his job, she couldn't see herself working there until retirement, but it was fine for now.

Lyric had a chunky bulldog named Bertram who might as well have been her child the way she doted on him. Tucker never had a pet growing up and was nervous the first time he met his new girlfriend's furry roommate. His anxiety was soothed as soon as Bertram greeted him with a slobbery kiss right on his mouth.

On Sunday mornings, the two of them would briefly go their separate ways. Lyric invited Tucker to church with her twice before she decided her new boyfriend wasn't going to join her any time soon. It took him a little longer to figure out that she wasn't going to skip her weekly worship to go to breakfast or have a lazy morning in with him.

Despite their differences, they found themselves spending more and more time together as the days turned to weeks.

One early morning, a couple of months after they met at the party, Tucker was letting Lyric sleep in and making them breakfast on an unfamiliar stove at her house. Bacon (for him) and eggs (for both of them) were sizzling on the stove when the alluring smell drew her from the bedroom. Even with no makeup, messy hair, sweatpants, and an oversized t-shirt, she was still way out of his league.

"Hey sleepy-head," said Tucker. "How do you want your eggs? Your choices are limited. There's scrambled or really scrambled." Eggs were one of the few exceptions she made to her vegetarianism.

"Good morning. You're making breakfast? What did I ever do to deserve you?"

"Karma. I'm a reward for something you did in a past life."

She leaned against the back of the couch and watched him. Nothing he was doing required any special talent or skill, but watching him do it, do it for her, made her eyes well up.

"There's, um, something I want to...say to you," she said. There was a tone to her voice, a seriousness that made him take the pans off the stove and turn around.

"What is it?"

"I've never been very good at putting things into words; saying how I feel." She folded her hands together and held them at her chest.

"I know. You have your own way of showing your feelings."

Lyric took a deep breath. "You make me so happy. Happier than I've ever been with anyone." Her normal, confident demeanor was hard to see through her nervousness. "My heart beats faster and I smile every time you walk into the room. It sounds silly, I know, but it's true. I feel so comfortable around you, so safe. I wasn't sure if I should tell you all this or not. Like, what if I ruin this good thing we have going?"

Tucker waited for her, the smell of breakfast slowly permeating the house. She seemed so small and vulnerable standing there with her heart on her sleeve.

"I love you," she finally said for the first time. "Hopelessly, totally, completely. I love you, Tucker Gibsen."

This wasn't the Lyric he knew. This Lyric was putting herself out there in a way she hadn't done before. He'd never seen her fidget like she was now. The expression on her face was a mixture of hope and trepidation.

"Do you remember," he began, his face giving away nothing, "a little while back, when we spent the weekend in Portland with those friends of yours from college? Tina and Michelle?"

She nodded and folded her arms across her stomach.

"After the show, we were hanging out in the hotel bar, just talking. I told a joke, not so much a joke but I said something funny, I really wish I could remember what it was. All three of you laughed but you laughed longer and louder than the others. You looked right at me and that laugh of yours…that's when I knew I was in trouble."

"Trouble? What do you mean trouble?"

Now it was Tucker's turn to take a deep breath. "That's when I realized how much I loved making you laugh. Seeing you looking at me like that - it just hit me right then.

Before that moment, I knew we had something, something special. After that night, I was sure I was in love with you so much it actually hurt a little." He tapped his chest with his finger. "And I knew I wanted to make you laugh like that as much as I possibly could."

Her hair hung over her right eye, hiding it from view. Her left eye misted over and threatened to spill down her cheek. Tucker went to her and took her hand in his.

"Wait a minute," said Lyric. "That trip to Portland was like, a month ago."

Tucker nodded.

"You're saying you knew you loved me a month ago and didn't tell me?"

Tucker nodded again.

"You dick." Lyric punched him in the chest. Tucker, in mock pain, staggered back a step. Now the tear fell down her face, leaving a glistening streak from her eye to her smile. "Why didn't you tell me before now?"

"Because I knew you were too good for me and I didn't want to do anything to rock the boat or screw things up." With one hand, Tucker gently brushed her hair away from her face.

"I want to kiss you so bad right now, but I haven't brushed my teeth," said Lyric, biting her lower lip.

"Me neither."

She buried her face in his chest as he wrapped his arms around her.

The shower was a quick one, but the bathroom was dense with steam by the time he was done. Tucker turned the knob all the way to the left, stifling a gasp as the icy water cascaded over him. His head still hurt, but it was a dull, manageable throb he thought he could deal with. The cold water helped him overcome his alcohol-induced malaise and felt like he could refocus.

"Lyric?" He raised his voice as he toweled off. "I'm sorry, I really am. You're right, I have been putting off talking to you since the other night. I didn't know what to say, you know, to make it better. Not sure there is anything I could say. I guess I was afraid that, if we had that talk, it would be our last talk. And I wanted to avoid that scenario, not avoid you."

Tucker came out into the hall wearing nothing but the towel. "I...I have other...stuff I have to deal with. I promise I'll tell you all about it, if you want to hear it. I should have told you about it before now but it's hard for me to talk about. It's from when I was a kid. Lyric?"

Hair still dripping, he went through the tiny apartment. She wasn't in the bedroom, living room, or kitchen. The place was empty except for him.

On the counter was a note written on stationary from Delbert J. Mahoney, Attorney at Law.

Found my sweatshirt. I didn't want to bother you any more today since you have more important things to do. Let me know when you can make time for me.

It was simply signed *L*. She usually included a *Love You* or a hand-drawn heart. Not this time. At least she hadn't left the key to his apartment behind. That was something.

Tucker let the note fall back to the counter. He plodded down to his bedroom to get dressed for work.

Chapter Seven

Spending mornings at the marina was Marshall Langford's favorite way to pass whatever time he had left. He'd wanted to make it there in time for sunrise but getting where you want to go when you're a little north of ninety-one years old takes longer than you think; even when you wake up early to get a head start.

He left his motorized cart at the open gate and maneuvered his walker off its rack. The ramp had a gradual decline and a textured, non-slip surface. Those two things made it possible for him to still make the journey to his and Janie's spot.

One agonizingly slow step at a time he went. His slip-on shoes shuffled along the ramp past the moored boats. Going too fast meant his walker might get too far out ahead of him, causing him to take a nasty fall. For Marshall, any fall could be disastrous.

"Okay, easy does it." He walked hunched over, a slight sweat forming on his forehead.

Marshall breathed a sigh of relief when he made it off the ramp and onto the flat surface of the dock. Still slow, but more sure-footed, he kept on. His goal was a blur through his bifocals. Even so, he knew he was close. He could have found it if he was completely blind.

Slip nineteen belonged to Mr. and Mrs. Langford. They had paid the rent on it, without fail, for nearly forty years. The last nine years Mr. Langford paid it by himself. It currently sat empty. It was hardly the only empty spot in the marina. Marshall saw several boats were already missing on this fine morning. Bill Jennings, in slip twenty, must be out in his thirty-two-foot Express

Fisherman. He could be out all day if he got a bite but would give up before noon if he hadn't caught anything by then.

He recognized other boats nearby, too. There was the Mallory's thirty-footer, the Dirty Birdie, tied up next to Ronald Longworth's Cabin Cruiser. Those folks were mostly weekend and holiday ocean-goers. They had families and jobs that kept them from enjoying their expensive hobby as much as they might like.

In the water where the Langfords once kept their sailboat was a large, floating rectangle, twenty feet long and ten feet wide. Technically it was a boat - it did float, after all - but there was no style to it. It was like a deck from someone's back yard had been dropped in to the water and tied to the dock. Thin metal sheets made up the deck's three walls and roof. Two chairs, cheap but comfortable lawn chairs, were the only items in the pseudo-boat.

Marshall stepped carefully over the narrow gap and onto the deck. With a grunt, he lowered himself into the chair. It squeaked back at him in response to his weight.

The sailboat had long since been sold. There was no reason to keep it other than nostalgia. He and Janie had spent many happy hours together out on the water. As they got older, they used the boat less and less. When they finally did pull the trigger and sell, they made sure it was to the right buyers. A young couple from down the coast got the boat for a little more than half of what it was worth. He hoped they still used it often. He hoped they were still a couple, even if they were no longer young.

Even without the sailboat, the marina remained a frequent stop for him and Janie. The sunsets they spent together were romantic and soothing to the soul. They kept the slip and had the floating dock built to replace the boat. The Langfords could sit and visit with their marina neighbors, enjoying each other's company along with the calming sway of the current beneath them and the fresh, salty air from across the bay.

"Well now, that's a pretty day." The risen sun was behind him, but its light made the water sparkle. Marshall looked at the empty chair next to him. "Your kind of day: clear sky, nice breeze, and none of those damned seagulls you hated so much."

Janie's dislike of birds was one thing about her he never did understand. It wouldn't be the Oregon coast without the cawing of gulls. That sound was embedded in the ambience of the area.

Marshall settled in. He had no further plans for the day. The dock rocked gently, almost hypnotically, and he knew he would catch at least one nap in the chair before he went back home. The marina fed directly into the bay and the bay fed directly into the ocean. A man in red shorts and a tank top gracefully windsurfed in the distance. Marshall zipped his sweatshirt up and put his hands in the front pouch.

"Good morning, Mr. Langford." A familiar voice called out. The man in a windbreaker and baseball cap waved as he walked by.

"Hello there, Charlie." Marshall waved back. "Are you taking the old girl out today?"

"Yep. Just a quick jaunt, though. Too nice of a day to stay on the shore."

"You enjoy yourself out there. Tell Laurie I said hello."

"Will do." With a tip of his hat, Charlie continued moving down the dock and out of sight.

"That Charlie," Marshall said to the empty chair, "he sure gets his money's worth out of that boat of his. Almost makes you think he doesn't want to go home."

The day went on. People came by; some stayed to chat, while others gave a polite nod and went on their way. One thing Marshall hadn't lost was his gift of gab. He greeted most of the people he spoke to by name.

"Warren, how's that son of yours doing? He's how old now?"

"Hello, Sandra. Good to see you up and around. Those kidney stones can be a real bear. I know from experience."

He laughed at his own jokes with his dry, raspy laugh that usually ended in a coughing fit. On those seldom occasions when he couldn't remember someone's name, Marshall would give them a "Hey there, buddy," or a "What's new, ace?"

He ate banana chips from a zip-loc bag. His doctor said his potassium was low. He dozed intermittently, fading out for a few minutes here or there. One of the perks of getting old, thought Marshall, was nobody thought you odd or drunk if you fell asleep sitting up in the middle of the day.

Snapping out of one of his short naps, Marshall saw movement through his sleepy haze.

Up ahead and to his left, a woman stood out on the bow of a tied-up trawler at the end of the dock. His vision wasn't what it used to be, and she was probably a good hundred feet away, but he could make out her slim figure and long, flowing blonde hair. He's never seen her out here before; he would have remembered. That boat, the thirty-seven-footer she stood on as she stretched her arms above her head, belonged to that one fella, what was his name? Had a pretty wife and two young boys he sometimes brought down to see the big boat he was fixing up.

The name finally popped into his head. He waved at the young lady to get her attention.

"Hello," he called out to her, "isn't that Greg's boat? You a friend of his?" He wasn't sure if she heard him over the wind but she turned his direction as he waved. She didn't wave back; just tilted her head and stared back at him. Marshall couldn't see her eyes, she could have been looking at something or someone else behind him, but he knew, he could feel, she was watching him. He stopped his waving and let his hand drop back to the armrest.

The woman briefly disappeared from view. When he saw her again, she was out of the boat and walking along the dock in his direction. She wore an untucked white t-shirt with the sleeves rolled up past her shoulders and black yoga pants. The shirt was tied in a knot on one side revealing a slim glimpse of her pale, flat stomach. Her blonde hair practically glowed in the sun. The sandals on her feet snapped against the wood with every step.

"Hello," she said to Marshall as she approached his floating refuge. "I saw you waving. Are you okay? Did you need some help?"

Marshall was uncharacteristically tongue-tied for a few moments. This woman was stunning. She was young, how young he wasn't quite sure. Late-teens or early-twenties perhaps. The way she looked at him, though, with those sky-blue eyes, made her look older.

There was a wisdom behind those eyes that made him think of his Janie.

"No, no, not at all, young lady. I was just being friendly, wishing you a good morning. I saw you there on Greg's boat and thought you might be a relative of his or something."

She frowned and for a moment Marshall thought he said something wrong. Maybe she wasn't a relative at all. Maybe Greg's wife didn't have a clue about the pretty girl down at the docks on her husband's boat.

"Oh, well good morning to you too." The frown quickly turned to a radiant smile. "Although, I think it's the afternoon now." She bent down and held her hand out. "I'm Charlotte."

"Marshall, Marshall Langford." He shook her hand, respectfully averting his eyes as the neckline of her shirt fell open, revealing smooth skin and cleavage. His face became hot all of a sudden. "Nice to meet you."

"This is a nice setup you have here," she said, admiring the sparsely furnished area. "All the cost of storing a boat with none of the benefits." Charlotte's smile and body language were pleasant enough. Her words and mocking tone caught him off guard. She was pretty, for sure, but Marshall had known a whole lot of pretty girls with mean hearts.

"Oh, I'm only kidding." She patted his hand. "This must be a special place to you. I mean, to go through all this trouble. Did you build this yourself?"

"No, no. We hired someone to do it. I'm not quite as handy as I used to be."

"I'm sure you're still plenty handy, Mr. Langford." Charlotte gave him a wink and let go of his hand. As she stood, Marshall caught the scent of strawberries wafting off of her. The smell was pleasant and his stomach growled in response. Before he realized what she was doing, Charlotte reached over and took hold of the empty lawn chair. Its metal legs scraped along the wood as she pulled it closer to Marshall's seat.

"You-you can't...that's not-"

"It's okay, Mr. Langford. I can manage. You don't need to pull the chair out for me or anything. You are such a gentleman for worrying." Charlotte sat at his right hand, facing him from only a couple of feet away. Black ink on her forearm in the shape of a star caught his attention. Were those snakes circling around it?

"So, Marshall - can I call you Marshall? - you got my attention. I noticed you. I don't notice people, not really. Generally, I'm aware of their presence but that's about it. Every once in a while, though, for whatever reason, someone catches my eye. You, Marshall, caught my eye."

"Well, I did wave you down."

Charlotte leaned forward, her elbows on her knees. "Yes, you did. But many others have done the same and I've paid them no mind. You, on the other hand, piqued my interest enough to come over and introduce myself."

"I always did have a way with the ladies." His initial protest at her occupying that chair was momentarily forgotten, as was his wariness. This young lady had a pretty smile, smelled nice, and wanted to know more about him.

"I'm sure you do." She looked around again at the three-walled structure where they sat. "What's the story with this, Marshall? You had this built and store it here instead of a boat?"

"There used to be a boat here. The Graceful Lady, we named her. A sailboat. It got to be too much, the upkeep and all, and we couldn't get it out as much as we wanted, so we sold her a few years ago."

"Ah, I see. You liked the waterfront so much you wanted to still spend time here even if you couldn't be on the water anymore."

"I guess I'm a sentimental old fool."

"Maybe." There was a gleam in her eye as she patted his knee. "But now you do it all by yourself. I'm not sure if that's romantic or pathetic."

He brushed his pant leg where her hand had been. "Now you're just being rude, miss. I don't need your approval for anything I do."

"Oh, I'm sorry, Marshall. I didn't mean to offend. You keep mentioning a 'we' even though you're out here alone. There was a Mrs. Langford? Is this her chair I'm sitting in?"

Marshall's mouth tightened and he looked away from her. The windsurfer was out there again. This time he was heading back the way he came.

"Let me make it up to you," said Charlotte, shifting her weight in the chair. "A long time ago, in another life, I used to tell people's fortunes. Reading palms, tarot cards, things like that. I can read you your future, Marshall. No charge."

"Not much left to my future, I'd say," he grumbled.

"You never know." She took his hand and turned it over to see his palm. He flinched in her grasp, but didn't try to pull away. "All these lines on your palm, you see, they tell a story. There's the heart line, the head line, the life line. But this one right here," she touched the middle of his palm with her thumb, "this is the fate line."

"I never went for any of that mumbo-jumbo," said Marshall, watching her out of the corner of his eye.

"Now I'm the one who's offended, Marshall." Charlotte placed her palm on his. "You shouldn't be so closed-minded. This 'mumbo-jumbo' can blow your mind if you let it."

"Sure, right," he scoffed. "You're going to tell me something I don't know? Nah, you'll tell me some fortune cookie prediction like 'good things will come your way' or 'someone you haven't heard from in a long time will call you soon.' New age mumbo-jumbo."

"You are one stubborn old man, Marshall. Nothing about this is new age. Just the opposite, actually." Charlotte traced patterns on his hand. "This, what I can do, is older than either of us." Her eyes met his. "There's really not much to your future. But you probably already knew that. I mean, at your age, you must wonder with each passing season if it's the last time you'll see that season."

"You're telling an old man he might not live much longer. Not very convincing, miss."

"Please, call me Charlotte." She looked back at his hand. "This empty chair belonged to your wife? She's gone now. Has been for years. That must be hard for you."

"Don't you talk about her." He tried to pull his hand away but she held it firmly in place.

"You console yourself. You tell yourself you'll see her again someday, someday soon. I'm sorry, Marshall but you're never going to see your wife again."

"What? What do-"

"You think there's some paradise you get to visit on the other side after you die? A place you can see your loved ones, maybe play with that dog you had when you were a kid? There isn't. After this, there is only darkness."

"To hell with you. Get off my boat."

"Not yet. You need to hear this, Marshall." Charlotte drew her thumb diagonally over his upturned hand. A thin line appeared on his liver-spotted skin as her nail sliced neatly through. Spots of blood seeped to the surface.

Marshall didn't feel any pain. His eyes widened at what she was doing to him, but he couldn't make himself move.

"Do you know why people cry when their loved ones die?" she asked. Mouth open and eyes glazed, Marshall nodded and stared. "No, you think you know. You think it's because they miss their friends, their family, the person they love most in the whole world. They won't be able to see them again, to hug them or kiss them or make love to them, until they join them again in the afterlife. How long were you married?"

"Sixty-three years and one month," he stammered.

"That's a long time. You want to see her again," Charlotte used both of her hands to spread the blood until it covered his palm. "But you won't. You see, the reason people get so upset when others die is because, deep down, they know there is nothing after this. Nothing at all. They don't cry when a parent or friend moves away because they know they're still around, even if they're thousands of miles away. But when someone dies, they know they're gone forever. Gone for good. Everything they ever were, all of their thoughts or feelings, hopes and dreams, winked out of existence the moment their heart stopped beating."

"You don't know that, you can't." His voice caught in his throat. Marshall could feel his heart breaking. They were only words, he tried to tell himself, but they cut him to his core. It was like he was losing her all over again.

"I do, though. Deep down, you know it too."

"Why are you doing this?"

Charlotte sat up straight and wiped her hands on her leg, leaving a faint streak of crimson in its wake. "Why? Because I noticed you. Our paths crossed. Out of all the possibilities and probabilities in this big old world, you and I ended up here at the same time and I noticed you."

Marshall shook his head and tried to speak. All he could muster was an inarticulate growl.

"You still don't understand, Marshall? It's hard to explain. It's more of an idea, a sensation. Picture an eclipse. You can see it, be affected by it, even if you're hundreds of miles away from it as the day turns darker. But those in the right place at the right time are affected the most. That's the path of totality, that line where the moon's shadow completely blocks the sun. The place where it's darkest."

Charlotte moved from her seat and got down on both knees in front of Marshall. He gripped the metal arm rests tight enough to turn his knuckles white.

"You can't control where the shadow falls, Marshall. That was decided ages ago. When it does fall, are you one of the lucky ones so far away it barely registers in your neat, orderly life? Or are you in that path of totality where nothing and no one is safe?"

He tried to stand but only managed to rock forward a few inches. After all the years, his body had finally betrayed him. Marshall Langford could only sit impotently and listen to Charlotte.

"This world is a cruel and arbitrary place, Marshall...."

The sun was setting by the time Chris Mathers made it to the marina. Hopefully, his wallet really was on the boat. It was the only place he hadn't looked, and he had taken her out yesterday. Chris' daughter, Annie, skipped along next to him as they made their way down the ramp.

"Look, Dad. Mr. Langford is here," she whispered. Annie complained when he told her she had to come with him. He wasn't sure if he was comfortable leaving a nine year old home alone, even if it was only for a few minutes. But she was always happy to see Mr. Langford. It probably had something to do with the fact that the old man had a seemingly endless supply of lollipops on him and never hesitated to give one to a particular little girl.

"Looks like it," said Chris. "You can say hello but we gotta be quick."

Annie skipped ahead and over to slip nineteen. "Hi, Mr. Langford." She gave him an exuberant wave. The old guy must be sleeping, Chris thought, that's why he's here so late.

Marshall Langford was slumped down in his usual chair; his chin resting on his chest.

"Annie, don't bother him if he's…" As he got closer, Chris could tell something was wrong. Mr. Langford's unblinking eyes stared straight down, focused on nothing. "Annie, go back to the truck. Now."

"Dad, he's bleeding." She pointed to his hand.

"Now."

Annie ran back down the dock and up the ramp. Chris approached the old man slowly.

Yes, he was bleeding from his hand. It wasn't bad, but the arm of the chair was covered in blood. He must have cut it on the metal, he thought. He wasn't moving at all. His chest remained still instead of rising and falling with each breath. He reached out to feel Mr. Langford's neck for a pulse like he'd seen on TV. Chris jerked his hand back as soon as he touched the old man. There was no need to check for a pulse, he was already cold to the touch.

"Aw, jeez," he said, pulling his phone out of his pocket and dialing 911. How long had he been sitting there like this? The poor guy must've croaked right here while he was taking in one last view of the ocean, he thought. At least it had been peaceful.

Behind Chris Mathers, further down the dock, there was the soft glow of a single light coming from behind a closed curtain inside the same trawler where Marshall Langford had first laid eyes on the pretty blonde girl, just a few hours before. By the time the EMT's got to the marina, all of the attention was on the recently departed. Nobody noticed as the light was extinguished, leaving that end of the marina in darkness.

Chapter Eight

Cheryl was on the phone when Tucker arrived at the office. He hurried past, avoiding the lecture but not the disapproving scowl as she not-so-subtly checked her watch and shook her head. Damn it, he thought, I even forgot to bring the coffee I promised her.

Further down the hall, Donnie exited the bathroom across from their shared office. "Oh, you're here." He pointed a rolled-up magazine at Tucker. "If I'd known you were coming in, I wouldn't have lit a match in there."

"Thanks. You're a pal." Tucker sank into his chair. The McGarrett file rested on his desk right where he left it.

"You look like shit, man. You sick or something?"

"I'll be fine," said Tucker, picking up the file. "Just caught a bit of what's going around."

"Dude, you can call in sick you know. Better than spreading it to the rest of us."

"Don't worry, princess, I'm not contagious."

Donnie shrugged and took his place at his computer monitor. Tucker leafed through the folder, unsure of what he was looking for. Reacquainting himself with the background of the case while fighting the urge to drop everything and rush over to the jail took all of his impaired concentration. Advil took the edge off his headache, but he still hadn't made the time to properly caffeinate yet. Prior experience told him a large coffee would reduce the pounding in his head to a more bearable level.

According to the case file, Greg McGarrett, seemingly out of nowhere, started watching, trading, and saving pornographic images of young children on his own personal laptop without anyone having a clue about his deviant behavior. It was a classic case of "No way Greg would do something like that," or "There must be some mistake. Greg? Not possible." When confronted with the harsh facts, as Tucker was doing for himself right now, those character references became muted.

The guy was guilty as hell; there was no way around it. Even so, Tucker truly believed the man deserved a proper defense in court. Innocent until proven guilty meant something to him but he had to admit the evidence was overwhelming. Like he told McGarrett in the interview room, the vast library of photos and videos found on that computer were damning. Add to that the webcam stills, captured at the same time an online photo swap was conducted, clearly show the clean-shaven face of the accused.

I'm not trying to prove his innocence, Tucker reminded himself. The end result of the case was irrelevant. Tucker's interest went beyond that.

This world is a cruel and arbitrary place

He heard the front door open and Cheryl greeting the visitor down the hall, but his eyes never left the papers in front of him. The quick, muffled conversation barely registered until he heard his own name spoken.

"...Tucker Gibsen." It was Cheryl. "I know he was working on that. Maybe he could help you."

He'd worked with Cheryl long enough to know what came next. She would raise her voice slightly and summon him from his comfortable chair. There would be a small amount of satisfaction in her voice; payback for being late and hung over.

Instead of waiting for the inevitable, Tucker got up and poked his head out into the hall. "Did I hear my name?" He tried to sound pleasant and professional.

The two women, Cheryl and the newcomer, turned to him. "Yes, Tucker," said Cheryl. "This young lady was hoping to get some more information on one of our clients, Greg McGarrett."

"Oh," said Tucker. "What-"

"Hi, I'm Donnie. How can I help you?" Tucker's office-mate elbowed past him and hustled down the hall with his hand held out. "And you are?"

"Rebekah." The visitor took Donnie's hand but her eyes barely even flickered his direction. She continued to stare at Tucker, puzzled, bright green eyes seemingly looking right through him.

Her hair, a dark shade of red, looked windblown, but not messy. A long-sleeved gray sweater was unbuttoned, revealing a V-neck white t-shirt beneath. She wore faded blue jeans with a hole in one knee. Her outfit made Tucker feel overdressed in his own workplace. A cloth tote bag hung across her body, the strap placed between and accentuating the shape of her breasts. Even with his co-worker's back to him, Tucker was positive Donnie was staring directly at the woman's chest.

"I need to speak with someone regarding Mr. McGarrett," said Rebekah.

"Of course," said Donnie. "Are you a member of the family?"

"I'm a friend of the family." Disdain, directed at Donnie, was oozing from her.

"Well then, if you follow me, we have a conference room where we can speak in private."

Rebekah didn't make a move to follow him. She nodded at Tucker. "Donnie, is it? I think I would prefer to speak with him."

Donnie snickered and flashed a smile. "Tucker? Sure, he could help you, but it would be my pleasure to address any concerns you have about your friend's case."

"I should speak with him," she repeated. Under normal circumstances the crestfallen look on Donnie's face would have made Tucker laugh. He tried so hard to be a womanizer; his usual tactic of casting a wide net and seeing what he could catch worked infrequently.

Most women saw right through his pseudo-slick exterior directly to the heart of a douchebag. Seeing it in person was a delight.

But this wasn't under normal circumstances. The woman, Rebekah with-no-last-name, looked at him with a mixture of intensity and fascination that made him uncomfortable.

The fact she was asking about the man who had quickly, but hopefully temporarily, become the focal point of his life only added to his unease.

The three of them waited for Tucker's response. "Right this way, ma'am," he managed to spit out. Tucker gestured and led her to the room directly across the hall from his workspace. This time, Rebekah followed close behind.

The small conference room, as it was referred to by the employees of Delbert J. Mahoney, was simple. A circular table rested at the center on the smooth wood floor. Three chairs surrounded the table and a potted plant sat on a shelf in one corner.

Rebekah took the chair furthest away and facing the hallway. Tucker briefly thought about leaving the door open but decided against it. He got the feeling this woman wanted privacy. She wouldn't speak freely in front of the other two.

Tucker sat down facing her, resting his hand protectively on the closed file and the stack of documents within. The boss took private meetings from important clients upstairs in his cavernous office. Donnie was normally the one who fielded questions and concerns from the less important clients or drop-ins like Rebekah. Not only was he good at pressing the flesh and putting people at ease with an off-color joke or feigned interest, he enjoyed doing it. Tucker, on the other hand, preferred to be left to his paperwork.

"Mr. Gibsen, right?" she said.

"Yes, that's me. Um, you said something about your friend's case. How exactly can I help you?"

She sat with her hands in her lap. "I know this is an odd request, but I was hoping you could help me see Mr. McGarrett. I need to speak with him as soon as possible."

"I'm not sure I understand. You mean like, visiting him? There are scheduled times you can go in and-"

"Yes, there are. But you need to be on a pre-approved list and even then, you have to wait until the right night of the week. I can't wait that long and I'm not on his list."

"Okay, well that's an easy fix. When he calls you just tell him to add you. In the meantime, I can see about passing along a message for him."

She shook her head. "That won't work. He doesn't have my phone number. To tell you the truth, he doesn't know my name either."

"Now I'm really confused. Out there you said you were a family friend."

"I am. Just not a friend they've met before."

This is a waste of time, thought Tucker. Whether she was a private investigator, reporter, wannabe-psychic, or a crazy lady off the street, it was clear she didn't have any official business here.

"I'm sorry, Rebekah but I'm very busy today. There's no way I can get you in to see Mr. McGarrett, so if there's nothing else I can help you with, I'll make sure Cheryl can see you out." Tucker stood and stepped away from the table, reaching for the door. He paused when he didn't hear her following him. Turning back to her, he could see she hadn't taken the hint. Rebekah still sat at the table. Her hands were folded neatly in front of her face. Her eyes peered at him over her fingers without expression.

"Greg McGarrett is innocent," she said. "He did not commit the crimes he is accused of. I am sure of it. I have to see him and talk to him in person. I have reason to believe he can help lead me to the one who set all of this in motion."

She was sure of herself. Her voice never wavered and her green eyes never left his.

"Please sit down, Mr. Gibsen."

A million questions ran through Tucker's mind as he struggled to make sense of what she'd just told him.

He sat back down. Rebekah reached across, took his hand in hers, and said, "I understand you're probably having a hard time believing me. Maybe you think I'm insane or some kind of ambulance chaser. I'm neither. Mr. McGarrett is a victim and I need your help or there will be more."

Rebekah's hands were warm but clammy, like she was nervous. Her body language, though, was all confidence. Leaning forward, jaw set, Tucker could feel the intensity coming off of her.

He took a deep breath. "Tell me what you know," he relented, "and I'll see what I can do." Vague assurance without promising anything. It was one of his tried and true strategies when dealing with difficult clients. He had to admit, this woman unnerved him. He wished he had gone straight to the jail instead of coming into work.

She sat up straight and looked over his shoulder at the wall behind him as if considering his offer. "No, that won't work. I've come this far and I'm so close I can feel it. But I need to see him myself." Her hands remained wrapped around his, her grip getting tighter with every passing second.

"If you have evidence that can aid in his defense then we are, without a doubt, the best people to talk to. It's our job to give him the best possible defense against these charges. You're convinced he's innocent? Then there has to be some other explanation for the mountains of evidence against him."

Tucker still didn't think she had any miraculous information that would save their client.

Something brought her here, though, exactly when this particular case was becoming the most maddening thing in his life. He couldn't bring himself to ignore that, even if she might be insane.

As he spoke, Rebekah's lips moved rapidly, murmuring words Tucker couldn't make out. "Rebekah? Are you all right?"

She bowed her head but didn't answer. Was she praying? This was just what he needed right now; some religious nut interjecting herself into something she knew nothing about.

He lowered his head out of respect but kept his eyes open. Hopefully she would be done soon and could he guide her gently out of the office.

Tucker's stomach growled. In the near silence of the conference room the low rumble drowned out Rebekah's whispers. He fought back against a wave of nausea and regretted his actions of the night before. The room started spinning. Shit, he thought, maybe I'm not as sober as I hoped. Tucker tried to calculate how much time had passed since his last drink but he kept losing focus. Surely it had been long enough to get it all out of his system. He squeezed his eyes shut and tried to will away the discomfort. When he opened them, he saw Rebekah regarding him from her chair. Her hands rested lightly on his.

"Mr. Gibsen, are you feeling all right?" she asked. Her words came out deep and slurred, like she was speaking through a narrow tube. Tucker had to concentrate to understand her.

"Please, call me Tucker." His reply took more effort than it should have. He braced himself against the table to keep from falling over.

"You don't look so good. Are you sick?" she said. Leaning forward, she whispered, "Are you drunk?"

Tucker slowly shook his head. "No," is what he said. Maybe, is what he thought.

"Do you need some air? We can step outside and continue our conversation there." He swallowed and nodded. That did sound like a good idea.

Rebekah got up and opened the conference room door. Tucker obediently followed, stumbling a little but managing to keep up as they went down the hall, past Cheryl's desk, and out the front door without a word. Neither of them so much as glanced in Cheryl's direction before the door closed behind them.

"Great," said Cheryl as the phone chirped at her, "now I have one more person to worry about."

Chapter Nine

Tucker handed his car keys over when she asked for them. He was in no shape to drive.

"Where are we going?" he asked, eyes glazed over.

"We're going to the jail, remember? To visit a client."

"Oh, yeah. We need to ask him how he knows what King said to me."

Rebekah didn't pay any mind to his words. The intoxicating effects would wear off soon. How soon varied from person to person, but she hadn't had to hit him with very much. Men in general were easily influenced, even without metaphysical aids. Younger men, like Mr. Gibsen, were even more susceptible to her charms.

She had to move the driver's seat back slightly. Rebekah was taller than Tucker by an inch or so and the car was smaller than she was used to. He flopped into the passenger seat next to her and struggled to manipulate the seat belt into place.

"What's the quickest way to the jail, Tucker?" Navigating the unfamiliar roads from behind the wheel of a car was entirely different than from hundreds of feet in the air.

He pointed out the window. "That way."

The drive didn't take long. Even with some wrong turns along the way, they pulled into the jail parking lot within ten minutes. Next to her, Tucker was shaking his head in short, rapid motions.

"Your head should clear up in just a minute," Rebekah said, placing a reassuring hand on his leg. Tucker looked at her and grinned, his eyes still unfocused.

Bringing someone else into this wasn't her original plan. Plans change, though, and she had to improvise. She had to get in the jail physically, not just her projection, and question the man she saw in the cell in a way only she could. Finding his lawyer's name and address was simple enough. A quick internet search told her he had a small office in town. His photo on the website showed him behind a desk with an open book in front of him. He was looking directly into the camera with an expression that was meant to be cool and calculating, but instead was more like an old man doing his best to look like Clint Eastwood in his prime. Behind those eyes, Rebekah could see the weakness and cowardice he tried so hard to hide.

That old man was her first choice. Convincing him to take her to see his client would have been easy and the added clout from being with an experienced, well-known attorney would smooth the way.

But he wasn't at work today.

The other two younger men were her remaining options. One of them, she couldn't remember his name now, was clearly more eager to help her for his own libidinous reasons but it was Tucker who claimed her attention the moment she saw him.

"Tucker? I need you to pay attention to what I'm saying."

"What was your name again?" His words were already clearer than when they left the office. Still slurred, but getting there.

"I'm Rebekah." He repeated her name softly to himself, committing it to memory. "Do you remember what we talked about? You said you'd help me get in to see your client. We were going to help him together. How can we do that?"

His eyes narrowed and he took a deep breath. "That shouldn't be too hard. We would go to the reception desk, I know most of them who work up front, and check in. If they ask, we can tell them you're a new assistant or," he paused, taking a look at her casual attire, "maybe an intern or something. You do look older than a normal college student though. You're what, thirty? Thirty-two?"

Rebekah smiled back at him, pleased with how effectively enthralled he was. She expected no less, of course. The spell was a simple one. "Older than that, Tucker."

"Really? Well, you look good."

"You're so sweet." She touched her fingertips to his cheek. The other effect of the spell was unflinching honesty, at least when speaking to her. "What happens if they don't believe us? If they ask for some sort of documentation?"

"They probably won't. Mr. Mahoney is the attorney of record on McGarrett's case. I'm his representative." He had to slowly enunciate the last word to get it out correctly. "I've been in to see him before so they won't even need to confirm any of that. It's just a matter of being convincing enough to get you in with me."

"What do I need to do?"

"Not much. They might ask for ID. Other than that, just let me do most of the talking. Maybe you could play at being the awkward new employee. I know these people. They like me."

Rebekah would have liked more assurance than that, but this plan was the best they had.

Necessity combined with time constraints made for taking calculated risks. Charlotte was here, not at the jail but somewhere nearby, but she wouldn't be for much longer.

Rebekah pushed the doubt out of her mind; the thoughts that crept in telling her she was already too late, that Charlotte didn't stick around this time, that she was a thousand miles away and yet another opportunity had slipped through her fingers.

This man next to her in the passenger seat looked too young to have a job with this much responsibility. She was sure he was older than she thought; her old eyes saw twenty-somethings as younger and younger with each passing year.

Even with his disheveled appearance, wrinkled clothes and barely combed hair, he radiated a vitality she possessed once upon a time but now only in her memories.

But that was not why she chose him.

Walking into the lawyer's office, she didn't know what she'd find. The woman she encountered first had a practiced pleasantness to her with a toughness below the surface.

The purple haze Rebekah saw surrounding certain citizens of the town glowed softly around the receptionist. It was faint, but it was there. This woman had been affected, either only slightly or long ago, by Charlotte's machinations.

The man who approached her, reeking of too much cologne and blatantly staring at her breasts, lacked any aura whatsoever. Still, Rebekah considered using him to get her into the jail. The lech could have been manipulated easily even without her special coaxing.

Then, Tucker stepped out into the hallway.

The purple glow surrounding him was ample, dark, and shimmering. Only the man she spied upon in the jail cell and his wife outside their house shone brighter. Somehow, this man had been, or soon would be, changed forever by powers beyond his understanding.

Rebekah believed in signs and omens. She was cautiously skeptical about them, not wanting to mistakenly see something that wasn't there, but the presence of such a man who was in a position to help her, and had a common enemy with was too powerful to ignore.

The fact that he was most likely unaware that such an enemy existed mattered not. This was kismet. Rebekah reminded herself kismet had a mind of its own and did not always smile upon her.

Tucker's sobering process was progressing nicely. While the inebriation wore off quickly, the suggestibility lasted longer. It wasn't really mind control. She couldn't make him jump off a cliff or choke his own mother or anything drastic like that. What she could do was gently nudge him in the right direction, make him do the things she needed him to do when he wouldn't normally do them.

The application of the charm was easy. Saliva, gained by surreptitiously licking her hands when Tucker turned away for a moment in the conference room, combined with skin-to-skin contact and a few words of power meant that his will was malleable in her hands for the next few hours.

"How are you feeling, Tucker?" She needed him to not appear drunk when they went in. That could complicate things.

"Feeling right as rain." He demonstrated by closing his eyes and touching his index finger to the tip of his nose. "See? Totally fine."

"I guess it's time then. Let's do this."

The building was ugly. Rebekah supposed it wasn't designed to be attractive to the eye.

It exuded practicality and strength. A squat, sturdy rectangle, four stories high, the county jail stood out like a sore thumb among the more aesthetically pleasing houses and businesses nearby. Reddish-brown brick made up most of the imposing walls. Windows crossed with metal bars lined each floor facing the parking lot, staring at them as they walked up the front steps. Rebekah could see a few faces staring out between the bars.

Whether or not they were looking at her, she couldn't tell.

She demurely let Tucker go ahead of her through the doors. The large reception desk, currently staffed by a young man and an older woman, blocked their way like a raised drawbridge. Rebekah had expected uniformed law enforcement to be their first encounter in the building. She was surprised to see that the pair at the front desk wore polo shirts and khakis.

The person at the computer, a skinny, baby-faced man with horn-rimmed glasses, greeted Rebekah and Tucker as they came through the heavy glass doors. His body language, stiff and gawky, and the thick open manuals in front of him marked him as a trainee. The woman sitting behind him damaged Rebekah's hope that an inept new employee might smooth their way. Her gray hair and keen gaze caused a glimmer of doubt to flare in her mind.

Looking past the unfamiliar face closest to him, Tucker waved. "Hi, Jenny. You training today?"

"Yeah," said the woman behind the desk. "Lucky me, teaching the next generation of disgruntled county employees."

"At least you can teach them the right way to do things. I bet you're a great teacher."

"Stop, Tucker. You're making me blush," Jenny said flatly. "Who's this you have with you?"

"Oh, you haven't met Rebekah? Jenny, this is our new office assistant in training, Rebekah. Rebekah, this is Jenny. She's the most helpful and knowledgeable person in this whole place."

Rebekah gave a subdued wave. Jenny nodded and grunted, "Mm-hm."

Tucker feigned a chuckle and ignored Jenny's frown. "Anyway, she's shadowing me today, learning how the whole process works. From arraignment to acquittal."

"Is she going in with you or did you just bring her by to say hello?" The unasked question behind the severe tone of voice almost made Rebekah wince. There was no Plan B so she started going down her list of options if this woman proved stubborn. There weren't many.

Tucker cleared his throat. "I was going to bring her in with me, see a defendant or two. She tagged along with Donnie the other day but he doesn't always set the best example." Jenny nodded in agreement. "So, I, the consummate professional, will be the one to show her how it's supposed to be done."

The lie would be an easy one to disprove. Cameras were everywhere and the log would confirm Rebekah had never physically set foot in the building before today. But that was a problem for tomorrow. Right now, Tucker was just trying to get them past this roadblock.

The trainee looked at the trainer, waiting for the word. Jenny gave a tiny nod. "Go ahead, let them in."

"Okay," he said, fingers resting on the keyboard, "who are you here to see?"

"We'll start with Greg McGarrett," said Tucker, trying not to let his relief show. "There's a few more, but I'm not sure how many we'll have time for."

Jenny and the trainee looked stunned, smiles disappearing from their faces. Perplexed frowns took their place, making Rebekah wonder what had gone wrong when everything seemed to be working so well.

"Is there a problem?" Tucker noticed the change in atmosphere as well.

"Hold on one second." Jenny picked up the phone and turned away from them. She spoke too softly for either of them to hear her.

Tucker leaned in and whispered, "We're busted. Maybe we should get out of here."

No, Rebekah thought. We stay. Something was definitely amiss, he was right about that, and her first impulse was to run, but the two of them had done nothing illegal. At worst, they'd been caught trying to circumvent the jail's policies on visitors and security clearance. If they were busted like Tucker said, they would be told to leave, perhaps even escorted out the doors. Tucker's employer would be contacted, and he would have a lot of explaining to do, but that wasn't her problem. No, they wouldn't be detained. There was no reason to run.

Jenny hung up the phone and turned back towards Tucker. "Sergeant Acosta wants to talk to you. She'll be right out. Can you hang out for a bit?"

"I don't know, Jenny. We're kind of in a hurry." Tucker rubbed the back of his sweaty neck.

"It'll just be a minute." Jenny turned her attention back to her trainee.

"Tucker, calm down," said Rebekah. She tugged at his sleeve. "There's nothing to worry about."

"If you say so. I don't feel so good." His skin was pale and he swayed back and forth slightly.

Almost three minutes passed by the time Sergeant Acosta emerged from the door behind the reception desk. "Hello," she said, shaking Tucker's hand and nodding at Rebekah. "You're McGarrett's lawyer?"

"Legal assistant to his attorney," corrected Tucker.

"I see." She hesitated a moment, weighing her next words. "My apologies, we thought notifications had been made, but apparently your office was missed. Mr. McGarrett was found in his cell early this morning. He tied his sheet around his neck and it appears he hanged himself. The deputies found him at breakfast. By then it was too late."

"No," Rebekah gasped.

"How does something..." Tucker began to say. He doubled over and ran for the nearby garbage can. Two steps were all he could manage before his stomach emptied all over the tiled floor. Vomit poured through his fingers and splattered against his shoes as he tried to cover his mouth.

"Sorry," he said. "Sorry, I didn't make it in time."

Chapter Ten

For the second time that day, Tucker stood in a hot shower. This one had cracks in the shower head and mildew collecting around the drain. The water ran down his face and steam surrounded him. Ever so slowly, he felt his wits returning. He replayed the events of the past couple of hours in his mind. He remembered almost everything very clearly; from waking up at his dad's house to the embarrassing episode at the jail. What he couldn't recall was why he went along with this woman at the expense of his better judgment. The lies he told at the jail would surely come back to bite him in the ass with his boss. Mr. Mahoney would demand an explanation and he wouldn't have one. Not one worth a damn, anyway.

Then, there was the disappointment. Greg McGarrett was dead; reportedly from suicide in the lonely darkness of his jail cell. The fact he did so shouldn't have been surprising to Tucker. He was looking at many years in prison; hard years of protective custody, constantly having to watch your back, and having the label of sex offender attached to your name for the rest of your life would be enough to cause the emotionally strongest of people to at least consider the permanent way out. Tucker thought back to his last words to his client. Not what McGarrett said to him that sent him on this insane quest, but what he said to the accused. Those harsh words could never be taken back and Tucker wondered if he had said something different, something compassionate or empathetic, if that would have made a difference. Now he would never know, just like he would never know the connection, if there was one, between this man and the man he met on the boat when he was a boy.

The woman with the red hair, though. She said he was innocent. She was sure of it.

Tucker could try to dismiss her as crazy, but she didn't talk or act like any of the crazies he'd dealt with before. Clear-eyed and confident, Rebekah's belief in her righteous cause was contagious. Contagious enough to sweep Tucker along with her.

"There will be an official investigation, of course." That's what the jail sergeant told them while Tucker sat on a bench with his head between his knees, the puddle of vomit discoloring the floor a few feet away. "Detectives from the state police will look into all aspects. We will make the final report available to your office."

Rebekah had taken charge by then, asking pointed questions at every opportunity. How do you know it was suicide? Who was the last person to see him? When? What did he do last evening? Sergeant Acosta couldn't answer most of her questions. She deflected as best she could, wary of misspeaking and giving ammunition for a possible wrongful death lawsuit.

The body was transported to the hospital. It would be there until the medical examiner's office completed their portion of the investigation. "This is common practice," she assured Rebekah. Any kind of in-custody, unexpected death was handled with the utmost transparency and care. In probably two to three days the deceased would be moved to a proper funeral home where the next-of-kin would arrange the appropriate services.

"Which hospital?" asked Rebekah.

"Hart Memorial. It's the only one in town."

"Right, of course." With that, she took Tucker by the arm and they were gone.

Tucker shut off the water and grabbed the ratty towel off of the bathroom counter. His dress shirt, stained with remnants of partially digested food, lay next to it. He couldn't wear that again without washing it five or six times.

The plain white undershirt remained unsoiled so Tucker put that back on along with his slacks. He couldn't see his shoes or socks in the small bathroom. This is quite the outfit, he thought as he looked himself over in the mirror.

The thin door with the broken lock opened into the motel room. Sunlight snuck through a narrow opening in the curtains on the far wall. The lights were off and the two queen beds were neatly made and empty. Rebekah sat at the tiny table next to the window. Her hair was tied back. On the table in front of her were two unlit candles, one black, one red, and an ice bucket half filled with water. Smoke was rising from the wicks in thin trails as if they'd just been blown out.

"Hey, are you feeling better?"

"Yeah, the shower really helped. Thanks. It was really nice of you to let me use your bathroom."

"Well, you were in bad shape. I didn't know where you lived and I thought you wouldn't want to go back to your office looking, or smelling, like that."

"You are right about that. I thank you again for your discretion," said Tucker. He was pretty out of it when they left the jail and got back into his car. Was he so sick he couldn't even get back home? "You helped me dodge a bullet there."

"I'm not sure if I helped as much as you think."

That much was true. He would still have a lot of explaining to do. Bringing him here instead of work might put it off, but not forever. Word of what happened at the jail would get back to Mr. Mahoney, if it hadn't already.

Tucker scratched his head. "Rebekah?" he said after a brief struggle to remember her name. "What, uh, what's going on? Why are you so involved in this case, wanting to get in to see him, if the family doesn't know you? It doesn't make any sense."

"It makes as much sense as anything else, Tucker."

"That's not an answer." Her green-eyed gaze made him feel naked, like she could see right through him. Standing there in this cheap motel room with peeling wallpaper, bare-footed on worn carpet, he matched her expression of determination. "Look, I could lose my job, I probably will lose my job, for helping you out. I'm not blaming you, I'm a big boy and I make my own decisions, but I did put myself out there for you. I think I'm entitled to some explanation."

Rebekah leaned back in her chair. "What does it matter anymore? The man's dead. Your part is over."

"It matters to me. This has been the weirdest couple of days of my life and your timing is extremely suspicious."

That got her attention. "Weirdest how?"

Tucker didn't know where to start. There was too much to say. Plus, he wasn't sure how much he should say to her anyway. He didn't know this woman. Why she might be interested in him or this case was still a mystery.

"Okay," Rebekah said, "let's back up a second. Let me ask you something else. Do you know a woman, blonde hair, blue eyes, thin, with a tattoo on her left arm?" She pointed to in the inside of her own forearm. "Looks early twenties, perhaps younger. Somebody maybe you've met recently, in the last month or so?"

He thought about it, mentally searching for anyone who might fit that description. "No, doesn't ring a bell. Could be someone I saw in passing, like a barista or something."

"You would remember her."

"Why do you ask? Who is she?"

"I've been looking for her for a very long time. I followed her here. She's the one who set up Greg McGarrett. She's responsible for his death. I have reason to believe you have been in contact with her or soon will be." She leaned forward, placing her clenched fist on the table. "I'm telling you this because I need you to understand how important it is that I find her. I need you to tell me if you've seen this woman. Anything you know, no matter how trivial it may seem, could be the break I need now that he's dead."

"No, okay? I've never met anyone like that. Why do you think I have?"

Rebekah's shoulders sagged, defeated. "I know she's still here. Somewhere in the city or the outskirts. She hasn't moved on yet, but she will soon."

"You didn't answer my question," Tucker said. "How is she responsible for his charges or his death? Do you think it wasn't suicide?" The possibility seemed unrealistic. The cells in the jail only held one inmate at a time.

"No, at least, I don't think so. If it was suicide, she pushed him to it. With her it's hard to be sure."

Tucker, standing there in a stranger's motel room, was suddenly struck by a familiar sensation. This dance he was doing with this woman took him back to a night he spent in Reno a few years back. Sitting at a poker table in the wee hours after midnight in a casino with framed black-and-white photos of cowboys on the walls, he was still playing long after his friends had moved on to the next casino and the next party.

Poker had never been Tucker's game of choice. On those rare occasions he did gamble, he stuck to blackjack or slots. That night was different. A streak of luck left him with a stack of chips like he'd never seen. Grumbling, mostly good-natured, came at him from all sides of the oval table as he caught card after card. One man in particular stood out to Tucker.

He wore a navy-blue windbreaker and glasses with thick lenses that sat half way down the bridge of his nose. Every hand, the man squinted down his nose at Tucker like he was trying to read his mind. The cat-and-mouse game was both exhausting and exhilarating at the same time.

That's what this felt like. The cheap motel room replaced the smoky poker table, but people's intentions were the same. Each of them wanted to know what was in the other's hand. Rebekah had shown a little of hers but not enough for him to get a good read.

"I don't know who this 'she' is you're talking about," said Tucker. "You needed my help and I gave it. Now you're asking questions I don't have the answers for."

This wasn't a poker game. Whatever this was, folding was not an option and sharing information didn't mean you busted out. Maybe there was a way they could both win.

"Time-out for a sec," said Tucker. "Let's start over. You keep being all cryptic and mysterious, which I get. You don't know me and you don't trust me." He sat down on the side of one of the queen beds, facing Rebekah, with the other bed between them. "But here I am and here you are in the same place searching for answers to different questions. I have my own reasons I needed to go see him today. Reasons important enough it couldn't even wait another day. I figure I have nothing to lose by showing you my hand."

He told her. Beginning with the day he went to the beach to dig for clams with his father, he told her the whole story. The derelict boat, seemingly deserted but with one nearly-dead sailor left on board, was the hardest part to relive. Years of repression made it difficult to dredge up the detail from the depths of his memory. He left out the gray seagull with bloody flesh hanging from its beak. The image in his mind was enough to make him wince and wish it away.

Wishing didn't work.

The conversation with Ray King in the belly of the boat, the ghoulish, almost poetic verse of the mass murderer, that unique feeling of knowing he was going to die before he could escape, the way nobody, not even his parents apparently, believed him when he told them what happened, it all came pouring out of him in one cathartic monologue. Rebekah didn't interrupt a single time. She sat, engrossed in the tale, not giving away an ounce of emotion.

"Then, when I saw him, spoke with him yesterday, and he said those same words to me, I had to know more." Tucker exhaled dramatically. "And they were the same words Ray King said to me on the boat when I was a kid. I'm sure of it."

Rebekah finally spoke. "But now he's dead."

"Yes, and now I may never know."

She stood and paced the width of the room, both of her hands slipping into her back pockets. Tucker waited. In the mirror on the wall, her reflection looked to him.

"Her name is Charlotte," said Rebekah. "Those are her words, burned into her victim's minds like a cattle brand. It doesn't happen like that every time, but they all take some piece of her with them, even if they don't realize it. She's the one I was asking you about; the one I've been searching for. Everywhere she goes, she leaves nothing but tragedy and death."

"Like framing people for crimes they didn't commit?"

"Like that, yes. That's one of her ploys."

"How does she do that? In either case, King or McGarrett, there's no way to fake that. I was there, I saw the knife in hand. And McGarrett's own laptop did him in. It's not like she planted a bloody glove and made an anonymous phone call." Knowing the case file as well as he did, it was practically inconceivable someone could have put those photos and videos on his personal computer without him knowing. Tucker was choosing his words carefully though. Rebekah was slowly opening up and he didn't want her to clam up.

"McGarrett is innocent, that much I know. What happened with you on the boat is an entirely different matter. She finds a way, usually a different way every time. Charlotte is very capable of coercing a person to do horrible things. It's part of the thrill for her. Even if it was Ray King's hand that killed those men, he wasn't responsible."

"I don't understand. She pushes one man to kill his own friends then, seventeen years later, she hacks into a random computer and puts criminally pornographic pics on it? Not to mention webcam photos, forum posts, all with time stamps stretching over weeks, sometimes months? How?"

"There are other ways to accomplish her goals. These two men are hardly her only victims. I have followed this woman all across the country. I've seen the aftermath, the broken lives she leaves in her wake. She can make people seem guilty of crimes they never would have committed; so guilty that even those closest to them, the ones who know them better than anyone, have no doubt. She can influence others to do things they would never have done of their own free will. In rare cases she will get her own hands dirty, murdering either directly or indirectly. Greg McGarrett was not her first. His life is over, but his family will have to deal with what she has done for the rest of their lives. There will be more if I don't find her and stop her."

"You know who she is. Have you called the police? Told them what you know?"

Rebekah was shaking her head before he finished his sentence. "With what evidence? There's never anything left behind. I can't even convince you, face-to-face, that any of this is real. How could I convince them?" Tucker nodded, considering her point. "Let me ask you something. In all of the McGarrett case file that you read, was there anything that would even suggest the possibility he might not be guilty? Anything at all?"

She was right. Tucker assumed his guilt even though his job was to look for holes in the prosecutor's case. It wasn't his fault, he told himself. The evidence was air-tight. There was no reason to doubt.

Now, however, he doubted. Now that it was too late to help the man who died alone while Tucker was sleeping off the bad decisions of the night before on his father's couch.

"How does she do it? If you're right that means she's ruined dozens of lives and gotten away with it every time. How?"

Rebekah stepped around the edge of the bed and sat down facing him. Their knees were almost touching. "How does she do it, Tucker? The same way I got you to take me to the jail with you."

"Got me to...?" he started to ask. "You drugged me? How..." Remembering the intoxicated feeling, too strong to be from his drinking the previous night, mixed with his completely out-of-character actions from his office to the jail made him confused, then angry, then nervous. What did he really know about this woman? He became very aware of her empty hands and scanned the room for anything she might use as a weapon.

"No, Tucker, I didn't drug you." She reached over and put a hand on his knee. "I nudged you in the right direction."

"Nudged how?"

"An old family recipe. It's almost nothing, really. Just a few whispered words, some positive energy manipulation, and practice. Maybe you could even do it someday."

"That doesn't make any sense."

"Hold on." She held up one finger. Next to her was the nightstand separating the two beds. Rebekah opened the drawer. In it was a Bible and a half-chewed yellow pencil. She took out the pencil and put it on the top of the nightstand, next to the broken digital alarm clock. "None of this makes a whole lot of sense, but I'm going to try to show you as best I can."

Rebekah held her hand over the pencil with her fingers stretched wide. She stared intently, whether it was at her hand or the pencil he couldn't tell. A hissing sound escaped her lips and she curled her fingers into a fist. Tucker's eyes widened as the pencil, synchronized with her hand motions, stood up by itself. It teetered there, balancing on its tip, sticking straight up and defying the laws of gravity.

"I still need your help, Tucker. I've never been as close as I am now and I can't afford to let her get away again. Too many lives depend on it."

Chapter Eleven

All things considered, Tucker was processing everything rather well. That was good. She didn't have the patience to hold his hand if he struggled. Mostly, he ran his hands through his hair, muttered to himself, and thoroughly investigated the diabolical pencil, still standing on its own point.

"Magnets," he said. "That's it." But he couldn't find any no matter how hard he looked.

Rebekah remembered that feeling of disbelief. The first time she saw the pencil trick she was as incredulous as Tucker was now. Something in the human mind made it unthinkable to accept the extraordinary at first glance. Maybe it was a survival mechanism from prehistory. Even eyewitnesses to the supernatural will invent perfectly reasonable explanations for the unexplainable. The shadows moving in the corner are simply the headlights of a passing car, the translucent figure at the back door is a reflection in the glass, the noise you heard is the old house settling on its foundation. Anything else would mean altering your worldview to an uncomfortable degree.

Working on the pencil problem kept him from becoming preoccupied with other, harder to explain events.

"What now?" said Tucker. "You said you know she's still around. Any idea where? Narrow it down a bit?" Rebekah could sense the question on the tip of his tongue. *How do you know?*

"No, I don't. He was my best bet. I'm sure he would have known exactly who I was talking about. He would have at least pointed me in the right direction. I do have a lead or two I'll have to try. It's better than driving around hoping I'll bump into her like she's a lost dog." She sounded like a detective on a case, and in a way she was, but she looked like she'd be more at home at a farmer's market or Grateful Dead concert.

"Why is it you think I've seen her? You were obviously disappointed when I said I hadn't, like you expected a different answer."

The question was expected, but she didn't seem sure how to answer. The truth? Maybe, but that came with extra risk and putting more trust in this young man than she already had.

"You may not have officially met her," Rebekah said, "but you have been touched by her. I can see it all around you, this cloud of despair. You have the aura, the same aura Greg McGarrett had. You're connected to her somehow. That's why I picked you."

"You can see..." Tucker brushed his hand down the front of his shirt.

"Yes, it's there. Proof she'd been here. It's how I know I'm on the right path."

"Because of what happened when I was a kid. She made that happen like she made this happen today." Tucker was talking to himself, trying to wrap his head around all of it.

"Not just from when you were a kid. The aura is too bright for that. There's something else too. Could be something yet to come."

"You don't know?"

"It's not an exact science, Tucker. Every time she touches a life, no matter how indirect, she leaves a trace behind. The fainter the aura, the more removed it is, either by age or intensity. Yours should be much more subdued after this much time." The ritual that allowed Rebekah to see the auras, the footprints Charlotte left behind, was something she had painstakingly created herself and improved upon over years of obsessing. It wasn't perfect by any means but until the effect wore off she could read and interpret each manifestation like a hunter tracking an animal through the woods.

Assuming he was correct and hadn't been near her recently, Tucker's aura told her he would encounter Charlotte in the near future. There was, of course, a chance she was wrong about that. Reading auras was like reading tea leaves or tarot cards. Differing interpretations and adjusting probabilities made predicting a bit touchy. She was betting on herself, that she was right about what the aura meant. If he was going to be near Charlotte in the next few hours or days, Rebekah was going to make sure she was here too.

Tucker was back sitting on the bed, studying the pencil. He reached out and poked at the eraser end with his finger. It tilted lazily to almost forty-five degrees for a second before rebounding back to its vertical position.

He looked up at Rebekah. "Witches?"

"If that's what you want to call us to make sense out of it. I don't like the term." That word could be dangerous. She'd seen bad things happen from casual use of it. Although this was a different time and place, such things were more accepted now, her old paranoia was hard to shake.

"What term do you use then?"

"I don't. I am who I am."

There was a tension in the room. He thought she wasn't telling him everything. She knew he was right about that.

"You said you had leads. What are they? What do we do now?"

Rebekah thought about that for a moment. "First, we should hit your place for a change of clothes. We'll talk about the next steps on the way."

They decided to wait until after dark. Correction, thought Tucker, he is the one who decided. He was doing his best to not ruin his previously normal life. Not completely losing his shit was a close second on that list. This tide he was swept up in made it hard to keep his head above water.

Currently, those rough waters brought him to the curb outside of the Hart Memorial Hospital. Rebekah sat next to him, munching on carrots out of a Ziploc bag. She wordlessly offered him some, but he declined. He wasn't very hungry right now. His plan to keep from digging his hole any deeper was about to hit a stiff challenge.

"There's no other way?" He asked for at least the fourth time since they left his apartment. The clothes he changed into while they were there, blue jeans, a black hooded sweatshirt, and a baseball cap, were more comfortable and smelled much better than the dress clothes he'd soiled at the jail.

"Possibly, but those ways are riskier and would take more time than we have." Rebekah wore the same outfit as before. Her bag rested in her lap. While Tucker had been changing at his apartment, she had helped herself to the meager offerings of his refrigerator and began to make a plan on how the two of them could sneak into the hospital.

"Riskier than this?" Tucker gestured out the car's open window at the hospital. "That's hard to believe."

Rebekah rubbed her eyes and popped her neck against the head rest. "I told you, you don't have to go in there. I do. You can drop me here and go. Maybe you should. I can meet up with you later."

He considered her offer yet again. It would be so easy to leave her here, climb back into his own bed, and start putting his life back together tomorrow; first with Lyric, then his job. Forget all about Rebekah, McGarrett, and that damn pencil. Except, he knew there was no way he would be able to sleep tonight. Even if he could summon the willpower to kick her out of his car, his own need for closure would keep him wide awake and staring at the ceiling above his bed well into the morning hours.

So here he was.

"Now I get to choose? You weren't so gracious before."

"I'm sorry, I really am. I didn't know if I could trust you, didn't know how you fit into all this. I also didn't know you'd get so sick. Mild nausea can be a side-effect but it's not usually that bad. It won't happen again."

Tucker didn't accept her apology but also didn't push it further. Rebekah might as well have drugged his drink the way she'd taken advantage of him. It wasn't exactly the same, no matter how much he tried to make the comparison in his own mind, but it was close enough to leave a bitter taste in his mouth. He didn't fully understand what was happening, but he was starting to believe her story. Belief was not the same as trust, however. Rebekah's motivation was not the same as his and he wondered how far was this woman willing to go to get what she was after.

"What's the plan?" Tucker asked, turning his attention back to the task at hand.

"We need to get in, get what we need, and get out without getting caught." She rested her chin on her hand and studied the hospital. "There's no lie that would make us look legitimate enough and nobody would believe the truth."

From the street, the single-story building looked more like an apartment complex than a medical center. The main entrance, automatic sliding glass doors with motion sensors, stood underneath a wide-shingled, A-frame roof. Lights lined the covered walkway, illuminating the cement.

Tucker could see part way into the lobby from where they sat. There were no signs of movement from within, but that didn't mean nobody was there. The night staff would be on shift by now and, while there would be fewer people to get in their way at this hour, all it would take would be one attentive employee to mess things up completely.

Rebekah pointed. "Look, there he is." The security guard appeared, coming through the front doors. He was short and stocky, wearing a dark jacket with patches on the shoulders.

The hat on his head read SECURITY in bright yellow letters. He held a long metal flashlight at his side, swinging in time with his stride. They could hear him whistling as his stubby legs took him down the walkway. He turned away from their car and continued down the sidewalk. The whistling grew fainter as they watched him disappear around the corner.

Rebekah checked her watch. "Forty-five minutes," she said. "That should be enough time."

"Unless there's more than just him."

"No," Rebekah gave a dismissive wave. "We would have seen them by now if there was more security than just him. This building isn't that big. If there's a second security guard he's probably posted at a desk inside, maybe checking ID's or something."

"ID's we don't have."

"We won't be going that way, then." She grinned at Tucker. He couldn't decide if that grin was amused or mocking. Digging through her bag, Rebekah produced a narrow ribbon of fabric and a metal lighter.

"What are those for?"

"Just making a little of our own luck." She coiled the fabric into a circle like a snake on her open palm. Rebekah closed her hand around it and held her fist to her forehead.

"I don't see-"

"Shh," she cut him off. "Don't be so dismissive." Her breathing slowed and she closed her eyes.

Her eyes opened along with her hand. The wad of fabric lay in her palm. With a flick of her thumb a low flame shot up from the lighter in her other hand. The ribbon caught fire with ease, sending smoke up and out in a steady stream. Rebekah wafted the smoke into her own face. She held it out to Tucker.

"Let it wash over you. Close your eyes, hold your breath if you want to."

"What is it?"

Smoke smelling of cedar continued to rise, filling the car and obscuring his vision.

Rebekah silently waited. Grudgingly, he followed her directions. If this was a trap of some sort, she was breathing it in the same as he was. The haze almost made him cough.

His breathing was steady and nothing irritated his lungs despite what his eyes were telling him. Tucker closed his eyes and brought the smoke towards him with a wave of his hand.

When he opened his eyes Rebekah's hand was empty, the flame having consumed the entire ribbon.

"We're not invisible," she said. "That's beyond what I can do. What this does is makes us more elusive. Easy to miss, easy to forget. We'll be at the edge of their awareness but, if we're careful, we won't be the focus of it."

"We're just going to walk in there?"

"Yep. Follow my lead, do what I do, and we will be fine." Before he could respond, she was out of the car and heading across the damp grass in the direction of the main entrance.

Leaping from the driver's seat, Tucker had to hustle to catch up to her.

"How do you know where we need to go?" he said as the automatic door whooshed open ahead of them. Crossing the threshold, Rebekah nodded hello to the young lady sitting at the circular information desk. The woman smiled and nodded back. Tucker put his hands in his pockets and looked at the floor. The two of them continued past without a word.

"I don't," Rebekah finally answered, "but it's not that big of a building. We should be able to find it." She tapped the bill of his hat. "And don't look so suspicious. You look like you've done something wrong already. Make eye contact if we pass someone. Act like we belong here and we know where we are going. People won't challenge us if we are confident. If you act shady, they'll be onto us. Fake it till you make it."

Tucker accepted it and adjusted his hat. He was acting guilty because he felt guilty.

True, they hadn't done anything illegal yet, but they weren't exactly here to visit a sick friend.

The directory at an intersection wasn't much more than a crude printed map with faded lettering that might have been blue at one point. "There, this is what we need."

Luckily, the hospital was small and designed with simplicity in mind. The map showed the rectangular building and a red star showing them where they were. Away from the main structure were various outbuildings used for maintenance, groundskeeping, and security.

Those could be ignored.

"I don't see it," Tucker said, scanning the map while Rebekah ran her index finger over the glass covering. He glanced up and down the corridor, tapping his foot. "Maybe it's not here. Maybe-"

"Right here." She poked the spot on the map aggressively. "Down that way. Two lefts and a right." Rebekah pointed further down the hall, the same direction they'd been heading.

Tucker squinted at her discovery. "I don't think that's it. That says-"

"It's the only place it could be." She didn't even spare Tucker a glance before turning and walking away.

"Okay?" he said as he trudged after her.

So far, he didn't think either of them had committed a crime. Criminal trespassing, maybe, but the hospital was open to the public and nobody had asked them to leave.

Cameras barely visible through tinted domes dotted the ceiling at every corner. Rebekah didn't seem concerned by them. Tucker and his paranoia imagined the person on the other end watching their every move. If that was the case, they were done before they even got started.

After the first left, they passed by a woman in maroon scrubs walking with a purpose in the opposite direction. She didn't look toward them and Tucker, despite Rebekah's advice, made it a point to not make eye contact. By the time they made their second left, they'd seen two more hospital employees. One was mopping the floor of an adjacent room and the other was emptying trash cans full of crumpled paper into a cart parked in the hall. The cart pusher gave them a brief glance but nothing else.

"Wait a sec." Rebekah stopped in front of him. Up ahead, two wide double-doors stood shut. The small pad on the wall at waist level beeped as a gray-haired woman in nurse's scrubs swiped her card over it. She was through the opening and down the corridor before the doors finished swinging outwards. "C'mon, let's go."

A quick stride allowed them both to easily get past before they closed again. On the other side of the doors, the hospital was quiet except for the faint hum of the fluorescent lights. With the nurse now out of sight, they were alone.

"Okay," said Rebekah. "We're here."

Chapter Twelve

"Multi-purpose room?" said Tucker, reading the carefully stenciled letters in front of him. "That's not what we're looking for."

"Yes, it is," she said, trying the lever-handle on the door. It barely moved. Locked. "People don't like to be reminded of unpleasant things. Hospitals, airports, prisons, they all use pleasant euphemisms to mask harsh reality."

"Euphemisms?"

"When you don't want your employees or clients thinking too much about what's on the other side of a door, sometimes a multi-purpose room," she tapped the door with a fingertip, "really houses the hospital's morgue."

Rebekah reached into her pocket and pulled out a metal object. The blade from the knife extended into place with the press of a button. She took a quick look to her right and left.

Reflexively, Tucker did the same. They were still alone. She took hold of the handle and pressed her weight against the door, moving it almost imperceptibly but enough to wedge the blade in between the door and the jamb. Gritting her teeth, she maneuvered the knife back and forth, up and down, until the combination of pressure, leverage, and expertise culminated in the satisfying click of the latch giving way. The door popped open a few inches, giving a partial view of the darkened room.

Tucker cringed, expecting an alarm to ring or a commanding voice ordering them to halt. He allowed himself to relax a little when neither happened. This was beyond trespassing. This had entered the realm of breaking and entering.

Sweat broke out on the back of his neck as he fought the urge to get the hell out of there. Instead, he followed Rebekah into the room.

"No windows," she said as Tucker eased the door closed behind them. "We can turn on the lights." Taking her suggestion as a request, Tucker flipped the switches on the wall, lighting the room up.

Rebekah was right about the room. The sterility and antiseptic smell of it made it look like an operating room. In a sense, that is exactly what it was. It was smaller than he expected, with a low counter and drawers lining the wall on the other side. The smooth, tiled floor looked freshly waxed. A stainless-steel table was centered in the room. There was nothing on it, but Tucker envisioned the pale bodies of the deceased being poked and prodded on top of the cold metal. A scale, like the ones in the produce section of the grocery store, hung above the table. To their left, next to the industrial-sized sink, was exactly what they were looking for.

Two matching steel doors, one on top of the other and both polished to a mirror finish, were set into the wall. The latches held the twin doors sealed shut like a refrigerator. They didn't seem big enough for someone to squeeze through, but appearances were deceiving. Those small doors were designed specifically to fit one person at a time.

As long as they were dead. Tucker shuddered.

"There's only two? I figured there'd be more," he said.

"My guess is this community rarely needs more than this. A confluence of population, relative remote location, and some luck. If that luck ever ran out, this hospital would quickly be overwhelmed."

Rebekah pulled at the latch of the highest door. Tucker held his breath as the sound of the seal broke and the door opened.

It was empty. "It's always the last one you check, right?" Tucker gave an uncomfortable laugh at his own lame joke. Rebekah ignored him.

She squatted down to reach the other latch, the one closest to the floor. Rebekah hesitated. "If he's not in this one...." When she finally opened the door, a relieved sigh escaped her. There was a black body bag, its contents forming a shapeless mass within, resting inside.

The table holding the body slid out smoothly on its tracks. The bag was unzipped, but only a couple of inches. Tucker readied himself. He'd last laid eyes on a dead man when he was ten. Years later, those men still haunted his memory.

The body in the bag before him was different. This was a man he'd spoken to, however briefly. He knew the names of his wife and his kids. He knew where he'd worked and how he died. Tucker keenly felt his own mortality in that moment in a way he'd never considered before.

Rebekah unzipped the black bag and pulled the plastic apart. Tucker was surprised and a little relieved when two feet, heels touching together to form a V, were revealed. He'd been expecting to see Greg McGarrett's face and head. He unclenched his hands and leaned on the table behind him.

"No eyes," he whispered.

"What was that?"

"Nothing." Tucker crossed his arms. "It's...I wasn't sure if his eyes would be open or not. I kind of didn't want to find out."

"Are you good now?"

"As good as I'm going to get."

She turned back to the body. The left leg had a red band around the ankle. Handwritten in black ink was MCGARRETT, GREGORY. Below that was his date of birth next to today's date.

"It's him," said Rebekah. "That's good. If he wasn't here, I'm not sure what our next step would be."

"Now what?"

Rebekah held up her knife to him, blade extended. "Now I do what I have to. Hold out your arm."

"You need mine?"

"Yes. Like I told you, we might only have one shot at this. We need to make it a good one."

Tucker gave her his left hand. She took it and, with one smooth motion, sliced across his open palm. He hissed in pain but managed to keep from yanking his arm away.

Immediately, blood filled his hand and trickled down his arm.

"Here." Rebekah took hold of his wrist and pointed his hand at the floor. "Just relax your arm."

Tucker felt his blood flow to his downturned fingertips. With her guidance the droplets fell to the floor in a circular pattern on the white floor as she manipulated his arm.

"Does this really help that much?" he asked.

"What I'm trying to do is challenging enough under normal conditions. This here," she gestured around the room, "is less than ideal. The blood enhances the incantation and I'll take any advantage I can."

Rebekah's explanation did little to reduce his uncertainty. On the floor near his feet, the crimson beads were slowly merging together.

"Okay, I think that will do." She released his arm and it fell to his side. "Put some pressure on that and hold it above your heart."

Tucker did as he was told, using the stretched sleeve of his sweatshirt to soak up the blood in his fist. Rebekah opened her own hand and pressed the knife's sharp edge to the tender flesh.

"My turn now," she said. Tucker watched as she cut herself the same way she'd cut him.

She repeated the circular motion she'd led Tucker through; her own blood mixing with his on the floor. The bloody circle was almost two feet in diameter by the time she was done.

Tucker never had an issue with blood but this, this was above and beyond. The throbbing pain in his hand, the way the life from the two of them spilled out until he couldn't tell what was his and what was hers, it was enough to make him feel light-headed. Rebekah, on the other hand, seemed perfectly at ease, like she'd done this many times before. The thought creeped him out. She turned to the pale feet sticking out of the bag next to her.

Taking the pinkie toe between two fingers, she cut into the meat of the foot. First down, then over, she sawed at the toe like she was trying to snap a leg off of a rotisserie chicken.

The crunch of breaking bone and tearing flesh made him groan and look away.

Abuse of a corpse in the first degree was also a felony. This felony would be harder to explain away than the others they've committed today. The list of crimes kept getting longer. Tucker did his best to forget about that. It was tomorrow's problem, he told himself.

Greg McGarrett's toe came off bloodlessly. Rebekah wiped the blade off on her sleeve and put the knife back in her pocket.

"All right," she said, digging through her bag until she pulled out a small, but powerful, flashlight. He'd seen the deputies in the jail with similar ones on their belts. "What I need you to do is turn out the lights. I need this room as dark as we can get it. And be silent. Find a spot, stand there, don't talk. No matter what happens. Got it?"

"Got it."

Rebekah tossed the toe into the middle of the blood circle. Thin rivulets stretched slowly inward like fingers reaching for the appendage. She set the flashlight on the floor on the far side of the circle and knelt next to the body. It was pointing at her, but was turned off.

"Hit the lights, Tucker."

He flipped the switch and plunged the room into blackness. The complete loss of light unsettled him. True darkness was a rarity. Ambient light, especially to a born and bred city boy like Tucker, was a constant, comforting presence. Street lamps bled through curtains in the evening. Moonlight and stars illuminated the night sky even if artificial light was far away. There was always something the eyes could adjust to in order to alleviate that feeling of the void. Not here, though. There were no windows and he might as well have been blind.

Tucker took a half-step backwards, pressing his back against the wall. For a few seconds there was silence. Only the whisper of air moving through ducts and the occasional sound of muted footsteps from the hall kept him from forgetting where he was. Then he could hear Rebekah. Slowly increasing in volume and frequency, her breaths came in quick gasps until they drowned out the other noises in the room.

"To do what I need to do I need absolute silence," she'd told him back at his apartment. "Fear, my fear, is a necessary component for this to work. I can put myself into a state of terror but it takes concentration, imagination, and most important, no distractions."

Rebekah had been stern on this point.

The rapid breathing turned to soft whimpers, like she was having a nightmare. Tucker tried to imagine how she would be able to work herself into a panic, much like an actor crying on demand, he guessed, even as his own fear crept up his spine like a frigid caress.

The seconds turned to minutes. How many, he wasn't sure. Time had become meaningless in the darkness of the morgue.

Finally, the moans ended and her voice broke through. "I have respectfully come to find one who has passed, but not yet passed beyond the veil. I seek knowledge and justice. Justice for the one who has wronged me and mine. Justice for the one who has wronged the one I seek." The effect of hearing but not seeing her was dreamlike. He thought he heard a slight tremor in her voice.

"Gregory Samuel McGarrett," she continued, "if you can hear me, if you have not already moved on, please show yourself to me. Please let me know if you're here."

Tucker could hear the beat of his own heart pounding in his ears. His own breathing was deafening. He started to count silently to himself after Rebekah received no reply to her plea, if only to measure the passage of time. He got up to twelve when the flashlight clicked on.

Rebekah, now visible with the white light shining at her, was still kneeling where she was the last time he saw her. He could see streaks running down her cheeks. Tears, already drying on her skin, glimmered out of the shadows. Then, as quickly as it came, the light vanished again.

"Thank you," said Rebekah. "Thank you for answering my call. If you can, turn on the light to answer my questions. Turn it on once for a yes? Leave if off for a no?"

The flashlight switched on for a beat, then switched off. The audible click both times made Tucker back up further against the wall. Something unseen was manipulating the physical world around it. Who, or what, pushed the button to answer Rebekah?

"That's good, we have an agreement then." She paused and inhaled sharply. "Am I speaking to Greg McGarrett?"

Click. Rebekah's hands rested in her lap. With her head down her face was hidden. *Click.*

"You're dead now. You know that, right?"

Click. Click.

"Do you remember the life you lived? Your friends and family? The events leading up to your death?"

There was a delay this time. A handful of seconds ticked by. Then, *click, click.*

"I need your help in an urgent manner. There is a woman I seek. Her name is Charlotte, although she may be using-"

Clickclick. Faster this time.

"You know who I'm referring to?"

Click. Click. The light showed Rebekah looking up now; leaning forward and staring intently at the flashlight. Tucker felt a cold draft sneak by him, raising goosebumps on his arm.

"Where is-" She caught herself. "Do you know where she is?" Yes or no questions only.

The light stayed silent. Tucker counted to himself again, one Mississippi at a time. He got to eight when Rebekah broke the silence.

"Okay, you don't know where she is now. Do you remember where you last saw her?"

Click. Click.

"That's great, Greg. Now I need you to reach through to me, before you're too far away from this world. I need to find her before she can hurt anyone else the way she hurt you. I know you weren't guilty of the crimes you were accused of. I know and, if I'm successful, your family will know, too. I think she got to you, influenced you." Her voice cracked, like she was choking back tears. The room remained dark.

"Can you tell me? However you can, I will listen for it. You'll find I'm an excellent listener. A whisper, a tug on my sleeve, something to point me in the right direction...please."

Click. The light switched back on. This time it stayed lit. Shadows can't exist without light and these ones were playing tricks on Tucker's eyes. He could have sworn he saw one of the feet on the slab move. Only a little bit, but it seemed like the leg was bending at the knee. In the fraction of a second it took for the light to come on, he saw the foot slide back into place. It happened so fast he couldn't tell if he imagined it or, against all reason, the body had actually been moving.

"Greg? I'm list-" *Click.* Blackness.

Less than a second passed and the flashlight came back on. Rebekah's furrowed brow was plainly visible. Then, as suddenly and unprompted as it turned on, it was off.

"I'm trying to understand, I am."

Clickclickclickclick

In rapid succession, the flashlight switched on and off so fast it made Rebekah shield her eyes. The strobe-like effect made Tucker dizzy. He forced himself to witness the spectacle even though every instinct in him told him to run away. Like a flip-book, he could see in millisecond snapshots. Rebekah with her hands up, pleading with the spirit to show her the answers. The body on the slab jerking upwards at the waist.

Shadows shifted as the flashlight teetered back and forth. Tucker squeezed his eyes shut tightly enough to see stars. When he opened them, the feet were motionless, just as they were before.

That didn't happen, he thought. *I'm only scaring myself.*

Rebekah shouted, "Greg, stop. I'm not understanding you. You're lashing out. Control yourself."

Something ice cold grabbed Tucker's wrists and yanked him forward. He leaned back and dug his heels in. The invisible grip tightened, bringing him to his knees.

"Don't resist, Tucker." Rebekah reached out to him even though he was too far away to touch. She was trying to help him, he realized. The light continued its staccato rhythm, throwing his senses into a confusing mass of chaos.

Tucker nodded back at her. He relaxed, allowing his arms to be guided further. "Oh, god, no," he moaned. His hand was being forced towards the blood circle and the detached toe within.

"Let it happen," Rebekah said. "This is how he's reaching through."

His hand, seemingly of its own accord, took the toe and dragged it through the puddle of blood. Tucker allowed his arm to be manipulated, creating sharp, violent streaks on the untouched portions of the morgue floor. He looked away, unable to bear the image of the toe between his fingers and the blood being used as an inkwell. A long, low grunt came out through gritted teeth until he thought he was going to pass out or lose his mind.

The phantom grip on his hands released, allowing him to fall over on his side. He struggled to catch his breath. It felt as if he'd sprinted a mile. The flashlight had stopped blinking, having locked itself into the on position. Rebekah appeared, standing over him but looking beyond him. Her concern wasn't for him, it was for the marks on the floor.

Tucker pushed himself up, his bloody hands leaving prints on the tile. He stared at his palm dazedly and wondered if the stains on it were from his blood or hers.

"You did good, Tucker," said Rebekah. "That's all we're going to get. We need to get out of here."

He followed her eyes to the words he'd unknowingly scrawled. Two words were crudely written, but plainly legible. He hoped they meant something to Rebekah because they were meaningless to him. Two words, one name.

MANDY LOU.

Chapter Thirteen

Two large coffees. One black, one with cream and sugar. The coffee stand in the empty grocery store parking lot was open early, beating the morning sun by at least two hours.

Rebekah walked the beverages over to the far corner of the lot where Tucker sat on the ground next to the Prius. Legs bent, his back rested against the passenger-side door and he was obsessively pouring through the stack of papers on his lap.

"Thought you could use this." She held out the steaming cup, the one with the cream and sugar. He paused his reading long enough to take it from her. He held the cup with both hands for warmth. There was still dried blood on them, under his fingernails and on his knuckles. He'd missed some despite the near-frantic way he'd wiped at them with his sweatshirt after leaving the hospital.

The sweatshirt was now crumpled up in the backseat. Wearing a thin t-shirt, Tucker shivered in the predawn coolness, his revulsion beating out his need for comfort.

He'd hardly spoken to her since the morgue. "You knew that would happen," was all he muttered as they made their way out of the hospital. He didn't object when she took the keys from him. He only talked to her enough to get her to stop at his office to retrieve the case file for Greg McGarrett.

Rebekah didn't respond to his accusation. She actually hadn't known what was going to happen when she tried to contact the spirit, but Tucker wouldn't have believed her if she told him that. She decided to keep silent and let him work through the trauma in his own way.

The fact was, the Ritual of Contact had worked better than she could have hoped for, especially given the ad hoc way she'd been forced to put it together. For a departed spirit to manifest like that, and with such intensity, was almost unheard of. The most she'd expected was maybe enough yes or no responses to narrow her search. Any help in that regard could prove to be the difference between success and failure. The way Tucker had been forced to do those things against his will told her how strong and vengeful the spirit still was.

Those words, that name written by a dead man in her own blood, didn't mean anything to her. They meant something to someone though. Now the two of them needed to decipher their only clue.

He looked up at her. "How do you do that? I mean, back there...I was there but I'm not sure what I saw. What was all that?"

"How? Practice, I guess, is the simplest answer. And a good teacher. The what is tougher to explain."

"Practice? Like, I could do what you do with enough practice?" Tucker sipped his coffee, but kept his eyes on her.

"Maybe," she paused, "but, honestly, probably not. Not many people can safely pull off what I did tonight." Rebekah knew that sounded arrogant, but it was true. "Contacting the other side can be dangerous. If you're not careful you can accidentally summon something that doesn't want to go back."

"So, you're some sort of prodigy? Nobody else is on your level?"

"That's not what I said. There are plenty older, wiser, and more skilled people than I am out there."

She sat down on the asphalt near him. This was good. Conversating like this would take his mind off of the events of the last few hours. With luck, he might stop blaming her.

"Plenty of people better at this than you? How many are there? People like you, I mean."

"People like me? That's another difficult question. There's no hard and fast answer that I know of. You might as well ask how many singers are there in the world. Do you count only those that call themselves singers? Everyone can sing. Some are better than others. Some are naturally gifted from birth with a melodic voice, setting them apart from their tone-deaf peers. Those born with the talent but never work at improving can only achieve so much. What sets the very best singers above the others is the will to be better. Natural talent plus work ethic will triumph over talent alone. If you're born without any talent though...." Rebekah shrugged.

"Are you the naturally gifted one?"

"Hardly, it took years of blood, sweat, and too many tears to get to where I'm at. Setbacks and disappointments, I almost quit dozens of times. But I stuck with it. None of this ever came easy to me. My learning process was a lot like I imagine banging my head against a wall would feel like."

"And her? What about her?" He didn't have to say her name.

"She's different. For her it's effortless, you can tell. I don't know where she came from or how she does what she does or why she is how she is. I do know she is the gifted singer whose voice is unlike any I've heard before. The things she can do, they're unbelievable. I wouldn't even know where to start if I attempted to emulate her, tried to replicate her abilities."

"She's better than you? But you're after her, hunting her. How is this going to go for you if you do catch up with her?"

Catching up to Charlotte. That was a scenario she'd imagined a thousand times with a thousand different outcomes. There were times when hope was the only thing that kept her going. "I have to try. If I don't, then she'll have gotten away with it. All of the broken hearts, the tortured souls, all of it."

"Like Ray King and Greg McGarrett and all the people they left behind with their lives damaged beyond repair."

Rebekah sipped her coffee. "I wanted to talk to him, ask him how he met Charlotte, where he saw her last. After he died it became much more difficult. But even in death, he helped point us in the right direction. I hope."

"Magic spells to talk to dead people." Tucker pressed the heel of his hand to his eye and rubbed. "You're really not kidding, are you?"

She opened her arms and held her hands out. "You were there, Tucker. You felt the loss of control of your own body. You tell me if I'm kidding."

He looked away.

"Tucker, have you ever had something happen to you that defied explanation? I'm not talking about these last couple of days. Something relatively mundane. Most people, if you ask them, have had an experience that gave them pause. A ghostly encounter? An alarm clock goes off in the middle of the night right after a distant loved one has died? Usually it's way more subtle. You have a song stuck in your head, then it comes on the radio. You're thinking of someone you haven't seen in a long time and you randomly run into them. Anything like that?"

He flicked at the lid of the cup with his thumb. "There was one time...no, it was nothing."

"It wasn't nothing. That's what I'm telling you. Simple things get overlooked or explained away as happenstance. It's not happenstance, it's you, briefly touching the potential we all have. What was it, Tucker?"

He leaned his head back until it touched the metal of the car door. "I've never been a believer, of much of anything really. Maybe ghosts. Never saw one personally, but I've heard enough stories from people who claimed they had. The first thing that came to mind when you asked was this time with my girlfriend – or ex-girlfriend now, I'm not real sure. Me and Lyric had only been dating a little while and I hadn't given her a key to my place yet. I was helping a friend move, had been at his house most of the day. By the time we were done I was sweaty and tired and ready to head home. About two blocks from my building it popped into my head."

"What did?"

"She was there waiting for me. Lyric. It wasn't a vision or some magical revelation. I was suddenly absolutely sure she was going to be there when I got home. That's why, when I got off the elevator and saw her standing there with her beaming smile and a bag of take-out, I wasn't surprised in the least. I never told anyone about that, not even her."

Rebekah reached over and put her hand on his leg. "There's a connection there, between you and her. You can brush it off as insignificant but you shouldn't. That was a moment when you experienced something more than the physical."

"You're saying I'm psychic?"

"No more or less than millions of others. That's what I've been saying. Anyone can sing."

The lights came on in the grocery store at the other end of the parking lot. Rebekah could see employees bustling back and forth, getting ready to open. Soon customers would be filling the empty parking spaces around them.

Tucker said, "She hurt you personally. That's why you've never quit."

Rebekah surprised herself when she felt tears welling in her eyes. She thought she was past that. Tucker's abruptness was unexpected. Willing the tears away, she managed a tight-lipped nod.

Tucker opened his mouth to ask the obvious question. How? She could see it on his face. Perhaps it was the look she gave him or an inner voice telling him he'd overstepped that shut him down before he could get it out. This was not the time.

Instead, she told him, "That's what she does is hurt people. Charlotte Disborough has marked herself as an instrument of Chaos and her goal is to sow discord, to cause despair, and to make the world a bit more miserable with every passing breath."

"That mantra you heard on the boat when you were a boy? The same one McGarrett said to you the other day? It's an incantation, a variation of an ancient one she translated and changed to make it her own. The incantation was designed to give respect and recognition to Chaos specifically. Chaos, the first to exist, emerging from the storm of creation. Charlotte is too proud to worship anything, not even a primordial deity. She seeks to mirror what she thinks Chaos is. Instead of embracing the beauty of disarray and random chance, she takes it upon herself to be the cause, the impetus for those things that true Chaos would leave to fate."

Now it was the look on Tucker's face that stopped her from speaking. This is too much for him, she thought. Even with all he's seen, this is enough to send him running for the hills to save his own sanity. He stared at her, silent and slack-jawed.

"I'm sorry," she said. "I've had a long time to come to terms with this. You haven't."

Rebekah would continue on without him if it came to that, but she knew her chances of success increased dramatically if she could keep him around.

There was more she could tell him. Maybe she would if this worked out the way she hoped. Tucker was close to snapping, she thought. Any more added straws might break his back. His life had been turned upside down; everything he thought he knew was wrong and his safe little world got a whole lot bigger and a lot more dangerous in a short amount of time. Even if she told him everything, he wouldn't understand. Not yet.

Tucker stood. "I found it. At least, I think I did." He placed the open folder on the hood of the car. Rebekah joined him, following along as he pointed at the papers. "Mandy Lou. My first thought was his wife, Amanda Louise McGarrett. Was that his nickname for her? It seemed like the obvious choice at first, that he was pointing us towards her like she would be able to help us. As much as I didn't want to do that, talking to a new widow about her husband's suicide, if she knew anything about Charlotte it'd be necessary."

Rebekah stopped him. "Wait a minute, you found this but held off telling me? You should have led with this." While she was babying him and patiently answering his questions, he had been withholding crucial information.

"I'm putting a lot on the line here." Tucker's tone matched hers. He was not in the mood to take orders. "Most likely, I'm past the point of no return. Following you into this craziness is going to cost me. We could be arrested. Nobody is going to believe the truth. I'm not sure I can believe it myself."

"That's how she's been able to escape without notice for so long. What she does is impossible so who could you tell without sounding insane?"

"Then maybe you should cut me some slack if I put my own questions ahead of yours one time."

That was fair. Finding Charlotte was far more important than coddling the young man but saying so out loud would be counterproductive. Rebekah put her hand on his shoulder in a silent apology.

"Okay, then." Tucker brought her attention back to the file. "We might still need to go see his wife. That's the most likely explanation. But I also found this." He handed her a single sheet of paper from the stack. "In order to get a court-appointed attorney, McGarrett had to fill out this financial form. Basic info: name, address, dependents, income and physical assets."

Rebekah saw what he was talking about. At the bottom of the form there were vehicles listed. Two cars were at the top. Underneath those was a dirt bike worth a few hundred bucks and a boat.

The trawler, according to the notes, was a thirty-seven-footer that was worth less than he owed on it. The form also included an additional detail that was most likely not required on a financial document.

The name of the boat.

MANDY LOU.

Chapter Fourteen

Spreading the sauce on the glass pan helped prevent the noodles from sticking. When the thick, meaty mixture covered the bottom, she began laying the extra-wide noodles on top.

Lyric was out of bed before the sun was up. She was awake long before that, fighting against her racing mind to get to sleep. Realizing she wasn't going to win that battle, she threw off the blankets and slumped out of her room, taking care not to wake her roommate.

Her faithful bulldog, Bertram, trotted along beside her.

The ingredients she needed were all readily available. She'd bought them last night, her subconscious making sure she was prepared for the meal she didn't know she was going to make. Lasagna. Her mother's recipe.

Early morning was not the ideal time for baking. This dish needed to be ready by lunch though, and it took almost two hours to complete from start to finish. The repetitive motions of cooking, mixing, and spreading helped soothe her. The oven beeped, signaling it was preheated to the appropriate temperature, as she spread the three-cheese blend over the noodles.

Why was she putting herself through this? No man, no cry. That was one of the rules she lived by. It was always a point of pride for her. No man was worth shedding a tear over.

There would forever be another one out there who wouldn't push you to be that emotional. Not since Brock Faulk in the tenth-grade had she broken that rule. Not once.

Lyric was able to walk away with a shrug if a relationship didn't work out. This past week was different. She'd cried, sobbed even, over a man.

The bags under her eyes were getting difficult to conceal with makeup. She tried unsuccessfully to stop obsessing over them every time she looked in a mirror.

Lyric replayed the conversation at Tucker's apartment and the words she'd left him in her note. Her tone had been harsh and, seemingly for the hundredth time, she wished she'd been more selective with her wording. She didn't go there intending on picking a fight. She should have said all of the things that had been keeping her up at night. Like how, even though she was hurt and pissed, she still loved him intensely.

It's what made all of this so hard.

Seeing Tucker yesterday morning, outside his apartment, made her momentarily forget how mad she was. When he came around the corner, he looked bedraggled, like he'd slept in his clothes. The stench of old booze came off of him in a cloud of foulness. She couldn't have missed it if she tried. Not wanting to start another fight, Lyric kept her comments to herself.

But where had he been all night? That question, like her comment about the drinking, remained unspoken. Whether this was a fight, a break, or a breakup, Tucker was dealing with it in his own way. One bottle at a time from the looks of it. She trusted him but there was a nibble of a doubt about where he'd been and who he'd been with while he consumed all of that liquor. He said he'd been at his father's house, but that seemed unlikely. Tucker and his dad were not close. They sure as hell weren't drinking buddies. "Guys mourn differently," is what her roommate April told her while they commiserated. Most women won't go out and hook up with some rando after a bad breakup. Men, on the other hand, will. She didn't know why it went like that but she knew it to be a fact of life.

"We didn't break up," she'd replied. Right? Honestly, those relationship-ending words weren't spoken but there was a sense of finality to their last real conversation.

The worst part had been his lack of give-a-shit when he saw that she was waiting for him. Maybe a flicker of surprise, but he didn't seem happy, that was for sure. That morning she felt like she didn't register as a priority to him in the slightest. In her heart of hearts, she had to admit she hoped he'd be happy to see her there, maybe give her a hug and apologize. Wishful thinking.

Italian sausage, spicy but not too spicy, was the special ingredient that made her mother's lasagna so irresistible. The sausage, mixed with ground sirloin and three different cheeses, cooked until thoroughly brown, went in to completing the dish. Some minced garlic, crushed red pepper, and diced tomatoes gave it that boost of flavor. The recipe, when completed, smelled almost good enough for Lyric to give up on her vegetarianism, at least temporarily.

Once it was ready, Lyric sprinkled parmesan cheese over the top and put it in the oven.

As she closed the door, she caught her blurry reflection in the microwave. Her necklace, a simple silver cross, glinted in the image. She took it delicately in her hand and sighed.

That necklace, a symbol of her unwavering faith, had been a gift from her parents on her twelfth birthday. It was the first piece of real jewelry she'd ever owned and she hardly went anywhere without it. If she wasn't sleeping or running, the cross rested comfortably on the thin chain around her neck.

Lyric grew up attending the small church a block from her house in Centralia. Her family of four were regulars every Sunday morning as well as an occasional Wednesday evening. The rest of the congregation was like an extended family for the Howards and Lyric felt at home in the pews of Trinity Methodist.

As an adult, she moved away from Centralia but not that far. Pine Harbor was hardly the big city but she found herself attending church services less and less. Nothing was quite like Trinity. After meeting Tucker, her Sunday morning worship usually took the form of a quick prayer after waking up and before she had breakfast.

She missed those days at Trinity, where her family wasn't limited to her parents and sister. When the entire congregation, all fifty or so, stood and sang hymns, Lyric could almost feel God listening and approving. Brought together in devotion, the people that made up the church were greater than the sum of their parts.

Asking Tucker to go to church with her, to share some of that feeling with her favorite person, had been a conversation she'd put off for a long time. She'd casually invited him a couple of times early on in the relationship, but he'd declined. As they got closer, it weighed on her more and more. It was necessary to bring it up again, she told herself, even though she couldn't shake the feeling that it had been a huge mistake. If she had it to do all over, would she still make the request? She wasn't sure.

Tucker was up front from the beginning. He didn't believe in God. Not one bit. He never tried to dissuade Lyric's enthusiasm or change her mind, but she always felt as though he was judging her any time the subject came up. That first date she told him, "This isn't going to work out." It was a joke at the time. Her own inner voice, the one that spoke with logic, told her it was a mistake to keep seeing him. He wasn't going to change and she shouldn't hope or expect him to.

Lyric listened to her heart instead.

He was so funny. That was the first thing she noticed. You wouldn't have known it at first glance. With his conservative attire and his short brown hair always immaculate, Tucker looked more like a young businessman than a jokester. It was an effortless sort of funny, not like he was trying too hard to make people laugh. That would have been annoying. Tucker wasn't mean either. He knew the difference between taking a little poke at someone and hitting below the belt. If he was ever rude, you could be sure that person deserved it.

His kindness stood out, even through his cynicism. Lyric blamed his job for the latter.

Dealing with liars and deadbeats day after day would take its toll on anyone. Tucker didn't let that stop him from having faith in people, even if that faith was tested frequently.

That innate kindness of his made the harsh words he spoke that much more unbearable.

Faith. Hers and his but different kinds. Tucker was definitely one of the Good Guys. She wished that was enough for her.

Tucker? I've been thinking about going to church more often. Maybe even going back to Centralia every once in a while.

She felt like a hypocrite or some sort of poser. To Tucker, this probably seemed out-of-nowhere. To Lyric, it was way overdue.

And I was hoping you would come with me.

It was important. If this was going to go somewhere, and Lyric was thinking it already was, they needed to be on the same page.

Lyric, I'm all for you going, as much as you want to. It's not for me. Never has been.

"Okay, okay. You've been patient. Here you go." She bent down and put a plate on the floor. Bertram wagged his stump of a tail and made quick work of the scraps of meat set aside just for him. "That's a good boy."

Why is this so important all of a sudden? I haven't gone to church since I was in elementary school. What's changed in the last couple of weeks?

I worry about us, our future together, if we stay the way we are. Can't you at least think about it?

Bertram followed Lyric to the couch and nuzzled up on the cushion beside her. "Sorry, little one. Mama upset your routine, huh? You're probably wondering what's wrong."

Lyric was wondering the same thing. The lasagna baking in the oven. What was that, an apology? No, she had nothing to apologize for. A peace offering, maybe? A desire to get back to some semblance of the way things were.

You think I haven't thought about it? I've probably thought about it more than you have.

What do you mean by that?

A few weeks ago, after they both slept through their alarm, Tucker had rushed off to work without breakfast or his lunch. "Don't worry, I'll grab something later," he told her.

Later that morning, Lyric took the time away from her own job to go to her house, get the leftover lasagna from the fridge, and take it to Tucker. She felt like it was something a good girlfriend would do, taking care of him when he was too stubborn to do it himself.

The reaction she got when she delivered his lunch was more than she expected.

Surprised and grateful, Tucker thanked her profusely. Lyric remembered how he held her hand and fawned over her all through lunch even as that co-worker of his, Donnie, teased them incessantly the entire time. She couldn't believe such a simple gesture meant so much to him.

That was the feeling she was trying to recreate.

Do we have a future together if we see this so differently? This is a big deal to me.

So now you're going to break up with me if I don't go to church? We just won't spend Sunday mornings together.

We're unequally yoked, Tucker. That's a recipe for disaster.

Unequally yoked? What does that even mean?

It's from the Bible. A warning, a command really, against a believer being in a relationship with an unbeliever.

Because we're not good enough. That's what you're saying? Your two-thousand-year-old magic book tells you to avoid unbelievers so you all can raise the next generation of good little brainwashed Christians?

The conversation took a dark turn after that. Lyric was shocked and hurt at Tucker's words. She thought she knew how he felt about God, Jesus, and religion but she was taken aback by the vitriol that came with his words. Magic book? Brainwashed Christians? Those words showed how little respect he had for her faith. How could he respect her as a person or partner if he looked down on her church like that?

The words she shot back at him were not well thought out. She was seeing red by then and forming a rational debate wasn't possible in that moment. The look in his eyes told her she'd cut him pretty deeply with her response. The fact that he started it was hardly an excuse. She should have been better that day. She wished she could take it all back. Tucker was one of the best people she'd ever known and his unbelief didn't change that.

It just meant they shouldn't be together.

The oven gave three short beeps, rescuing Lyric from her own thoughts.

"Food's done, Bertram," she said. The dog perked his ears up and tilted his head at the sound of his name. Lyric scratched Bertram's head. "Mama's gotta go see if she can figure out if she should follow her head or her heart."

Lyric stood at the door of the Mahoney Law Office. The pan of lasagna was still warm in her hands and foil covered the top. Every time she visited Tucker's work she hesitated before going in. It was a house, so she felt like she should knock. It was also a place of business, so she felt like she should be able to walk in without being invited. As always, she overcame the urge to knock and opened the door with her free hand.

Cheryl's smiling face was the first thing she saw. Her eyes got wider when she recognized the face coming through the door. The smile faltered, but only a little.

"Hey there, hon," said Cheryl. "Good to see you. It's been a while."

"Hi, Cheryl. Yeah, sorry I haven't been by. Things have been..." Lyric didn't know how to finish her sentence. Cheryl had always been so friendly to her, taking the time to get to know what was going on in her life, not just going through the motions because she was Tucker's girlfriend. But, at the end of the day, Cheryl was more Tucker's friend than hers and Lyric wondered how much the older lady already knew.

"It's okay, sweetie. Don't you worry about it." Cheryl's look was sympathetic with a tinge of worry. Her eyes darted to the back office, where Tucker worked with Donnie. "He's not here today. Was there something I could help you with?"

"Oh," said Lyric, surprised. "Did he call in sick?" Now she was embarrassed. She hoped Cheryl knew some of the story. Tucker having the day off was something his girlfriend should have known.

Cheryl's eyes softened and she leaned forward. Her lips formed a tight line. Lyric, fearing the worst, cringed inwardly in anticipation. "I shouldn't say anything," Cheryl whispered. "The boss doesn't even know he's not here. It's none of my business what's going on with you two, I know that. But I notice when things aren't right. You," she pointed at Lyric with her pen, "you're good for him. I've seen you together and you're like two peas in a pod."

Lyric blushed. "Thanks, Cheryl. I feel that way too. It's not-"

Cheryl cut her off. "I'm worried about him. He hasn't been his normal self. His behavior has been odd to say the least. At first, I thought he was just having a tough go of things, seeing as how you stopped coming by around the same time."

Lyric gave a tiny nod, blinking away the beginnings of tears.

"But I didn't ask." Cheryl put her hands up. "Figured he would tell me if he wanted to."

She straightened up in her chair and put her hand on Lyric's. "He didn't come in today. Didn't call in sick, didn't ask for the day off. Tucker just didn't show up. He's never done that before. I've been trying to call him all morning and he's not answering his phone. I can only cover with the boss for so long, but eventually even that one will get wise. There's already been calls from the jail wanting to speak with Mr. Mahoney; Tucker made quite the spectacle yesterday. I've managed to run interference, but pretty soon I'm going to have to pass along those messages."

"What do you mean, spectacle?" Lyric hadn't considered the possibility that Tucker had more issues than what was going on between the two of them. Cheryl was worried about him and she wasn't one to overreact. That concern was contagious.

Cheryl paused, frowning. "You're going to have to hear about that part from him. I only know what I heard. I wasn't there. He could be in some decent trouble here, sweetie, and I'm sure seeing a friendly face like yours would be helpful for him."

"But you're not sure where he is?" She'd come here to be the friendly face Cheryl wanted her to be. She could have called ahead, but the surprise was a big part of the plan.

Now, after talking to Cheryl, Lyric thought her butting in might not be as helpful as she imagined. "And he's not answering his phone."

"I hope he's at home, sitting on the couch watching game shows. Lord knows we all need a mental health day from time to time. And no, not answering calls or texts. Donnie and I both tried him several times."

"Okay then. I guess I'll swing by his place." Mistake or not, Lyric needed to see him. If there was even a remote chance she could help, she had to try. Not too long ago, it had been Tucker and Lyric against the world. She missed that. The gnawing feeling of trepidation in her stomach made her doubt that course of action. She pushed it down, the dread of what might come.

"Thank you, Cheryl, for everything. You were always so nice to me."

"You're welcome, honey. But you make it sound like we won't be seeing each other again. Kind of doomy and gloomy."

"I didn't mean it like that. I'll see you around. This town isn't that big." Cheryl patted Lyric's hand before the young woman turned to leave.

"Don't forget your dish." The foil-covered pan sat alone on Cheryl's desk.

"Oh, it's yours if you want it. Lasagna. My mother's recipe. Please, take it. Share it with the office. It's too much for one person."

"Okay, I'll clean the pan after and you can come pick it up. Gives you a reason to visit."

"Sounds good, Cheryl."

Lyric walked out the front door, pulled out her phone, and dialed Tucker's number.

CHAPTER FIFTEEN

In the dream, Tucker was walking with Lyric down a long, endless hallway. The words exchanged between them were nice in a way they hadn't been for too long. He was sorry, she was sorry, and they were able to move past it together, hand-in-hand. The shirt she wore was his. It was too big for her. He knew it belonged to him instinctually, even though he couldn't have said for sure what was on the front or when he wore it last.

Then they were on a boat in the ocean. The water was rough and spray from crashing waves soaked him and stung his eyes. Lyric stood near the bow, just out of arm's reach.

She wore the same shirt, but it was now wet and clinging to her body. A mask hid her face from him. It was a simple mask, solid white with a vicious grin, giving her the look of an evil mime. Her eyes pleaded with him through holes in the mask.

Tucker touched the mask. He wanted to take it off, wanted to see her face again. Lyric swatted his hand away. He moved to take the mask with his other hand but she dodged.

She hit him, first with open hands, then with fists. The blows rained down on him in a flurry, forcing him to throw his arms up to protect his face.

He took hold of her wrists but still she struggled and flailed. The boat vanished beneath them, plunging the couple into the cold, churning water. Lyric kept fighting him even as the waves crashed over them. Tucker lost his grip and she disappeared into the darkness of the sea.

Suddenly, he was standing on the beach in ankle-deep water. People strolled along in the sand; couples, families, and the occasional dog-walker passed by without noticing Tucker. Up ahead, beyond the high-tide mark, was Rebekah. Her hands tied behind her back; she was bound to a thick wooden stake. Driftwood was stacked all around her feet, hiding most of her legs from view. Looking at the sky, her head was pressed against the wood behind her. Her wet hair was plastered to her face.

As if sensing he was there, Rebekah lowered her head and looked at Tucker. He began to walk to her, to free her, but he sank deeper into the sand with every step. Time slowed.

The distance between them never changed. Slowly and methodically, Rebekah shook her head back and forth.

"No?" said Tucker. "No, what?"

Flames sprung up around Rebekah, engulfing her body and tickling at her chin. She closed her eyes and turned her face back to the heavens.

Tucker screamed.

The barking dog jolted Tucker from sleep. Outside, a black and white terrier pulled mightily against its harness, trying to get at the seagulls circling above. The elderly couple out for a walk scolded him apathetically. "Aw, quit yer yappin'."

It took Tucker a moment to gather his wits. Rebekah sat in the driver's seat. The car was turned off.

"This is it," she said.

There were eleven marinas within city limits where the boat could have been stored.

That number was much higher if you added in the ones within thirty miles or so. Boats on the coast were plentiful; finding the one they were looking for was like finding one specific tree in a forest.

Hitting the first four on the list took most of the morning. The last thing Tucker remembered before drifting off was Rebekah yawning as she drove the two of them to the fifth location.

"It's here? Are you sure?" Half-asleep, he pressed his fingers to his eyes and rubbed hard enough to see bright spots. His sliced palm throbbed with a dull pain. The impromptu cloth bandage was soaked through, threatening to drip onto the seat.

"Yes. I've been waiting for you to wake up. You needed the rest. Besides, there's only one entrance and exit." She pointed to the chain-link door blocking the ramp leading down to the water. "I can see anyone coming or going from here."

"Then how do you...never mind." He decided not to finish his question. Rebekah said this is the place so this must be the place. He probably wouldn't understand how she knew that information anyway.

Tucker got out of the car and stretched, feeling more clear-headed with every passing moment. Rebekah joined him and they proceeded to the Northpoint Marina gate. This time of day, the gate was left unlocked allowing paying members to come and go as they pleased. It wouldn't be locked again until after dark. She led the way down the ramp and Tucker followed.

Rebekah clomped along the wooden dock ahead of him, swiftly bypassing the smaller boats. The one they were looking for was listed in the court paperwork as a thirty-seven-foot trawler. Most of the ones they passed were much smaller than that. The larger boats were parked in slips at the end of T-shaped rows, parallel to the shore. She stopped suddenly, allowing Tucker to catch up.

"What is it?" he asked. She stared at the empty slip next to them, absorbed by the two unoccupied law chairs resting there.

"Nothing. It's...nothing." Rebekah moved on, setting a quick pace once again. She drew a bead on her target, one of the larger trawlers at the end of a row, and went straight for it.

Tucker could see they were in the right place. From a hundred feet away, he could make out the name elegantly painted on the side underneath the cabin: MANDY LOU. The quality of the paint job belied the current condition of the rest of the boat. Spots of rust, bent rails, and barnacles near the waterline made the trawler look downright derelict. A carefully hung blue tarp covered the openings where glass should have been in the cabin's windows.

A closer look showed more. Cans of paint and workman's tools were visible on the deck. An awning, brand new from the looks of it, stuck out off the stern, offering shade for potential loungers or swimmers. This was a work in progress.

The name on the side, though; someone had gone to a great deal of trouble to make it look perfect. Someone made sure that part was done before the barnacles were even scraped off the hull. The name had meant something to Greg McGarrett.

"Something's here," said Rebekah. "Something worth telling us about from beyond death."

"Or we could be wasting our time."

"Is that what you think? You were the one who found the name of the boat. That's what brought us here."

Tucker looked down and stuck his hands in his pockets. No, he didn't think they were in the wrong place. It had been written in blood right in front of him: Mandy Lou, not Amanda Louise. The spirit wanted them here. He was being contentious out of spite, just like in the parking lot earlier that morning.

Rebekah waved at the three steps leading up from the dock to the boat's deck. "After you, then. If we're searching in the wrong place you don't need me to go in first."

"Fine." Her reaction was to challenge, and perhaps shame, him. Tucker walked around her and took the first step. Immediately, a sinking feeling of dread hit him in the pit of his stomach. The feeling came out of nowhere, quickly moving down to his legs, making them wobbly and weak. The panic, though unfounded and confusing, grew, forcing him to recall the first time he was on a boat close to this size.

This world is a cruel and arbitrary place

With Ray King close behind, he thought he was going to die that day. This was worse. He was a kid then. Now he was a full-grown man with nothing to be afraid of. Nobody but Rebekah was anywhere near him. There was no reason he should feel this way. He fought back a whimper and took a second step. One more and he would be standing triumphantly on the deck. Every sense told him to run, that moving forward or staying where he was would be the end of him. All he could hear was the pounding of his heart.

Survival instinct won out. Light-headed and breathing heavily, Tucker retreated the two steps back to the safety of the dock. Relieved but embarrassed, he squeaked, "What the hell?"

Rebekah moved to his side. "Like I said, something is here. Something important enough to need protection. The charm on this boat will repel any curious or nefarious people who might want to look too closely."

"Like us?"

"Yes, exactly like us." Rebekah stepped to the base of the stairs. Raising her arms, she said, "Fear is one of the oldest of emotions, maybe the oldest, and one of the easiest to tap into. We're hardwired from birth with fear as a survival mechanism. It's what keeps us alive when danger is near. A fog of fear surrounds this boat. She did this, but I can undo it."

With her arms in the air, eyes closed, and face to the sky, she looked as if she was in a revival tent, listening to a sermon only she could hear. Tucker was silent, afraid of making any noise that might disrupt her concentration. Without warning, Rebekah dropped her arms and blew, exhaling through pursed lips like she was blowing out birthday candles. A haze, enveloping the boat so faintly Tucker had barely seen it, was scattered into the wind.

When she finished, she turned to him.

"Follow me," she said. "Stay close. It should be better now." There wasn't much time to consider his options. Rebekah went up and onto the boat without hesitation. Tucker hurriedly got in behind her, bracing himself in anticipation of the crippling anxiety from before. When it failed to arrive, he was so astonished he didn't notice Rebekah had stopped in front of him on the narrow walkway. He ran right into her, earning a look of irritation.

"Sorry," said Tucker.

They moved into the main cabin. It was bare, even the boat's wheel was missing.

Everything else had been torn out. Rebekah ran her hands over every available surface as she meandered through, leaving footprints on the dusty floor.

"Looks like this hasn't been running in a long time," said Tucker.

"No, it runs. He had it purring – that's what he called it, purring – a couple of days before he was arrested." She felt at the air around her and tilted her head, listening to the silent rhythm of the vessel.

Tucker listened too, not hearing anything but the water lapping against the hull. He accepted what she was saying, but that didn't mean he was without questions. Now was not the time, however.

"This," she continued, "was a labor of love, his dream. He got a 'sweet deal' on it because of the condition it was in." She smiled. "He called the boat a 'she', not an 'it'."

Tarps covering the empty windows flapped in the breeze. Underneath, a short stairway led down into the belly of the boat. This boat was smaller than the gruesome Coast Guard vessel from his childhood, but the design was similar enough to make Tucker uneasy.

Unlike before, he was able to overcome this anxiety.

Rebekah went down the steps, hand out, feeling her way through unseen currents. "He repaired the hull first. She was barely floating when he got her. No use fixing anything else before making sure she wouldn't end up sinking on her first trip out. Charter fishing and whale watching, that's how he was going to make money. Hopefully enough money to quit his day job, but he wasn't too optimistic about that." Her expression turned somber. "He didn't have much faith in himself."

Down the stairs she went, pausing for a few seconds with each step. The living area was more spacious than Tucker assumed it was. The low ceiling made him feel a tad claustrophobic. Like the upstairs, most of it was torn out, but there was still a kitchen, bathroom, and queen-sized bed alongside the disarray of McGarrett's unfinished remodeling project.

"Someone's been here," said Tucker, "recently." On the counter in the partial kitchen was a loaf of bread and a jar of peanut butter, but it was the bananas that caught his eye.

They still had a green tint to them.

"He let her stay here," said Rebekah, examining the bed. It had been slept in and was left unmade. A small duffle bag rested on the floor by the headboard. Tucker could see a pair of jeans and some shirts stuffed inside. On the wall, hanging from a towel bar, was a short black dress and two bras.

"Like, live here? Why would he...oh." Tucker's question was answered in the form of a slinky red teddy Rebekah took out of the duffle and held up for inspection.

"I cannot sense her, not directly. It's as if she's shrouded herself." Rebekah let the garment fall to the bed.

"Except for those things, she seems gone."

"Yes, physical evidence of her presence. She's been here. By the looks of things, she'll be back unless she's long gone and left these behind to make us think she's coming back." Rebekah shook her head. "But I should be able to get a read on her. All I can see of her right now is through him. How he saw her.

"He was ashamed of himself, the way she made him weak. He knew he shouldn't be with her, but he couldn't help it. He tried, time and time again, but he always found his way back to her." She looked at Tucker and he thought he saw a glimmer of a tear. "McGarrett couldn't have known it wasn't a personal weakness. It was her, manipulating, corrupting, both physically and spiritually. He didn't have a chance."

How hard had the man really fought? Tucker knew too many who would have jumped at the chance to have a fantasy girl on his own private boat. A boat named after his wife, no less.

Rebekah seemed to read his mind. "He loved his family. I can feel that much. Charlotte made this happen. All of it."

Tucker kept his doubts to himself. It wasn't worth arguing about. Rebekah was going over the living area with a fine-tooth comb. If there was something to be found, she was going to find it.

"So what's the plan, then?" he asked.

She stopped searching and considered the question. "We need to be ready if she returns. She left her belongings behind, but it's not like her to stay in one place for long. Once the damage has been done, she's on the road to her next project. If she is already gone, there has to be something she left behind that would give a clue about where she went."

"And you'd follow her?"

"Yes, of course I would. I've come too far to fail. You would do the same in my place."

"I don't know about that."

"Perhaps you wouldn't. Maybe you could sleep at night knowing what she's done and what she's going to keep doing."

"I don't deserve that, Rebekah." Her tone was biting and condescending. Tucker fought the urge to mirror it. "I'm a volunteer here, trying to help."

"You're right, you don't need to be here. You know where the door is if you want to leave."

They stared at each other for a long moment. Was she bluffing? Rebekah had sought him out, not the other way around. Something convinced her he would be of help. Tucker never seriously considered leaving. He was too far in.

"I know where the door is. I'm staying. What do you want me to do?"

"Go up top, I'll stay down here. Keep an eye out for anything of hers. She should have a book, a valuable book. Probably large, too large to carry around with her wherever she goes. You'll know it if you see it. If that book is here, she'll be coming back for it. Other than that, look for anything out of place. You never know what could give us our next break."

"Okay, will do." Tucker gave a thumbs up and retreated back up the stairs. The chances of finding anything out on the deck were slim, he thought. Any valuables would be tucked away in some secret corner, not out in the light of day. Rebekah wanted him out of her way. That was fine with him. It was getting a little cramped down there.

The sunlight made him squint when he emerged from the cabin. He made his way clockwise around the boat as he half-heartedly searched. There wasn't enough room for two people to move side-by-side on the walkway from the rear of the boat. The surface was thin in places, giving way a little as he passed over.

On the deck, forward of the cabin, that's where there was room for sunbathing or maybe even a barbecue setup. Tucker could envision the potential here. McGarrett could never have afforded a boat like this unless it was a fix-er-upper. Cans of paint sat partially covered by a tarp. A worn tool belt hung from one of the sawhorses; its owner planning on returning, never imagining that day would be the last day he ever set foot aboard his boat. We always think there will be more time.

A vibration from his pocket reminded him of all the trouble he was trying to put off.

"Shit," he said, pulling out the phone. Several calls from Cheryl, most of them he'd seen and ignored earlier, he could understand. By now she had to have heard about his behavior at the jail. Knowing her, she was doing all she could to keep the boss from finding out.

Tucker never failed to show up for work without having a damn good reason. If he listened to the voicemails, he knew he would hear how worried she was.

The more recent messages surprised him and made him curse out loud. Three texts and two voicemails, all from Lyric. Had Cheryl called her after he couldn't be reached? Tucker opened the first text; it was a long one. Before he could finish the first sentence, he saw her out of the corner of his eye.

The girl looked to be around sixteen. Her platinum blonde hair was pulled tightly back in a single braid. On her back was a plain green drawstring pack. She wore a short white sundress with sandals and clutched a plastic sack of groceries to her chest.

"Hi, there," she said, flashing Tucker a disarming smile. "This is Greg's boat. Are you a friend of his?"

"Hi, yeah, um, sort of. I'm a legal assistant with-" Tucker caught himself before his made-up excuse left his mouth. The girl watched him from the dock by the Mandy Lou's stairs. She had been about to come up when he spotted her. Was that when she saw him?

Everything about her appearance said she was the teenager he assumed she was: the makeup, the hairstyle, even the bubbly way she greeted him.

The way she stood, the way she held the sack low on her hip, and most of all, the way he could feel the weight of her scrutiny in the intensity of her gaze, it all tickled at the back of his brain, warning him. She wasn't a young girl, but she wanted others to think she was.

The pieces fell into place.

"Charlotte?" Tucker didn't intend to speak out loud.

For a split-second her smile faltered. She recovered promptly, hiding again like a chameleon. "I'm afraid you have me at a disadvantage. You know my name but I don't know yours."

Chapter Sixteen

Charlotte had to be coming back. The signs told Rebekah she'd been living here and wasn't yet done with the place. But she'd been wrong about that before. If Charlotte's therimoire was still here, that would eliminate any doubt. That's the one thing she wouldn't permanently leave behind. Rebekah's own was tucked away safely in a drawer back in her motel room. To lose it would be disastrous. More than just a journal, a therimoire represented the sum total of her mystical journey. From basic initial lessons to more advanced recipes and magic, Rebekah's Book contained invaluable and irreplaceable learnings. Some of those lessons came from teachers who no longer walked this plane of existence. On those rare occasions she had to leave it behind, no matter how temporarily, she felt naked.

Charlotte had to have one just like it. Hers was most likely larger or thicker but the principle was the same.

So far, though, Rebekah had gone through the place and found nothing of the sort. The bed's mattress was now bare, the bedding itself in a pile on the floor, and the few hiding places in the bare living space were all vacant. Rebekah fell back on the bed and tried to plan her next course of action.

"Shit," she said aloud. To be this close and not know made her want to scream to the heavens. The bed might as well have been warm from Charlotte's body heat. They hadn't missed each other by very much. Now Rebekah had to guess. Was she coming back or was she already hundreds of miles away?

Guessing wasn't something Rebekah usually needed to do. The myriad of methods she had at her disposal to divine the future were useless when it came to Charlotte Disborough.

Whether it was an intentional precaution or not, there was a sort of black hole in Rebekah's second sight, allowing her to only detect Charlotte from the way she affected things around her.

The way she could see and feel through Greg McGarrett was the only way she could even tell Charlotte spent time here. He came through to her easily – his emotions, his thoughts – because this was a special place to him. The time he spent here was cathartic; the work he put in was for his family's future.

And then he met Charlotte.

She couldn't see how they met. Probably happenstance, something McGarrett could have avoided if he'd only known; a seemingly benign conversation in line for coffee, bumping into each other at a grocery store, or perhaps even out here at his boat while he was doing a weekend remodeling project. Embracing the chaos that is life, she left everything to chance.

In her mind's eye, Rebekah could see Charlotte lounging on the bed. Then she was sitting on the kitchen counter. Then she was giggling at something he'd said, tousling his hair and turning him to putty in her hands. All of this was from McGarrett's point of view.

Rebekah closed her eyes and concentrated. She wanted to dig deeper than these surface echoes. Sifting through them was unpleasant, especially so given the way things ended for him. The two of them eating dinner up on the deck, her doing a graceful pirouette in the morning sun, him walking in on her unexpectedly when she-

There it was. In the vision she saw Charlotte looking startled at his sudden appearance.

Her hand was hidden from view before she quickly tucked it behind her back. McGarrett felt suspicion but only for a moment. Her smile and the spell she had over him made him forget all about it.

The bed frame was built into the floor. The headboard was part of the back wall. This way it couldn't slide around even if the boat encountered rough seas. The mattress was not secured in the same way.

"Of course." Rebekah was disappointed in herself for not thinking to look there before.

Now it seemed obvious. The mattress was heavy but she barely noticed. Flipping it over exposed four flat, metal crossbars running across the frame. Underneath, laying on the floor, Rebekah could see a corner edge of brown leather through the gap. "It has to be...."

Her arms fit through the bars with room to spare. She slid the book through them and held it in both hands. Scanning the pages quickly, she confirmed this was what she'd been searching for.

Excited and appalled at the same time, Rebekah ran her fingers over the basket-weave pattern on the cover. There were no words printed on the front, only the familiar eight-pointed star embossed into the leather. Here it was, in her hands, physical evidence of the ghost of a woman she'd chased for so long. These pages were filled with her horrific and vile practices, enough to make her skin crawl just thinking about them. She gripped it tighter as if it might melt away before her eyes.

Voices drifted in through the hull. Rebekah was vaguely aware of them for some time but only focused on them now as they got louder. The muffled words escaped her. She tried to picture the outside dock and how close the speakers were.

The distinctly female giggle, along with a male voice that had to be Tucker's, made her freeze. Perfectly natural groans from the boat camouflaged the faint conversation, aggravating Rebekah. She hurried out of the half-done bedroom and up the stairs, Charlotte's therimoire cradled under one arm. Who was Tucker talking to? Hope and trepidation rose within her equally. It couldn't be her, could it?

Tucker caught her eye first. He was supposed to still be on the boat, checking for any sign of Charlotte. Standing on the dock, he had his back to her as she came out of the cabin.

Tucker wasn't a large man, but he was big enough to shield the person he was speaking with from view. Hands in his pockets, he appeared at ease with whoever this was.

The top step creaked beneath her foot. Tucker turned around lazily. Glassy-eyed with an idiotic grin, he looked to be intoxicated even from twenty feet away. Rebekah knew that look immediately. It was very much like the stuporous state he was in yesterday as the two of them went to the jail. Only this was worse.

"Hey, Rebekah," he said, waving limply. "I was looking like you told me but she walked up and I didn't want to be rude."

"She?" But she already knew. In an instant, Rebekah recognized the woman leaning out past Tucker's shoulder. The playful look she gave was the same as it was the first time she laid eyes on her at Mirror Lake. That was a lifetime ago for Rebekah, but with a glance she was transported back to that summer.

"Hi there," said Charlotte. "Who's your friend, Tucker?" She looked Rebekah over head-to-toe as she caressed Tucker's arm. "Do you know Greg, too?" she asked Rebekah.

Tucker answered, swaying as he spoke. "Sorry, I forgot to mention she was here with me. This is my...this is Rebekah. Rebekah, this is Charlotte. You were right, she did come back to the boat."

Charlotte lightly slapped Tucker's shoulder. "Yes, you should have told me. That was very forgetful of you." Her expression hardened. "How did your friend know I'd be coming back? You didn't come here looking for me, did you?"

"Yeah," Tucker replied, "it's a funny story. See, I was at work-"

"Shut up, Tucker." Rebekah's firm voice silenced him. It wasn't his fault, she told herself. Charlotte's touch had charmed him like her own had the day before. The tendrils now affecting his mind would have taken hold even easier given his recent experience.

Charlotte couldn't possibly know that. As far as she knew, Tucker was simply more susceptible to her abilities.

"That was rude, talking to my friend Tucker like that. Almost as rude as taking things that don't belong to you. That book is mine."

Rebekah held the book tighter to her side. So preoccupied was she with Charlotte and Tucker, she'd forgotten she even had it.

"Is this yours?" Rebekah felt light-headed. Her hands shook as she adjusted her grip.

Was this a trick of Charlotte's, some unseen force extending out to disrupt and debilitate?

No, she thought. This was not her doing. Adrenaline was coursing through her body, quickening her pulse and making her hyperventilate. Focus on the task before you. Her old mentor drummed the mantra into her from day one: slow down, one step at a time, do it right, no mistakes.

Her heartbeat slowed as she calmed herself. This was the moment she'd fantasized about, the stuff of daydreams when hope became fleeting. Seeing Charlotte again, in the flesh, out of arms reach but close enough to see the stray hairs on the top of her head flutter in the ocean breeze. In moments of weakness, Rebekah sometimes doubted she'd ever lay eyes on her again.

In all of her imaginings of how this meeting would go, she never planned for this scenario. The dock ended a few feet behind Rebekah so she was surrounded by water on three sides. Somebody else might have felt trapped, but her main worry wasn't being cornered by Charlotte, it was Charlotte fleeing before Rebekah could snare her.

"Yes, ma'am, that is my book. I'm sure you know it's not yours so I don't know why you're trying to leave with it."

An ad hoc plan began to form. Rebekah stood up straight, shoulders back, chin held high. "Leave him alone. He has nothing to do with this." She took a step forward.

"I'm afraid I don't know what you mean. Whatever this is, he seems to be right in the middle of it." Charlotte wrapped her arm through Tucker's. The way they stood, arm-in-arm, they looked as if they were posing for a photo at a high school dance. She also moved a step, not backward but sideways, putting more of Tucker between her and Rebekah. She was definitely wary.

"No, he's not. It's me. I'm the one who's right in the middle. He's just some poor sap I convinced to help me."

"Help how?"

"Help me find you." Tucker's eyes went back and forth between them like he was watching a tennis match. His vacant expression made Rebekah doubt he understood much of what was being said.

"Oh, I'm flattered." Charlotte placed her hand on her chest. "I hope you haven't gone through too much trouble."

"More than you know."

"May I ask why you've gone to so much trouble to find me? I haven't exactly been hiding. Have we met before? You don't look familiar."

"I'm older now, even though somehow you're not."

"That sounded a tad judgmental. I don't think I'm the only one who's bent the rules a bit to keep the wrinkles at bay." Charlotte winked at her.

Rebekah's face reddened and her hands started to shake again. "Bent the rules. That's putting it mildly."

"Tucker, I think I touched a nerve with your friend here. What did you say your name was? Rebekah? No, I think I'd remember if I ever met a Rebekah."

"New Jersey. A long time ago." She couldn't have forgotten. Rebekah was forced to remember every single day.

Charlotte put a finger to her lips in contemplation. "That's a long ways away. No, I don't recall ever visiting there. Sorry."

Anger flared, but Rebekah pushed it away, refusing to be baited. It didn't matter. Charlotte would pay for what she'd done whether she remembered doing it or not.

"Tucker, though," said Charlotte, "he and I clicked right away. I wonder if we've encountered each other before, maybe in a prior life." She giggled. "If you believe in that sort of thing. I like him. He's the sort of person who has the potential to make a difference in the world, know what I mean? I enjoy that particular type of person."

She ran her hand down Tucker's arm. He didn't seem to hear her. Blinking rapidly, as if he had a piece of dirt in his eye, Tucker was no longer a part of their conversation. It was almost time.

"I know exactly what you mean. Just how many people like that have you known?"

"I don't keep count. It's not a contest. A lot, that's for sure. They're more common than you would think. I seem to find one wherever I go."

"You're not from around here," Rebekah said. Tucker rubbed at his eyes with his free hand.

"No, but I think you know that. My hometown doesn't exist anymore. It died slowly like those little towns tend to do. The price of progress, I guess. That's okay, though. It was a shithole, full of hypocrites and degenerates." Charlotte shrugged. "I'm a citizen of the world. Traveling, meeting new people, realizing over and over again they're really all the same if you dig down deep enough. That's my passion."

"I think what you mean is ruining lives and spreading-"

"I'm bored with this now. You have something that belongs to me. I'll take that back and be on my way. Do it nicely and I won't leave you something to remember me by." Charlotte's easy-going demeanor was gone. Rebekah steeled herself against the invisible tendrils reaching out to touch her mind.

"You stay right there," Charlotte commanded. "Tucker, be my hero and get me my book back. I would be most appreciative."

Rebekah took a step forward. "No, bitch," said Charlotte. "I told you to stay put. Tucker, don't just stand there. I said-"

The look on Tucker's face cut her off. Perplexed but clear-eyed, he turned to Rebekah. "Wait a sec, what is it we're here for?"

It was her ace-in-the-hole; the thing Charlotte couldn't possibly know. Her influence over Tucker, while effective, was fleeting. His previous exposure from the day before made him easier to dominate initially, but it wore off in a fraction of the usual time.

Rebekah shouted, "Tucker! It's Charlotte, grab her, now!"

Chapter Seventeen

Rebekah's cry spurred them both into action. Charlotte reacted faster than Tucker. She pulled away from him as he fumbled for her arm. The fog in his mind had lifted somewhat, but not completely. The last thing he remembered clearly was Charlotte playing with his hair and telling him how handsome he was. Everything between then and now was a dream-like haze.

Her mouth contorted to a snarl as she avoided his grasp. Charlotte slapped him across his face with an open hand, catching his ear and blurring his vision. Instead of pulling her hand back after the slap, she raked her fingernails down his cheek all the way to his mouth, drawing blood and leaving bit of ragged flesh hanging. The ringing in his ear and the stinging in his cheek cleared his head just in time for Charlotte to bring her foot up into his groin. The force of the kick doubled him over and sent him to his knees.

"Don't touch me," Charlotte screamed, sounding every bit like a damsel in distress. She spun towards Rebekah. "Give me my book back, bitch."

Rebekah stopped in her tracks as Tucker crumpled to the ground. Their two-to-one advantage was temporarily eliminated. She met Charlotte's icy stare with one of her own.

"Come and take it. Do your own dirty work for once."

Rage glinted in Charlotte's eyes. The two women faced off from a few feet away. Charlotte tensed as if to leap at Rebekah when a voice came from a boat three slips down. "Hey, what's going on over there?"

Then a different one said, "Linda, call the police."

Charlotte and Rebekah glanced back down the dock. Several onlookers, some standing atop boats of their own, stopped what they were doing and turned their attention toward the confrontation.

"Somebody, help me!" Charlotte transformed right there in front of them. Standing there, demanding her property be returned to her, she was ready and able to destroy anyone standing in her way. Rebekah looked intimidated, thought Tucker. He didn't know that was possible. Then, as if sensing an easier way out, Charlotte instantly changed into the perfect victim. Her features softened and took on a look of fear. She backed away from Tucker, her hand covering her face. Impossibly, she seemed to get smaller, more vulnerable.

"They're trying to take me," she yelled to the closest witness, a man in shorts and a tank top. Charlotte's high-pitched plea for help surely sounded legitimate enough to fool the concerned bystanders.

Charlotte tore off down the dock, running past the tank top man and his outstretched arms. "No, don't let her go," Rebekah groaned as she chased after her. The book, no longer as important now that she had her real target so close, fell out of her hands and hit the wood with a deep thump. She moved past Tucker, struggling to get to his feet, without a second thought.

Rebekah dodged the first man who tried to stop her from pursuing. It was the older couple a short distance down who deliberately blocked the walkway in an attempt to keep her from Charlotte. Watching all this through waves of pain, Tucker was very aware of how this whole thing must look to ignorant onlookers. To them, Charlotte was the vulnerable victim being accosted by two crazies. These were good samaritans trying to help.

He couldn't worry about that now.

Lowering her shoulder like a running back, Rebekah blew through the obstacle, knocking the gray-haired wife onto her backside and sending the husband reeling. Charlotte kicked off one sandal and was in the process of getting rid of the other one when Rebekah caught her by her hair. They both shrieked; Charlotte in pain, Rebekah in triumph.

A bearded man in mirrored sunglasses intervened, wedging himself in between them, trying to separate the two women. Rebekah held fast, even as Charlotte twisted around to face her. "You're not getting away this time."

"Hey, hey, hey, break it up," said the bearded man. One hand wrapped in blonde hair; Rebekah held up her bandaged hand to Charlotte's face.

"*Somnum*," she said, focusing her energies into her adversary.

The man pushing them apart collapsed instantly. He landed, shoulder-first, and laid still.

Charlotte's grip on Rebekah's wrist relaxed and she started to fall into her arms. It almost worked; Charlotte was milliseconds away from unconsciousness. Rebekah's arms were out to catch her but Charlotte caught herself. Their faces were inches apart.

"Close, but not good enough," Charlotte said, her face a mask of ferociousness. "You won't get another chance." She grabbed Rebekah by her forearms, closed her eyes, and murmured, "*Astrapi*."

The shock of pure electricity hit her like a freight train. All over her body her muscles seized. Rebekah's hands locked up into claws. "Gh, gh, gh," was all she could get out.

Charlotte released her hold and Rebekah fell limply to the dock next to the bearded man.

The smell of burnt hair wafted around them. Charlotte staggered and stumbled away from the bodies at her feet. Dazed, Rebekah fought to regain the coordination necessary to get up.

"Watch out, she's got a taser." It was a woman's voice screaming. The crowd of witnesses had grown to more than a dozen.

"Help me, someone," Charlotte begged, fake tears shining in her eyes.

Doubled over, Tucker managed to make his way past the concerned citizens to Rebekah. "C'mon," he said, reaching down to help her up, "she's getting away."

Seemingly in slow-motion, she took both of his hands and got up, first to her knees, then to her shaky feet. Tucker put an arm around her waist for support. Up ahead, Charlotte wobbled on unsteady feet up the ramp to the marina exit.

"Can't let her get away," Rebekah wheezed.

A voice behind them tore their attention from the escaping woman. "Hold it right there, you two. Stay right there. You leave that girl be and we'll let the police handle it from here." Backing up his words was the gun pointed at them from three feet away. It seemed out of place in his hand. Wearing khaki shorts, thick glasses, and a sweatshirt, he was dressed more for a stroll on the beach than an intervention in a crime-in-progress.

Tucker froze in place, hypnotized by the gentle sway of the dark muzzle of the pistol. His eyes fixated on the front sight and the gaping hole below it. The man behind the gun had his finger on the trigger. Just a few pounds of pressure and a bullet would tear through him.

"Get on the ground," said the man, gesturing with the weapon. He looked to be about fifty, his hair was more gray than brown. It was clearly a command but it lacked intensity. There was a tremor in his voice as he gave the order. This wasn't someone who was used to putting himself in the middle of a crisis. Great, thought Tucker, an off-duty mall security guard trying to be a hero. He could ruin everything.

"No, no, no." Rebekah locked eyes with the gunman. "You don't understand. None of you do." She spread her arms wide and leaned forward on the balls of her feet, the gun now aimed directly at her throat. "I don't have the time to explain or convince but I will not be denied by any of you."

Slowly, she brought her hands up and in to the pistol. Tucker winced in anticipation of the inevitable explosion when the trigger was finally pulled. The man in the khaki shorts glanced around at the others for some sign of how he should proceed. Rebekah touched the cold metal with one hand, then the other.

"Get, stay back," he stammered. "Stop or-"

"I won't. I can't. Not ever." She gently pulled down on the hands holding the gun with one long, smooth motion. The barrel traced its way from her neck to her chest to her stomach until it was pointing straight down between her feet. "Tucker, go. Find her."

Nobody tried to stop him. They were all in awe of Rebekah as much as he was. Tucker dodged around the people of the marina until he reached the gate. Charlotte was nowhere in sight as he reached the small parking lot and the Prius. A car horn in the distance caused him to turn. Her shining hair was unmistakable even from this distance. There she was, narrowly avoiding being run down by an orange pickup as she fled through the intersection.

He reached into his pocket for the car keys, then cursed out loud when he remembered Rebekah had them. Charlotte made it safely across the road, ducked behind a convenience store, and disappeared into an apartment complex close to a hundred yards away. Tucker grimaced and took off after her, heading for the spot where he saw her last. The ache in his groin was subsiding, but not fast enough for his liking. Blood ran down his cheek and neck from the fingernail wounds. He tried to fight through the pain and focus on putting one foot in front of the other. Tucker's run was ungainly, doubled over as he was. He covered the distance quickly, though, his will trumped his discomfort.

The concrete sidewalk behind the store led him into the breezeway of the weathered complex. Four distinct buildings were separated by walkways and surrounded a courtyard of foliage and a small playground. Standing outside Apartment 3, Tucker scanned the grounds. Charlotte was gone, but which way did she go?

"Fuck." There were too many possibilities. He picked one and started jogging. With no sign of her, the lull in action allowed Tucker time to assess his situation. Appearances were not on his side. Here he was, chasing a scared young woman across traffic. He couldn't blame anyone who tried to help her. What was he going to do if he did catch up to her? Up until now he'd been operating on reflex; Charlotte's influence, much like Rebekah's, left him foggy, like waking from a deep sleep.

He tried to think of a plan. Could he throw Charlotte over his shoulder, kicking and screaming, and haul her back to the car? Not likely. Someone, maybe even the police, would stop him. What was Rebekah going to do if they were able to incapacitate her? Tucker thought he knew the answer to that one, but didn't want to think about it.

A wailing siren passed close by on the other side of the building. Police? Fire? He sensed he was walking a fine line where a misstep could send him plunging into a chasm. Maybe he was already doomed.

"What am I doing?" Tucker took in the cloudy sky and considered walking away and trying his best to forget all about Rebekah, Charlotte, and the last couple of days. If only he could go back to the blissful ignorance of last week, when the biggest stress in his life was his relationship.

It would be easy. The office was nearby and, if he didn't feel like going there, home was only a few more miles. Walking distance, even if it took him a while. Tucker would have to come back to get the Prius; maybe he could avoid the police but probably not. Questions would need answers. The truth was not an option, nobody would believe it. Concoct a story and, unless they found Charlotte to be cooperative, he would get past this, legally speaking.

Going further didn't seem worth it anymore. Tucker could learn to live with his own remaining questions.

Movement from the playground, a wisp of white fabric seen through a gap in the bushes, flashed and then was hidden. Tentatively, he went down the walkway, the row of closed doors to his left, the empty play area to his right. Tucker slowly circled the entire area. There was no one.

"Tucker." The whisper came from the air itself. Over by Apartment 3 – the white sundress again – a blur of blonde hair and the patter of bare feet on pavement appeared and disappeared. Behind him, the air moved as if someone ran past him. He wheeled around in a complete circle but didn't see anyone.

"Oh, Jesus," he said, holding his hands to his head. Colors dulled and the air itself took on a grayish hue. His mind was slipping and he doubted his own senses. Tucker caught the faint scent of strawberries in a breath of wind. There was no sound in the courtyard. For a split-second, he saw Charlotte facing him on an upstairs balcony, her face hidden behind her hair. He blinked and she was gone.

Then she appeared in a first-floor doorway on the other side of the playground. Tucker stared and her voice whispered to him from behind. "I meant what I said. I do like you, Tucker. You stand out in a way most people can't see. I see you. I see you very well."

This world is a cruel and arbitrary place

Cold hands slid up his back and reached over his shoulders, covering his eyes and mouth. Tucker shouted in surprise. A sultry voice in his ear said, "Know. Understand. See."

At once he was taken away from the present. As if in a dream, he could see through another's eyes.

A woman, driving a minivan, is stopped at a busy intersection. She sees the light turn green and puts her foot gently on the gas pedal. The vehicle that hits her is a utility truck on its way back to the city lot after a day of work. It rams directly into the driver's door doing forty-five. She is killed instantly. Her eight-year-old son in the back survives but will walk with a limp and battle anger problems for the rest of his life. The driver of the truck is able to walk away but the trauma forces him into early retirement. He, along with everyone else who witnesses the accident, swears her light was red when she pulled forward.

Then

A man, given so many painkillers he can barely remember his own name, is in a hospital bed surrounded by loved ones. Six weeks ago, he was preparing for a 10k race and worrying about a leak in the roof. Now, he is breathing his final breaths. The doctors have never seen a brain tumor come on so fast. The treatments were aggressive, but ultimately ineffective. He'd put off marriage until three years ago. His wife, by his side and looking haggard and withdrawn, is the one holding his hand as his chest hitches once...twice...then lies still. He was forty-three.

Then

A young man in his late-teens stops to pick up a hitchhiker in his souped-up Mustang that he purchased with cash after he was drafted in the third round by the Arizona Diamondbacks. On his way to Geneva, Illinois and the team's Class A minor league club, he decides to stop on the side of a deserted road with his lovely young passenger. Charlotte sits next to the youthful pitcher, listening with rapt attention to tales of his exploits on the mound. She spins a baseball in her hand with a practiced ease. The ball picks up speed and levitates above her fingertips.

"Whoa, that's a cool trick. How do you do that?" Charlotte smiles. The cowhide sphere flies from her hand twice as fast as he's ever thrown in his entire life. His face is obliterated, the ball striking him below his right eye. He is found in his car the next day. There is no trace of the passenger.

Then

A girl, fourteen years old, is walking down the side of a highway outside of town. Long, greasy, dirty blonde hair hangs down around her face. She can't remember when she showered last. Her tears have been all used up in the past few days and her eyes burn. All she has in her possession are a few groceries from a mini mart stuffed into a backpack. All of these things are stolen; something she wouldn't have dreamed of doing a week ago. Now, it's about surviving from one day to the next.

How many days has it been since she walked in the door of the house she grew up in? Her own mother didn't recognize her. At first, she thought it was a prank. "Knock it off, Mom, you're freaking me out."

"Oh, dear," Mom said in her customary soothing tone, "I think you need some help. I'm not your mother, sweetie."

The photos on the mantle were all changed. She was missing from every single one of them. Her bedroom, the one she left that morning for school, was now being used for storage. When the police came, her parents stood on the porch. "I feel for the poor girl, I do, but I don't know why she thinks she lives here. We don't have a daughter and our son is away at college."

The worst, though, was Molly, her stringy-haired gray mutt. The dog who slept in her bed almost every night and who shivered with fear at thunderstorms, didn't know who she was. Molly showed her teeth and growled if she even tried to get close.

That was too much. Either she was crazy or the rest of the world was. She ran out the back door, crawled through the hole in the fence, and headed out into the world, alone and scared. Nonexistent.

All of these went by in a blink. Tucker could see beyond, into the river of past images of ruin Charlotte had wrought. The scope was mind-boggling. "Why?" he shouted. Why did she do it? Why was she showing him? "Why?"

Two apartments down, a door creaked open and two women stuck their heads out. They seemed real. Their expressions of worry mixed with a tinge of fear sure looked real. Tucker cautiously took a look at his surroundings, expecting her to appear again at any moment. He was on his knees in front of Apartment 3.

He put his hands on the wall to stop the world from spinning and waved absently at the women to show he was okay. Charlotte was gone.

The sound of more approaching sirens set him off limping as fast as he could in the opposite direction, away from the marina, his car, and Rebekah. Whatever happened next, he couldn't afford to be detained.

Charlotte was still close, and she had to be stopped.

Chapter Eighteen

A book, in and of itself, is neither evil nor good. It is a repository of information. Documentation recording events, stories, or instructions used throughout the ages. This book held a malevolence to it. She couldn't shake that feeling, no matter how illogical it was. It was her own prejudice telling her the inanimate object was anything more than what it seemed. Would Rebekah view it the same way if she was unaware of who the owner was?

Her path back to the motel room was fraught with close calls. Had she been wrong about him, the man with the gun could have ended things right there. Rebekah had read him, not with any special abilities, but with her own natural senses. She'd bet her life, along with Tucker's, that he wouldn't use lethal force to keep them from leaving the marina. He'd only gone as far as he did to justify his own sense of self. He wanted to be the hero, imagining himself swooping in and saving the day, but that wasn't who he was deep down.

Her gentle but firm response completely defused his violent potential.

His gun rested on the bed next to where she sat cross-legged. Charlotte's book was in front of her, unopened.

Going back to get Charlotte's therimoire was a must. If Tucker couldn't catch up to her, the book was their only chance. Rebekah didn't hold out much hope that Tucker could get the job done. She feared Charlotte would feast on his too-pleasant nature if he was lucky enough to get to her before she vanished again.

The people at the marina gawked at her as she got back to the car. That was all they did; none of them stood in her way. Gun tucked into the back of her jeans, Rebekah did not stick around and give them a chance to change their minds.

The Prius was waiting for her right where she'd left it. She assumed the police were on the way. The car was the quickest way to leave the scene before they arrived. Rebekah ditched it, keys and all, a couple of blocks from her motel. Hopefully someone would steal it. The thief could explain to the authorities why he was driving a car involved in an earlier attempted kidnapping and theft of a firearm. Tucker would have to find himself another means of transportation.

When she finally opened the book, she was surprised at the feeling of guilt coming over her. The invasion of privacy she was committing was a violation on a most personal level.

In her own book was everything from basic lessons to advanced techniques to her innermost thoughts and dreams. It was more than a journal, more than an instruction manual. The thought of anybody casually leafing through it made her shudder.

But this was Charlotte's book. Charlotte, the destroyer of lives. Normal etiquette or respect for boundaries didn't apply to her. She deserved far worse.

A soft pounding at the door followed by a firm voice from the other side told her Tucker had made it back. They hadn't discussed a plan on where to meet up if things went wrong so his only option, besides giving up altogether, was to head back to the only place he associated with her.

Tucker didn't wait for an invitation, he pushed past her into the room. "I was hoping you'd be here and not lying in a ditch somewhere," he said.

"I had the same hope for you." Rebekah told him what she'd done with his car and her reasoning for it.

Tucker's head bobbed up and down. "Yeah, that's smart. One of those marina-people had to have jotted down the plate. They'll run it, connect it to me...fuck. I'll jump off that bridge when I come to it."

"What happened with Charlotte?"

Tucker put his hands on his hips and looked at the floor. "Yeah, well, obviously she's not here with me." He put his hands in his pockets. "Chasing after her like I did, I felt like a dog chasing a squirrel. Have you ever seen a dog catch one? I haven't. Seen plenty of chases but not one catch. That was me, chasing the squirrel and not knowing what I was going to do if I caught it. You know what you would do, though. Don't you?"

"Tucker, I-"

"I'm not judging or accusing. We didn't talk about it, we let it go as one of those unspoken things." He paused. "I did catch up to her, not too far from where I left you. I shouldn't have, looking back on it. She should have been farther away by the time I got there. She caught me, you could say."

"What do you mean? What happened?"

"I was about to quit on you. You should know that. I saw my way out. I'd lost her, Charlotte got away clean. All I had to do was forget I ever met you or her, forget everything you showed me, forget about that day on the Coast Guard boat with my dad, and just go back to my life and try to clean up the mess I made. I almost did it, too."

Rebekah folded her arms over her chest. "But you're here."

"Yeah. I'm here. I'll probably regret it. I think I'll regret it more if I quit."

"What happened, Tucker?"

"She caught me. Here I was, here we were, trying to catch her and I ran right into her arms. Charlotte showed me. Showed me what she's done. It was horrible, Rebekah."

"I know. She has no conscience."

"You think you know but have you seen? I don't think you've seen like I have. So many, countless victims, and for what? Her own fucked up idea of playing god?"

"You don't know what I've seen. Don't presume." She'd seen more than enough and she'd lost more than he could imagine.

"No, I don't. Because you won't tell me." Tucker snapped. "Can you explain why Charlotte opened up and showed me her resume like she did? Like she was proud of her accomplishments? Wouldn't it have made more sense if she'd just killed me? One less potential threat to worry about."

Yes, that would have made more sense, but Charlotte had a tendency to do the unexpected. It was one of the reasons Rebekah had never caught up to her until today. One thing she was sure of; if Charlotte wanted Tucker dead, she'd have killed him when she had the chance.

"She has a plan for you, that must be it."

"Yeah, well now we need a new plan for her. One that ends with her head on a pike."

There it was, out in the open. The words sounded out of place coming from Tucker, the mild-mannered legal assistant. Neither of them had said it out loud until now. Charlotte dead was the only way to be sure she couldn't hurt anybody ever again.

"And you're okay with that? You're willing to go that far?" There was a reason Rebekah avoided asking the question until now. Tucker was no killer. His moral compass could be a hindrance.

"I am now. I understand what she is. She likes it, Rebekah. I could feel it through the visions she made me see. Her mission is to spread chaos, like it's her calling, but she enjoys her work. It's sickening."

"Okay, good. We're in agreement then." Rebekah picked up the book from the bed. "Charlotte will come for this. She has to. We missed this chance but we'll make sure we get another."

"We can't sit around in a crappy hotel room, waiting for her to show her face. She's not that stupid."

"No, she's not, and we're not going to sit around. Here, look." Rebekah opened the book and leafed through the pages. Tucker looked over her shoulder at the glyphs, letters, and images. "This is the best lead we have, a window into her thoughts, secrets, everything."

"That's not English," Tucker said.

"No, not entirely." The passages that were in English were more common in the beginning of the book. As it went on, those became fewer and fewer. Some were in languages she recognized but wasn't fluent in – Greek, Latin, Spanish – while others were completely indecipherable. Parsed throughout, at random intervals, were hand-drawn pictures. Crude sketches but with an obvious talent showing in each one.

"What is that?" Tucker pointed at one such drawing. It was done in pencil. The detail and shading were exquisite. A small crowd of five were gathered at the base of a wooden gallows that was the focus of the piece. Three people stood with their hands bound behind their backs and a noose around each of their necks. Two of them – men, judging by the way they were dressed – were hooded but the third, a dark-haired woman in a long dress, was not. She stared defiantly at the man with one hand on the lever that would send her to her death. The executioner wore a six-shooter on his hip and a cowboy hat on his head.

"A memory, I think, of something long ago." She touched the paper with the tip of her finger.

"A memory? This is something out of the wild west." Tucker paused a moment before asking, "How old is Charlotte?"

"Older than she looks."

"I figured that much out. How does she pull that off? Is she like a vampire?"

"Dark rituals. The kind that no being with a soul should ever attempt." She slammed the book shut and dropped it on the mattress.

"The kind of rituals you would never try?" Tucker snatched the book back up and opened it.

"Certain ceremonies take a toll on you, stain your soul even. Stains that don't come out no matter how much you try to make amends. Some souls have been dyed black by their actions. Others are like a small blemish on a white dress. You can see it from across the room and it won't ever go away, but the good outweighs the bad."

Tucker sat and laid the open book in his lap. "How stained is your dress, Rebekah?"

"That's irrelevant. I've made sacrifices to get this far. I have regrets, too. Stopping Charlotte will make those sacrifices and regrets worth it."

"The ends justify the means."

"Overly simplified but, in this case, yes."

He slowly turned the pages. Tucker couldn't have understood more than a sliver of what he was looking at on the paper. His attention was on Rebekah. He had questions and perhaps the time had come for answers.

She said, "I'm not proud of everything I've done but I'll be proud when I finish what I've set out to do." Rebekah stood in front of Tucker, her hands balled into fists. He looked up from the book. "Charlotte is old, I don't know how old. Older than you and me combined."

"You're older than you look too. Aren't you?"

They'd switched roles. Tucker was calm and composed, patiently waiting for Rebekah to say what she needed to say. She was far from flustered, but the words came out faster the more she talked. So much time had gone by since she'd last spoken to a real person about this.

"There are spirits among us, all around us. Most are the untethered souls of human beings, the last remnants of our family and friends, those who came before us. Those souls, like ours, are eternal, even if they aren't recognizable as the person they were. A smaller number of spirits have never known corporeal form. Through the ages they've been referred to as angels, demons, djinn, fairies, the list goes on. Beseeching these spirits for favors comes with a price. Turning back the hands of time, bringing youth to old age, is one of those favors. Among those like me, it is taboo to do so because the price is too high."

"Who decides what's taboo and what isn't?"

"Centuries of harsh lessons, passed down from one generation to the next." Thankfully, Tucker didn't press the question. The real answer was harder to explain to the average person. There were no laws nor law enforcement for this kind of thing. Peer pressure where applicable plus the desire to not draw attention decided what practices were acceptable.

Drawing attention meant creating fear. Fear led to trials and then burnings.

Rebekah continued. "The ceremony involved for recovering lost youth makes it possible to reach into the ether and grab a soul from its rightful place. One soul out of the hundred billion who have died since the world began turning doesn't seem like a big deal. The soul, the eternal flame, is completely consumed in the process. Forever destroyed. You asked if she was a vampire?

She is, of a sort. Killing that which should be forever is an affront to the natural order. We are meant to continue into the next life. Charlotte steals that in exchange for a few more years on the mortal plane."

"Whoever that was ceases to exist. She stays young forever."

"Not forever. It's temporary. Charlotte has to repeat the process over and over again. The way she casually throws away something so precious is obscene."

"What about you?"

"Me?" The denial was on the tip of her tongue but she stopped. At this point there was no reason to hold anything back. "I've made mistakes, done things I'm not proud of. I felt the years going by too fast and, in a moment of weakness, I pushed my scruples aside. I turned back my own clock to buy more time with the hope it would be enough. I meant what I said about the stain on your soul. I know about it firsthand."

"The ends justify the means." Was that sarcasm? Contempt?

"I wasn't about to let her get away with her wickedness just because I'd gotten too old and gray. If I die before she gets her justice it won't be the passage of time that does me in. I won't let my body fail me."

"So, you'd do it again?"

"If I-" Rebekah stopped mid-sentence. The book in Tucker's lap was opened to a page with tiny writing on one side, a drawing on the other. It was the drawing that caught her attention and left her speechless.

Like the gallows picture, it was done in pencil. This one was an outdoor scene devoid of people. The view was of the end of a narrow dock overlooking a large pond; this kind of dock wasn't built for boats but for lazy days of fishing with your feet dangling in the water. With the tall grass along the edges and wooded area in the background, the idyllic setting would have been right at home in a Norman Rockwell collection.

"What is it? Rebekah?" Tucker asked as she took the book from him to study it. "Have you seen this before?"

"Yes," she replied, "and no. Not since I was young. I know this place, not the drawing. This is where I grew up. This is where..." She was breathing hard. This was unexpected. "Charlotte memorialized her time in my hometown. Wrote it in her damn diary."

"That's where you know her from."

"This place specifically…is where it all started for me." She looked away from the paper and into Tucker's eyes. "Okay, for you to understand, before you judge me, you need to hear what I have to say."

CHAPTER NINETEEN

Rebekah's Story Part One

I was born to Charles and Laura Goodwright in Independence Corner, New Jersey. Our town was small and friendly in a way you'd have to experience to believe. The nearest town over, Walker Township, had around fifteen-thousand people or so. We were about half that size so if you didn't know someone, you probably had a friend in common at the very least.

My dad knew everyone. He ran the grocery store in town, Goodwright Grocery. Not a very creative name, I guess, but he wasn't a very imaginative man. Charles Goodwright was hardworking, loyal, and honest but he was no poet. I still remember when Mrs. Greene was a little short of money for how much she put up on the counter at the store. He told her not to worry about it and that she could pay for it in her own time. She cried and six-year-old me wondered out loud about how somebody could forget to bring enough money to buy food for their family.

"We don't judge, Rebekah," he told me. "We don't know their struggles so we don't judge." I can still picture his face, stern but not mad. I thought he was the wisest man in the world.

Laura Goodwright, my mother, was cut from the same cloth as her husband. They married very young, most people did in those days, and I wish I could have known them then. Were they always so much alike or did each of them, over the years spent together, assume the temperament and demeanor of their spouse?

Mom handled the bookkeeping duties at the store. If my dad was the heart and smile of the operation, then my mom was the brains and the behind-the-scenes stage manager of the whole thing. Dad used to always joke that he was the only married man who could get away with sleeping with his secretary. Mom would roll her eyes and laugh every single time he said it. We all knew the truth, though. The store and, by extension the whole family, would be a lost cause without Mom steering the ship.

Even though they married young, I didn't come along for a few years. Mom told me once that she had given up on having any children, that it just wasn't God's plan for them.

I was their Miracle Baby, she said. Dad was so excited when I was born that he changed the name of the store to Goodwright and Daughter Grocery. He made the new sign himself.

This sign displayed the name of the store in larger, three-foot high letters for all to see.

It was still hanging proudly five years later when my little brother, Evan, was born. I guess one miracle wasn't enough for my mother. Dad didn't hesitate to make another sign proclaiming the store was now Goodwright and Daughter and Son Grocery. Evan was adorable when he was little. Nobody was sure where his mop of blonde hair came from because Mom and Dad were both brunettes. One of his eyes was green, the other was gray.

I'd never even heard of such a thing at the time. We were a family of four living in our little blue house on the edge of town.

Evan and I got along from the start. Maybe we wouldn't have if we had been born closer together. Most of my friends couldn't stand to be around their siblings. I doted over him, even when he was a baby. When it came to Evan, anything my mom needed help with I cheerfully volunteered for.

I taught him to play tic-tac-toe, then jacks, then hide-and-seek as he got older. He always tagged along with me if I went anywhere with my friends. I never minded and my friends adored him so much that they welcomed him too.

With open fields and wooded areas surrounding our house, it was easy to find something to do when we weren't in school or helping at the store. Mirror Lake, though, that was our favorite. Us kids called it Mirror Lake because sometimes, on a clear and sunny day, it perfectly reflected the sky and trees. We never did learn if that was what the rest of the world had called it. It was more of a pond than a lake. The water level would rise and fall with the seasons but there was always enough water to swim. Mirror Lake wasn't the only place to hang out at in Independence Corner, but it was the most popular because no adults ever made the trek out that far.

During the summer, we would spend all day at the lake. After breakfast and chores, Evan and I would head down there at least three or four times a week. Mom and Dad only insisted that I keep an eye on him if he were to come with me. "He's your little brother. It's your job to keep him safe and out of trouble." I took that responsibility seriously.

We were hardly ever the first ones to arrive. Other kids from town either got up earlier or didn't have as many chores as we did. I look back and wonder at how we could spend day after day, with kids of all ages, skipping rocks, swimming, or throwing a Frisbee, and not once do I remember being bored at the lake.

Richard Clausen was one of the boys I often saw there. He was two years older than me.

Evan liked him right away. Richard let Even hang out with him and watch the older boys do cannonballs off the end of the wooden dock. Evan liked him so I liked him too.

It wasn't long before Richard and I started taking walks around the lake, just the two of us. Walking all the way around took twenty minutes or so. It wasn't very big. He was so nice and polite, more than any of the other boys. On one of those walks, he grabbed my hand and held it in his for the first time. He was awkward and abrupt about it, I could tell, like he had been thinking about doing it for a long time but had to work up the nerve to actually do it. I felt my face turn red but I held his hand right back. Richard was fourteen and I was twelve the summer we first walked together and held hands at the lake. That was the same summer we met Charlotte.

She was already there one afternoon in July, sitting alongside the edge of the dock, her toes making lazy circles in the water below. Evan and I noticed her right away. "Who is that?" he asked. We'd never seen her before, at the lake or anywhere else. Was she new here? I hadn't heard of any families recently moving to Independence Corner but it was possible I had missed the news.

The first thing I noticed about her was how pretty she was. Her pale skin and blonde hair seemed to glow in the sun. As we drew closer, I saw her lips were an unnatural shade of red that reminded me of blood. I was envious, my father wouldn't let me wear lipstick yet. Even if he did let me, I would not have been bold enough to wear that color.

My envy turned to jealousy when I finally turned my attention from her to the boy she was talking to.

Richard, my Richard, was sitting right next to her, so engrossed in this new girl that he didn't even see us walk up.

"Hi, Richard," I said, interrupting their conversation. I was speaking to him but looking at her. This wasn't an attempt to intimidate or anything, not that I could have if I wanted to, I just was immediately fascinated by her. Her hair was pulled back in a ponytail. She wore a white tank top and denim shorts that were cut way too short to be considered decent.

Richard's eyes drifted to her thighs every time she glanced away from him. She made me feel frumpy, angry, and jealous all at the same time.

She met my gaze with a sly smile, like she knew what I was thinking.

"Oh, hey, Rebekah. Hey, Evan." He stood to greet us. Richard was clearly startled, his face flushed with embarrassment. "This is Charlotte, she just moved here. Charlotte, these are my friends, Evan and Rebekah."

Friend, he called me. I'm not sure what exactly we were to each other at that point, but the way he said it gave me a sinking feeling in my stomach.

Charlotte was sixteen, she told us. Looking at her, I thought she looked sixteen, but I also thought she could have passed for twenty-five if she wanted to. She was thin, but she had the curves of a woman. That day, at Mirror Lake, she was sixteen. Charlotte was vague about where her house was or where she lived before coming to Independence Corner. Her father, she claimed, got a new job nearby, forcing them to move, but she deftly avoided saying exactly where his job was. She lived "on the other side of town" and none of us, including me, pressed her for more specifics.

Sometimes I think back to that day, the day we met her. She made me uneasy and I disliked her right away. I couldn't have told you why at the time. What if I had taken Evan, gone back home, and avoided the lake the rest of the summer? Everything would have ended differently. I did almost leave out of spite, out of jealousy, but I didn't. I stayed, and now all I have is what ifs.

"What's that on your arm?" Evan asked, pointing at Charlotte.

"It's a tattoo, little one." She held it out so we could see better. I was amazed; I think we all were. I didn't even know a kid could get a tattoo. The only people I knew who had them were adults. Even then, they normally had them in places that could be covered up with a t-shirt. Hers was plain to see, on the inside of her left forearm, jet black against her pale skin.

"What is it? A star?" my brother asked again. "With snakes?"

It was a star, an eight-pointed star. Snakes wrapped around and through each of the points. The scales and eyes were so detailed I felt like they could have jumped right off of her arm.

"Serpents, not snakes," Charlotte said.

"Why do you have that?" I asked.

"Because I like serpents and stars." She lowered her arm back down to her side and smiled at Richard. It seemed to me like I was suddenly an unwanted third wheel. Neither of them objected as I excused myself and took Evan over to play with the other kids.

The next day, I made sure to get there early. There were ominous clouds in the sky, but I didn't care. If Richard was going to be there, I wanted every minute with him I could get without her.

He did show up, along with his usual band of friends. I don't know if he was aware that I was upset or not. He would have to have been pretty dense not to know, but he was just a boy after all. We picked back up where we left off, talking and laughing just like before. What made it even better was Charlotte didn't come to the lake that day.

Unfortunately, she didn't stay away. Every couple of days she would make an appearance. I tried to avoid her, but the lake wasn't that big. Richard didn't avoid her. He also didn't go out of his way to seek her out, though, which

I appreciated. Maybe he wasn't as dense as I thought. Whenever Charlotte was around, she seemed content to lie in the sun and watch. She never swam, she never played any of the games. Watching everyone was her entertainment. Looking back, I think she was looking for the right someone.

That someone was my brother. I don't know why she chose him out of all of the others that summer. He was seven. I thought he was young enough to need supervision, but old enough that it didn't have to be constant. I was wrong.

Richard and I were pretty much back to normal again. I kept a worried eye out every time Charlotte was around, which was less and less as the summer drew to a close. We held hands all of the time now, not just when nobody could see.

One day, Richard seemed nervous, more nervous than usual. He kept stumbling over his words and was so distracted that he wasn't listening to a single word I said.

"You want to walk around the lake?" he asked me.

"Sure." I checked to see that Evan was okay. He was standing by water; his pants were wet near his ankles even though I had rolled them up for him. A small pile of rocks rested by his feet. One at a time, he threw them into the water. He watched the ripples from the stone expand, then gradually dissipate before he took another one from the pile. This could keep him occupied for the foreseeable future.

We walked hand-in-hand like we had done a dozen or more times already. Richard's palm was sweaty and his step was quicker than normal. I was suspicious, but didn't think much of it. When we reached the other side, exactly opposite from where we started, he stopped. He turned towards me and I looked up at him with my back to the water.

Richard took a deep breath, leaned down, and kissed me right on the lips.

The kiss surprised me and sent my heart racing. It was my first kiss. The only way I can describe it is magically innocent. We held it for several seconds, his hands gently gripped my arms just below my shoulders. When he finally pulled back, we stared at each other, both of us looking for a reaction from the other. I laughed as I felt my face turning red. He smiled back at me. If the day had ended right then, right there, it probably would have been the best day of my life.

Out of nowhere, it started raining. It was just a sprinkle at first but it turned heavy very quickly. There wasn't much in the way of cover out by the lake.

"Oh, no. Where's Evan? He's probably a mess already." Even with the rain making a mess of me, my first thought was of my little brother covered in mud.

"Let's go find him. I'm sure he's having a great time."

Richard and I made our way back around to where we started. Most of the kids were packing up as fast as they could and were heading home. The rain was a warm summer rain but it wasn't letting up. I figured I would have to get Evan and get us home soon or I would get an earful from my mom.

Except Evan was nowhere to be seen.

I scanned the water line where I last saw him throwing rocks. I looked at the retreating throng of kids leaving the lake, hoping to catch a glimpse of him with one of his friends. Nothing.

I was scared. I ran around the water's edge, yelling his name. Evan could swim, but not well. My imagination conjured up images of him swimming out too far and not being able to make it back. His little head sinking below the water as he desperately hoped his big sister would rescue him.

"He's gotta be around here somewhere," said Richard. "Keep looking, I'll go catch up with the others and see if he left with them." He put on a brave face, probably because he could see how close I was to losing it, but I could tell he was worried too.

Richard ran off, chasing after the retreating children. I watched him leave, hoping Evan was walking along with one of his friends. I would scold him when I caught up to him and tell him how worried he made me and how I would tell Mom and Dad when we got home. Before I told him all that, I would give him a big hug.

Already drenched and trying to avoid panic, I turned back to the lake. Rain continued to pour, plastering my hair to my head. There was no sign of him anywhere in the water.

The area around was nothing but grass and dirt with thin forest maybe a quarter-mile off. I didn't think he would have made it that far so fast.

A flash of movement and a faint light caught my eye. Down by the water, not far away from where I was standing, there was a big patch of cattails and tall grass. I couldn't see over them, the grass was taller than I was, but the pounding rain moved the blades enough for me to catch a glimpse through.

Somebody was down there.

Hope and relief flooded through me. Surely, it was Evan down there, still playing and getting dirty, not minding the rain one bit.

I ran over to the place I'd seen the light. The ground was slick with the dirt turning to mud. Pushing through the thinnest part of the grass, I almost shouted with excitement. Evan was there. Immediately, I knew something wasn't right and I stopped myself from calling out to him.

Charlotte was with him.

He was facing me, but clearly didn't see me. His eyes were glassy and his mouth was hanging part-way open. Ankle-deep in the water, he was oblivious to anything around him.

Charlotte knelt in the water in front of him. She had her back to me. Even on her knees, she was as tall as my brother. Her soaking wet hair ran down her back like a waterfall and her left hand rested on Evan's chest. A pulsing green glow surrounded her hand and bled onto Evan's torso. I could see her tattoo; it seemed to move on its own in the arcane light.

I stood there, frozen. I don't know if it was from fear, surprise, or something else entirely, but my feet felt like stone, rooting me to one spot. If I could have stopped her sooner...I'll never know for sure.

"Stop!" My voice and my legs started working at the same time. I wrapped my arms around Evan, shoving her away and pulling him towards me in one motion. "What are you doing?" I screamed. Charlotte smirked. She wasn't one bit surprised to see that I was there.

After I separated them, Evan still stared right through me. There was no expression in his face. I ineffectively wiped rain drops off of his face with my wet hand.

"Evan? Can you hear me? Come on, little buddy." I took him by the shoulder and shook him. The panic I felt when I thought he was lost returned with a vengeance. This was worse, though. I knew something was very wrong with him, but I wasn't sure what I could do about it.

Finally, after what seemed an eternity, Evan blinked. Then he blinked again and his eyes came into focus on me. Confused, he frowned and reached up to touch the top of his head.

"It's raining," he said.

"Oh, thank God." It was only then that I remembered Charlotte. I spun around and she was gone. I spotted her quickly, walking away in the same direction Richard had run. Actually, she was strolling away, like she didn't have a care in the world.

My fear, which had turned to relief, now became anger. That anger gave me a courage that overwhelmed my sense of self-preservation. I left Evan by the water and ran after her. She hadn't made it very far and I swiftly caught up to her.

I grabbed her by the arm and yanked her around to face me.

"What did you do to him? What did you do?" I yelled at her. Charlotte was taller than me, I barely reached her chin, but I didn't care. I was mad enough to fight her right then and there.

There was a glint in her eye that made me take an involuntary step back. I had expected hostility or irritation, but what I saw was joy. Charlotte's eyes lit up with pure glee.

"What did I do? That's the best part. I don't even know. You'll just have to wait and see. I wish I could see it for myself but..." She shrugged her shoulders and patted me on the cheek. Then she turned and sauntered away, leaving me with nothing but more questions. I stood there, impotently, not having a clue what had happened or what she meant by those words.

Later, much later, I did come to understand. I just wish to God that I hadn't.

CHAPTER TWENTY

Rebekah's Story Part Two

None of us saw Charlotte again that summer. She might as well have vanished off the face of the Earth. We carried on like she'd never been there. Richard never mentioned her absence around me. The rest of the summer flew by.

I didn't tell anyone about what I saw that day. Evan said he couldn't remember anything after the rain started until he woke to me shaking him. It was so fantastical, glowing appendages and a semi-comatose brother, that I began to question myself. Did I really see what I thought I saw? I could have told my parents about it, but what then? The police? For what crime? Evan was home, safe and sound, so I decided to keep it to myself.

After school started back up things got back to a normal routine. The store and our studies took up most of our time. Richard and I hardly saw each other anymore, unless it was in passing while we were out with our families since I was younger and he and I went to different schools. Maybe our thing, whatever it was, had been a summer thing, not to be continued in the real world.

Evan seemed fine...at first. He never went back to the lake, though. The rest of that summer, and every summer after, he always made some excuse as to why he couldn't. Eventually we stopped asking.

Time passed, like it always does. Evan and I got older every day while the rest of the town stayed the same. Dad lost a little more hair and Mom got grayer in hers but they were a constant. Always supportive, always there. Our town, too, was a constant for us. No matter how much time went by, it stayed our familiar home. Even now, all these years later, I bet it still only has the one stop-light.

I'm not sure when I first noticed the change in Evan. He was the sweetest kid I'd ever met. Never did he have anything mean to say to anybody. Everyone in town liked him, both children and adults. Whenever Dad needed help fixing something around the house or the store, Evan would be right by his side handing him the right tools like a miniature surgeon's assistant.

It was in the fourth grade, I think, when he first got sent home from school.

"Evan, tell me what happened." Mom heard the story from the principal but wanted to hear her son's side of things.

"I'm sorry, okay? It's just, um, Tim was picking on us, you know, because he's bigger. He told Stacey her dress was ugly and she cried. Then he tried to push me down and I punched him back. Dad always said to stand up to bullies."

He cried as he told his story to Mom. She hugged him and told him it was going to be all right. Laura Goodwright always saw the best in people. This was especially true of her only son. Her sweet boy couldn't have started the fight, so it had to have been the other boy's fault.

I didn't speak up and tell Mom what I thought about it. First, that I was friends with Tim's sister, Dorothy Macklin, so I knew that Tim wasn't a big kid at all. I was pretty sure Evan was the larger of the two boys. Second, the part of the story Evan conveniently left out was where he had bitten Tim on his arm hard enough to make him bleed. But I let it go; I wasn't there when it happened so, like Mom, I decided to believe Evan.

Little things, suspicious things, kept happening around Evan. They seem bigger in hindsight but at the time we all made excuses and explained it away. Cash from Mom's purse went missing, only to be found in his dresser drawer. He got into more trouble at school. Fighting and talking back to teachers. In the fifth grade he got suspended for telling Miss Strickland to fuck off. Dad took his belt to him for that one. My parents never used language like that and had no patience for those that did.

When Dad was done, Evan pulled his pants back up. "That hurt me more than it hurt you but you have to learn. That sort of language is for lowlifes and idiots," he told his son.

Evan was crying or, I should say, he had tears streaming down his face. The look he had in his eyes wasn't what I expected. He wasn't cowed or ashamed, he was mad.

The look he had was cold rage.

I learned to walk on eggshells around Evan. Our house wasn't that big and he developed a short fuse as he got older. I wasn't the only one. Mom was careful about what she said and how she said it when speaking to him. Dad refused to give him any kind of special treatment. "This is my house and no son of mine will be disrespectful to his parents. If he does, he can find another place to live."

By the time I reached high school I was already putting in late hours almost every night at the store. It wasn't easy juggling those responsibilities, but I didn't complain. We were a team and we all helped each other.

Foreign language was a requirement at my school. My sophomore year I chose to take German. Richard, my Richard from the lake, was in the same class.

"Hey there, stranger," he said with a wink.

He was a senior, practically a grown man now, but I could still see the boy who held my hand and walked with me. It was a small school and we'd crossed paths before, but nothing like this. With him sitting in front of me, I was guaranteed to be distracted for the entire semester.

"You know," he said one day in class, "I am horrible at foreign languages. French, Spanish, German, it doesn't matter. I'm hopeless."

"I could probably help you study." I wasn't sure if I was any better than he was, but I wasn't about to pass up on a golden opportunity.

So, we studied. My house, his house, it didn't matter. Soon, we were spending time together without school books between us. When he asked me to go to the Senior Prom with him it took all of my self-control to be cool, hide my excitement, and calmly tell him yes.

During our last dance that night he leaned down and whispered in my ear.

"I never did need any help in German."

I whispered back, "I know."

While my social life was heading in the right direction, things at home were strained. Evan repeatedly got sent home from school for his behavior. My parents were at their wit's end. He barely spoke to me, spending most of his time in his bedroom during his continuous groundings. Richard even tried to engage him in conversation when he was over, but all he got in return was a cold shoulder.

There was a Saturday during my junior year. I was working at the store with Mom. Dad and Evan stayed home, planning on fixing a leak in the roof. Evan was not happy about being drafted into the roof repair business but Dad was adamant. My brother's attitude had gone from bad to worse. More and more, he and Dad would argue loudly. He was only twelve, but was already almost as big as our dad. I was shocked at some of the language that came out of Evan's mouth during those fights. The thought of speaking to any adult like that, let alone our parents, would never have even entered my mind.

Dad didn't take his belt to Evan anymore. That might have been because Dad thought Evan was too old to be disciplined like that. I think it was because Evan had grown too big and, honestly, too scary. He got a look sometimes, when he got angry, that reminded me of a shaken soda about to explode.

The weather was cool and clear. It was slow at work so I was able to stare out the front window and lose myself in the beautiful day.

"What? Evan, slow down." My mom was on the phone nearby. Her worried tone immediately snapped me out of my daydream. "Oh, my goodness. Where is he? Who else is there? Okay, I'll be right there." The tears in my mom's eyes made me scared.

"Mom? What is it?"

"I need you to stay here Rebekah. There's been an accident, Dad fell. Don't worry."

She rushed out the door, leaving me behind, scared and alone.

Those next couple of hours were torturous for me. I didn't know much and nobody called to tell me more. Dad fell, she had said. Fell from the roof? Fell off the front porch?

I made an executive decision to close the store early that day. Mom had left the keys behind so at least I had that option. No sooner had I locked the front doors than a car pulled up behind me.

"Rebekah?" It was Mr. Williamson, our neighbor. Mom had sent him to get me. That's when I knew it was bad. Dad hadn't just fallen off the front porch.

Dad's back was broken, he told me on the way to the hospital. He didn't know exactly how bad because the doctors didn't know yet. Dad and Evan were on the roof together when it happened. It could have been worse; he fell from the roof of the first floor, just in front of the bedroom windows. If he had been on the second floor, we'd probably be making funeral plans.

I'll never forget seeing my dad lying in that hospital bed for the first time. What I can't remember is the last time I saw him walk on his own two feet.

Dad was conscious and alone when I came in but the pain meds had obviously taken effect. His eyes were glassy as he turned his head towards me.

"Hello, princess." He tried to manage a smile but couldn't quite pull it off.

I ran over to him, crying but afraid to touch him. I thought that touching him might hurt him worse somehow. It was stupid of me; the damage had already been done.

"Don't cry, baby girl. I'm okay. Your dad's tough." Only he didn't look tough laying there in the hospital bed. He looked so old to me, old and withered. Dad reached over and held me by my arm. He looked at me with those kind eyes.

"Where is everybody," I asked.

"I'm sure they're around here somewhere. I've kind of been in and-" He stopped mid-sentence and stared over my shoulder. I looked back and Evan was standing there in the doorway. Neither of them said anything but I could feel the tension between them even if I didn't know why. Dad's expression was one of anger and hurt, his eyes no longer kind. Evan's was blank and unreadable.

"Charles, you're awake." Mom pushed past her son and rushed over to her husband, oblivious to the hostile mood she'd walked in on.

Surgeries and physical therapy helped, but only slightly. Dad never walked again. The best he could manage was a wiggle of his big toe. All things considered, he adjusted well.

It took him time to find acceptance. He would, at first, tell anyone who would listen that the doctors didn't know what they were talking about. He would walk again and that was that.

Dad and Evan's relationship noticeably changed. It was bad before; it was nonexistent now. Mom, now with so much more on her plate taking care of Dad as well as the store, didn't seem to notice but I did. Whenever the two of them were in the same room, which wasn't often, they completely ignored each other. Any time I attempted to dig, to find the source of their newer rift, I was met with a wall of resistance. Neither of them had anything to say. Not to me, at least.

We had a ramp put in, replacing the front steps, to accommodate Dad's wheelchair. For other people, those who lived outside our home, Dad put on a brave face. They would visit bearing gifts and sympathy. He would greet them, either from his bed or wheelchair, with a smile and a joke. When they left, that's when I could tell. He wasn't his old self. The fall had taken more than his ability to walk. Dad seemed beaten, the glint in his eye gone. In its place was pessimism and depression.

Given time, people can adapt to almost anything. We were no exception. All three of us, even Evan, had to bust our asses to make up for his inability to do what he used to: shelf stocking, yard work, unloading delivery trucks, fixing leaks, the list went on. He tried to help with what he could but there just wasn't much he could realistically help with anymore.

Richard and I saw more and more of each other. He was the bright spot in my life as my home became chaotic and stressful. He usually had to come see me at my house or work since my free-time was now taken up with familial responsibilities. I knew I was in love with him after that magical prom night. When he said it to me, I got so light-headed I thought I might pass out. To this day, I have never felt that overwhelming kind of joy as I did when Richard Clausen told me he loved me.

After graduation, he got a job in Walker Township at his uncle's hardware store. Those tools and his know-how really came in handy every weekend when he would come to the house and fix whatever was broken. He truly was a godsend for us. If not for him, I swear the house would have fallen down around us one piece at a time.

I tried to make the best of things. Instead of going away to college after I graduated, I stayed home to take care of Dad. When I told Mom about my decision, she said all the right things, "Don't worry about us, think about your own future, it's not your job to take care of us," but I could tell her heart wasn't in it. She needed me to stay and we both knew it.

Potentially sacrificing my future for the sake of my family was my call, but there were days when I wondered if it was worth it. Being a caregiver for a paraplegic, even your own father, requires a patience and understanding that I didn't always possess. Add that to missing Richard terribly between his weekend visits and wondering what I would have been doing right then if I'd been more selfish and left home. The result was I sometimes had more than I could handle.

When it got to be too much, I would go out to the back porch. It was covered and got very dark at night. I waited until the rest of the house was asleep because I wanted to be alone.

I never wanted anyone to see me cry.

Some nights it was so bad I would sit on the back steps, sob, and silently curse my self-centeredness. I was overwhelmed with guilt at my resentment. Mom and Dad had taken care of us; they had accepted, even welcomed, that burden. What I was doing was hardly comparable.

But I was twenty-two and I still lived with my parents in the house I grew up in. Everyone I knew from school became an adult in the normal fashion: moving out, going to college, getting married. My life was anything but normal and I didn't know how much longer I could do it.

One summer night on the porch, as I cried and felt sorry for myself, I was startled to find I wasn't alone.

"Hey, sis." I jumped even as I recognized the voice.

"Holy crap, Evan. You scared the hell out of me."

He sat in the darkened corner where the moonlight couldn't reach. The faint red glow of a cigarette was the only way I could tell someone was there.

"Sorry, didn't mean to."

I wiped my eyes with my sleeve. "What are you doing out here?"

"Same as you, probably."

"Mom will be pissed if she finds you smoking. How did you even get those anyway?"

It sounded stupid as soon as I said it. Evan was only seventeen, but I knew he had been smoking for a while.

"You come out here a lot," he said. "But only after Mom and Dad are asleep. Almost like you're hiding something."

Despite our blood relationship, he was a stranger to me. I never thought about it like that until right then. My brother, this young man sitting with me, had grown up in the same house with me, but I didn't know who he was.

"Evan, do you remember when we were little? How you and me got along? What happened to us? We used to joke and laugh. Even though I was older we always found something in common we could talk about."

He took another long drag from his cigarette. Maybe I caught him off guard with my heartfelt question instead of a verbal attack. Evan was used to being attacked and certainly wasn't used to honest communication.

A small pile of butts littered the porch by his feet. He had been there for quite some time.

"What happened was that Dad fell off the fucking roof and got himself crippled." Evan dropped his finished cigarette in front of him with the others and put it out with his booted foot.

"No, that might have been the big catastrophe for us as a family but with us - between me and you – things were different before that."

"Dunno, sis. Maybe I just got older and didn't need you on my ass anymore."

I didn't respond. I'd seen him do the same thing to Mom and Dad. He tried to pick fights and knew what buttons to push to do it.

We sat in silence for a long time, listening to crickets and gazing at the moon. Evan lit another cigarette.

"I still dream about her," he said softly.

"What? Dream about who?" I honestly had no idea what he was talking about. His tone was different, I noticed, not antagonistic or snarky. He almost sounded nervous.

"Her. Charlotte. From the lake."

I hadn't thought of that girl or that summer in years. Those memories must have been close to the surface because as soon as he mentioned her name it all came back in a flash.

"I remember her. That was a long time ago." Ten years had passed but I could still see her in my mind like it was yesterday; that glow around her hand, her excited smile when I confronted her. I shivered involuntarily.

"Doesn't seem like that long ago."

Something was wrong. He wanted to talk to someone, maybe anyone, but was apprehensive. Evan had burned so many bridges that he didn't have anyone he could turn to. I realized I was probably his best option. This was him trying to reach out.

"I've dreamed about her for so long it's like I've known her my whole life. Sometimes I think I dreamed of her before we even met her that day at the lake. That's crazy, I know. It's not possible."

"What happens in the dream?" I asked. This was a different side of my brother I was seeing and I didn't want to break the spell.

"Nothing special, that's what's weird. It's usually me, going about my business. Maybe reliving a day, something I'd done before. She's in the background, like an extra in a movie, in my movie. If I'm riding my bike, she's on the bench waiting for a bus as I go by. If I'm at a camp out with friends, she's sitting across the fire from me. She looks at me and smiles but we never speak. She's just there."

They're just dreams, I wanted to tell him; be the good, supportive big sister for the first time in years. But I kept silent, thinking back to that day at the lake. Maybe there was more to it like I thought.

"Mom thinks I pushed Dad off the roof."

The statement caught me off-guard. It came out of nowhere. A question formed in my mind, then stopped before it left my mouth. *Why do you think that?* A second question, also unspoken, jumped ahead of that one. *Did you?* Before that moment I never once thought Dad's fall was anything other than an accident. I was a little horrified that I found the possibility even remotely plausible.

His eyes were on me. Even in the dark I could feel them. Maybe I wasn't the only one afraid to ask the tough questions.

"Up on the roof with Dad, just him and me. He was trying to teach me, trying to reach out to me. I realized what he was doing but couldn't find it in me to care."

I had to remind myself to breathe. I wanted him to stop talking. Wherever he was going with this, I knew I didn't want to hear how the story ended.

"She wasn't there - Charlotte I mean - but I swear I could see her, feel her. Dad started getting on me. Said I wasn't paying attention. 'Stop lollygagging,' I think he said. He was right on the edge, where the gutter ends right underneath your room. Below him was the fence. He was bent over, nails held between his teeth, hammer in his hand-"

"Stop it," I said. "Just stop." I covered my ears but he had already gone quiet. If he didn't finish telling me, I thought I could still pretend this conversation never happened.

Evan flicked his cigarette off the porch and into the night. He stood.

"G'nite, sis," he said and went inside.

The worst night of my life came less than a week later. I barely even saw Evan in those days after our talk on the porch. If I did run into him, it was only for brief moments. He refused to even look me in the eye, choosing instead to find any excuse to leave the house.

It was late, almost closing time at the store, and there were only a couple customers left.

I was glad. Seemingly half the town had been through my line that day and I was tired.

Richard was with me, keeping me company and helping where he could. He was lightly spraying the produce with the hose. "You have to do this regularly, Beck," he said. "Helps keep them fresh." He wasn't getting paid, didn't even officially work at the store, but there he was, lending a hand. I couldn't help but love him.

The phone rang at the empty front manager's station. I ran over from my spot at the cash register.

"Rebekah?" It was Mom calling from home.

"Yeah, Mom. What's going on?" I could hear yelling in the background. Male voices. Dad and Evan fighting. "Everything okay?"

"They're at each other again. They haven't argued like this for a long time. Evan is asking for you, specifically you, but he won't say why. Is it busy there?"

Mom sounded worried but not scared. The yelling was muffled now and I pictured her cupping her hand over the receiver.

"No, not really. We have a couple stragglers still shopping but that's it. It would only take me a few minutes to shoo people out and lock up." I was more than a little confused.

Evan asking for me? Thinking back to our talk on the porch made my stomach hurt but I couldn't imagine any reason he would need to see me immediately.

"No, I don't think you need to do that. He'll just have to wait for you to get home. That is what started the yelling, though. Evan asked where you were. Daddy told him you were working. Then he - Evan, I mean - started cursing. He was upset because you weren't scheduled to work today. He said you were supposed to be here."

"That's really weird, Mom. Even for Evan."

"I know, that's why I called. Don't worry, dear. Whatever it is can-" With an audible click, the call was abruptly cut off.

"Mom?" The timing of the hang-up was odd and I swore I heard a male voice right before we disconnected.

"Who are you talking to?" The voice had been Evan's.

I called back but only got a busy signal. Then I waited impatiently for her to call again, thinking maybe we were calling each other at the same time.

"What's wrong?" Richard asked, putting his hand on my shoulder.

"Probably nothing. Dad and Evan are at it again, but Mom hung up in the middle of a sentence. Now it's busy."

"You want me to go check it out? Make sure it's all quieted down?"

"No, you don't have to do that. I'm not sure that's such a good idea anyways. If Evan's all fired up, he might need me to talk him down." Evan might not respond well to Richard showing up unannounced. I was already fearing the worst, but even the worst my imagination conjured up was nothing compared to what reality had in store.

"Then you go. I can watch things here."

"Yeah, right."

"Why not? I can ring people up and make change. They're almost done shopping anyways. Even if my math is bad, I can't screw things up that much." He smiled that crooked smile at me. Richard was right. I could go and be back in maybe thirty minutes. Just check in and make sure everything was all right.

"Okay," I said. "But I'll be right back. You shouldn't have to do much."

"That's good. I like not doing much."

"Thank you. You're the best." I reached up and kissed his cheek.

"Love you," he said.

"Love you more."

There were two ways to get to my house from the store and both of them took about the same amount of time. Taking Main Street, paved and well-lit, was easier on the car. That was the way I usually went. Pulling out of the little parking lot that night, I made the turn to take the more direct route. Shorter as the crow flies but most of the way was unpaved gravel. That's why I normally avoided it. As I turned from Main onto Lark Road, I saw a car's headlights heading towards me. If I had kept going that way instead of turning, I would have passed right by it. I don't know for sure who was in that particular car, it was dark and too far away, but something tells me I would have recognized the driver. It was that close of a thing, a seemingly innocuous sequence of events, when taking a different path would have altered my future.

As it was, I didn't see another soul on the drive home. I wasn't worried, not really. Maybe this fight was bad, but we had all been through Evan's bad times before. The worst I expected was a kicked in door or a hole in the drywall. Nothing that couldn't be fixed.

The first thing I noticed, pulling up the driveway, was every light in the house was off. Little warning bells started going off in my head. That was not normal at all. Even if everyone was gone or asleep, Mom always at least left the porch light on. Still, nothing seemed out of place so I dismissed it as paranoia.

The front door was unlocked. I felt around and turned on the hall light. Everything looked fine; no sign of anything out of the ordinary.

"Mom? Dad?" I walked slowly through the house, turning on lights as I went. Nothing in the living room. The bathroom was clean as a whistle. Given the choice between the upstairs bedrooms and the kitchen, I chose the kitchen.

That's where I found them.

When I turned on the kitchen light, Mom was on the floor at my feet. I covered my mouth to stifle a scream. A bed sheet covered her face and most of her body. Her bare feet stuck out from the bottom of the sheet.

Dad was in his wheelchair, pushed up against the back door. A butcher knife had been driven into his stomach all the way to the hilt. Blood soaked the entire lower half of his body and pooled on the floor under his shoes. His arms hung lifeless at his sides.

It's funny what goes through your head when faced with a horror like that. My mind was racing, trying to make sense of the scene in front of me. For a split second, I was worried for Evan. I wanted to find him and make sure he was okay, that whoever had done this to Mom and Dad hadn't hurt him too. Then I remembered the phone call that brought me home. I remembered Evan's voice before Mom was disconnected.

Then I was afraid. Evan did this. Did he stab Dad in a fit of rage before turning his attention to Mom? Did Dad watch Mom die while he bled out, trapped in his chair?

I wasn't even aware I was crying when I bent down and pulled the sheet from Mom's face. I had to be sure. Her eyes, cloudy now and bright red around the irises, stared up at me without blinking. Horrible bruises, thin like fingers, encircled her throat.

I steadied myself and took a deep breath. Where was Evan now? Upstairs? Out back on the porch, watching me right now?

The phone was gone. The cord had been ripped right out of the wall. Getting help would mean having to leave my parents in the kitchen. They were beyond help. I had to worry about me now.

Dad's body was blocking the nearest exit and I couldn't bring myself to put my hands on his wheelchair or walk through his blood. I chose instead to retrace my steps and go back out the way I came in. Moving slower and quieter than when I arrived, I made my way down the hall and past the stairs. I paused at the bottom and looked up to where Evan and I had slept in neighboring bedrooms ever since he was born. Nothing moved up there. Every step seemed unbearably loud to me. If Evan was still in the house, there was no way he didn't know I was there too.

My nerve finally broke. I ran the last few steps, threw open the door, and scrambled down the front steps into the yard. I cringed with every passing second, expecting Evan to emerge from the shadows and stop me. I jumped into the car and started it up on the first try. Hands shaking, I locked all the car doors and checked the backseat. It was empty.

No boogeyman wearing the face of my brother jumped out of the shadows to stop me. I tore out of there as fast as I could. Fishtailing and throwing gravel into the air, I sped down the driveway, into the street, and towards the store. Richard was there. Whatever happened now, I had to see him first. We needed to find Evan. The police needed to find Evan. Mom and Dad were dead. Dead on the floor of their own house.

Mom and Dad were dead. Murdered.

The weight of it all, the recognition of how my life had just been changed forever, came crashing down on me in an avalanche of emotion. Grief, fear, guilt, anger and confusion all swirled together in a storm, threatening to overwhelm me completely.

I pulled over to the side of the road. The darkness of Main Street was only broken by the headlights of passing vehicles. I was barely able to get the car door open before vomiting all over the pavement. It felt like everything I had eaten for the past week erupted out of me right then and there. Dry heaves and sobbing followed for what seemed like an eternity.

Leaning out of the car, I stared at the ground, breathing deeply and gathering my courage.

Bright lights from an oncoming car snapped me out of my trance. The car was pulling up right in front of mine, facing the wrong way for the flow of traffic.

"Rebekah?" A familiar voice called to me. It was Mr. Williamson, the same neighbor who delivered the bad news about Dad's fall all those years ago. "Is that you? I was heading to your house to find your parents and saw the car pulled over here. Are you okay?" He cringed when he saw the vomit on the ground. He was breathing heavily and his face was flushed.

"Mr. Williamson, we have to get the police. Mom and Dad-"

"Police are on their way, honey. Fire department is already there but I'm afraid there's not much they can do."

"What?"

"The store. That's where you're going, right? The fire's spread. The whole building is one big inferno. I wanted to be the one who told your dad. Does he already know?"

The fire's spread...the whole building...inferno.

I slammed the door in Mr. Williamson's face and put the car back in gear. The store was on fire? That wasn't possible, I was just there. I didn't know what time it was, but I couldn't have been gone that long. Richard stayed when I went to check on the house.

Richard was at the store.

The broken lines in the middle of the road flew by. I saw the light and commotion up ahead before I saw the blaze. The dark smoke blended with the night sky. What would have been obvious from miles away during the day was hidden from me until I was on top of it.

Two fire engines and more than a dozen firefighters worked the hoses. Water sprayed impotently at the fully engulfed building as I screeched to a halt across the street. A small crowd had gathered, hypnotized by the dancing flames. One by one, their murmurs became louder when they saw me. Most of the faces were familiar and the looks of sympathy they gave me made this all too real. I searched through the faces in the crowd for Richard's but he wasn't there.

The sign on the front of the store, the one I had looked at thousands of times, was obscured by smoke and fire. I could still make out the "Daughter" through the flames before it, too, was destroyed forever.

I was numb, probably in shock. Everyone there seemed resigned to the fact that the store was lost. Even the firefighters were going through the motions with no real sense of urgency.

"Thank god nobody was in there," someone in the crowd said.

"How did it start?" chimed in another voice.

"That's a damn shame. I hope Charles has good insurance."

"Oh, my god. There's someone in there!" Screams and shouts filled the air. Fingers pointed at the front doors of the burning store. A shadow in the shape of a man moved inside those glass doors. The orange and red flames hid the figure's features as he stumbled into view. He had to have been in impossible agony. A hand reached up and pressed against the glass. I watched, horrified, as the man fell to his knees. His hand slid down, trailing slowly behind him. Finally, he collapsed to the ground and I couldn't see him anymore.

Of all the things I have seen in my life, including the lifeless, murdered bodies of my parents, that is the image I still see when I close my eyes. The burning, stumbling man with his hand pressed against the glass.

My scream was just one of a dozen in the parking lot that night. The world turned dark and I fainted into unconsciousness as the firefighters scrambled all around me to try and save the burning man. It was pointless. The fire burned too hot and the damage was already done.

I don't remember anything after that.

Chapter Twenty-One

The act of confession, if that's what it was, lifted a weight from her. It was visible as she wrapped up her tale. Enthralled as he was, Tucker kept silent the entire time. He was afraid of tripping her up if he interjected, like she would somehow forget where she was in the story and not be able to continue. Logically, that was ridiculous. No matter how much time passed, Rebekah would never forget.

"That's horrible." It wasn't enough, not by a long shot, but it's all he could say.

"I didn't stay in town long after the fire. I couldn't. Everywhere I looked there was a memory of murder and loss. For the longest time I couldn't get over the fact that I didn't know who it was I saw burning at the entrance to the store. Was it my brother or Richard? In the end it shouldn't matter, both bodies were found in there after the fire burned itself out, but it mattered to me."

Tucker shivered. Burning alive had to be one of the worst ways to die.

Rebekah said, "The funerals were only a few days later. I spent those days in a fog, going through the motions of what I thought a normal person should do. As soon as my family was in the ground, I was out of there. I didn't care what happened to the house or the store. Jesus, the store was nothing but a charred tragedy anyway."

Outside, a person-shaped shadow moved past the drawn curtains. Rebekah and Tucker turned towards the door. The staggered sounds of footsteps didn't stop in front of their room. Instead, the sounds receded as whoever they belonged to kept moving.

Tucker let out a breath. "I guess we're both a little jumpy."

"With good reason. We both know what she's capable of."

"How did you know," said Tucker, "that it was her, I mean? You couldn't have known for sure."

"I didn't, not at first and not consciously. Subconsciously, I think I suspected right away, but it was all so hard to come to terms with."

Tucker could sympathize with that feeling. He was getting more familiar with it by the hour.

"Dreams," Rebekah continued. "Dreams of fire, then of her, standing over the bodies. Years later, when I found my first teacher, he showed me how to focus and delve. He showed me the true nature of things."

"He?"

"Yes, my teacher was a man. Does that surprise you?"

"Maybe, I guess. I hadn't thought about it, just assumed because you and Charlotte..."

"Men have the aptitude as much as women. They tend to not follow it as much, though. I don't know why. Maybe something ingrained from a young age."

Tucker rubbed his face with his hands and winced. The scratches Charlotte left on his cheek had stopped bleeding but were tender to the touch. He stared at the wall through his fingers. That was something new she could bewilder him with. Male witches. Of course there were male witches. It shouldn't have come as a surprise but, in his current exhausted state, the revelation astonished him.

"Okay, that's enough for now. You need to get some sleep." Rebekah grabbed the gun and tucked it away in the small of her back. "You look ready to fall over onto the floor."

Tucker was ready to do just that. "You don't look much better. No offense."

"I'm fine. Get some rest. I'll stay up and keep a watch. Charlotte won't be able to find us, not yet. I've warded and cloaked the room and everything in it."

Sure, he thought. Why would Rebekah need to stand watch with a pistol if Charlotte couldn't find them? Tucker reluctantly gave in to the need for sleep. He fell back onto the lumpy mattress. "Fine, but wake me in an hour. Then I'll take my turn."

He didn't bother to take his shoes off. The last thing he heard before fading out was Rebekah. "Okay, Tucker. Whatever you say."

The last thing to go through his mind were those messages from Lyric and how he forgot to call her back.

"I'm sorry, boy. You thought we were going to the park, huh?" Lyric scratched her dog behind the ears. Bertram answered by licking her on the wrist. "That's where we should be going. Screw all this other stuff. Just me and you, fetch and belly rubs. Nobody else, not even Tucker." The dog perked his ears up and looked out the windshield at the sound of the familiar name. "Yeah, you love Tucker. That's part of the problem."

They sat in Lyric's SUV, parked down the street from the sketchy looking motel they'd been watching for the past hour and a half. Anger, worry, disbelief, and a thousand other emotions coursed through her. The sun made it warm in the car even though the temperature outside was cool. A breeze occasionally came through the open windows on both sides.

Bertram tightly circled twice before curling up in the passenger seat. He looked up at Lyric with questioning eyes.

"I don't know why we're here either," she said. After leaving Tucker's office, Lyric went to his apartment. There was no sign of him there, even his car was missing. Several text messages went unreturned so she moved to voicemails. "Tucker, it's me. I stopped by the office and talked to Cheryl. She's worried...we're worried. Please call me back and let me know you're okay." She tried not to sound desperate or needy but this wasn't like him. The optimistic side of her said it was an impromptu road trip, a quick getaway to clear his mind and decompress. God only knew she could use some solo time, maybe he did too.

Her realistic side told her it was something else. Was Tucker avoiding her? Surely he wouldn't ghost her. Ghosting was for casual relationships or one-night stands. They meant more to each other than that, right? Even if it was over between them, the break up should be in person with no questions left unanswered.

At least, that's how Lyric felt.

Was he in trouble? Something completely unrelated to her? That possibility kept running through her mind. When Cheryl confided in her about Tucker's odd behavior, worry leapt ahead of anger. Why was he acting this way?

There was one more thing she could try but she was loathe to use it. A couple months back, Lyric lost her phone while she was out for a jog. Somewhere along her miles-long route it had worked its way out of the tight pocket of her running pants. If she'd been listening to her music, she would have noticed the missing phone right away. As it was, she carefully retraced her steps twice before accepting the fact she'd need to buy a new one. It was Tucker's idea to get the app for both of their phones, "It'll be easier to find in case you ever misplace another gadget worth hundreds of dollars," he said, teasing her. He was hesitant, she could tell, like he was unsure how she would react.

The phone tracker app was free and they both downloaded it. "We don't have to if you don't want to," he kept reassuring her.

"No, it's a good idea." Lyric needed no reassurance when it came to Tucker. She only intended to use it in an emergency and she knew him well enough to know he wasn't the controlling type. He wouldn't waste his time randomly checking her whereabouts.

Since then, Lyric hadn't so much as opened the app to see if it was still working. Earlier in the day, when she did give in and open it up, she would not have been surprised to find Tucker in some out of town locale. His actual location, when the blinking blue dot finally came up, confused her.

The dot on her phone's screen showed he was in a part of town she didn't recognize.

Zooming out allowed her to spot familiar street names. Tucker, or his phone, was on a dead-end street two blocks off of Highway 101. Lyric tried to picture the area in her head. All she could remember was the gas station on the corner.

Now she, along with her faithful Bertram, sat in the gas station's parking lot staring at the tiny, no-tell motel that the app told her Tucker was in. Her face wrinkled in disgust.

This was the kind of place she expected would offer cheap weekly rates or hourly rates for a discreet rendezvous.

And Tucker was in one of those rooms.

That's where she'd been for the past ninety minutes, weighing her options. Lyric knew the second she took her eyes of the motel she would miss Tucker coming out of one of the rooms. Of the eight rooms she could see from her stakeout point, six of them had their curtains open and appeared vacant. Housekeeping had been in and out of each one during her watch, readying them for the next guests. The other two had curtains drawn and doors shut.

Unfortunately, the tracking app could only narrow down Tucker's location; it couldn't pinpoint it exactly. The circle around the blue dot covered the motel and part of the parking spaces in front of the rooms. The margin of error was greater than she would've liked.

A battered Volkswagen bus took up a spot next to one of the closed curtain rooms. Lyric leaned forward and squinted as the door to the room opened. A man with curly gray hair and mustache to match came out. His tie-dyed shirt was almost big enough to cover the ample belly hanging over his belt. Scratching his butt through dirty jeans, he walked with a slight limp over to the closet-sized motel office staffed by a single employee.

"Not that one," said Lyric. Volkswagen Bus Man looked like he hadn't bathed in a few days. Not exactly the type of person Tucker would hang out with in a cheap motel room.

But could she say that with any certainty? Tucker had been acting very out of character lately. That's why she was creeping around a gas station parking lot like a stalker.

The other room's occupants remained a mystery.

"We can't wait all day, Bertram. We have to decide." It wasn't much of a decision to make. Lyric couldn't walk away not knowing if Tucker was in there or who he might be with.

"You stay here, be good. Mama will be right back." She gave the dog a quick pat and got out.

Crossing the intersection diagonally, Lyric put one hand in her purse. The pepper spray cylinder fit in her palm comfortably. Her thumb slipped under the flip-top safety. It wouldn't take much pressure to activate it, sending disabling orange foam into the face of a potential threat. She didn't know what was on the other side of that door, but she was going to take any precautions to mitigate the risk of her impulsive plan.

Her purposeful strides swiftly took her down the sidewalk and through the cracked and disheveled motel parking spaces. Behind her in the SUV, Bertram whined, not once looking away from his favorite person. To her left, Volkswagen Bus Man watched her walk, his eyes running up and down her body.

Lyric stood before the door with a plastic 4 centered above it. The number was set crooked and metallic paint was peeling off of it, fitting right in with the rest of the place.

The three thudding knocks were followed immediately by three more. Rebekah shot out of her chair where she'd been studying Charlotte's book. Tucker didn't move a muscle. He'd been sleeping like the dead for almost two hours and only his faint snoring let her know he was still alive. His feet were flat on the floor, his arms spread wide in the same position as when he first laid down.

"Hello?" came the voice from outside, then three more rapid knocks. It was a woman, but didn't sound like Charlotte.

Rebekah put one hand around the pistol grip in her back waistband. Probably housekeeping, she thought, ignoring the Do Not Disturb sign and rudely coming by with fresh towels. She put one eye to the peephole. All she could see was a vague shadowy form. "No, thanks," said Rebekah, "we're good in here."

Three additional knocks, more aggressive this time. The woman outside said something Rebekah couldn't make out. Cautiously, she put one hand on the door knob. Was she being paranoid? Surely Charlotte couldn't have caught up with them so soon. Rebekah chastised herself. She was the hunter, not the hunted. The missed opportunity at the marina didn't change that. Charlotte knew she was being pursued, though. How much more dangerous did that make her?

"Only one way to find out," Rebekah said, opening the door.

The room didn't seem dark until daylight spilled in. It took a second for her eyes to adjust. The young woman in front of her was not a motel employee. She was shorter than Rebekah with her dark hair pulled tightly back. The little makeup she wore had been smeared slightly around her eyes. It looked as if she'd had a rough day. Rebekah knew what that felt like.

"Can I help you?" Rebekah was terse. The woman jerked backward as the door was opened like she was expecting someone else to answer.

Whoever she was, she composed herself quickly. "I need to speak to Tucker." No, the stranger wasn't surprised anymore. Now she was angry.

"Sorry, nobody here by that name." Rebekah kept the door partially closed with her body blocking the view into the room.

"Look, I know he's in there and I know he's in trouble. I don't care who you are, but I'm not leaving until I see him." Her voice trembled and tears welled in her eyes.

Rebekah's heart went out to this woman at the door. She was obviously upset and kind, comforting words were on the tip of her tongue. Then she noticed the woman's hand tucked into her purse.

"Let me see your hands, slowly." Her grip on the gun tightened but she didn't draw it. Even to her own ears she sounded like a cop giving orders to a suspect.

The woman stiffened and moved her right foot back a few inches. A fighting stance, thought Rebekah. How could she have been so stupid? This was a trap. Tucker had to have been followed. She couldn't believe she'd let her guard down. Whether willingly or not, this person was in league with Charlotte.

"I will not. Let me see Tucker." Her demeanor changed rapidly from brokenhearted victim to that of a fierce adversary, further convincing Rebekah of her intentions. "You're not keeping me out."

Her hand came out of her purse holding a dark metal object. Rebekah's mind screamed, "Knife!"

She stepped forward to meet the threat, drawing the gun with her right hand while grabbing a handful of hair with her left. The woman gave a yelp as Rebekah yanked her head down and pulled her into the room.

A spray of orange coated the wall in a wide line. The object in her hand wasn't a knife, Rebekah now saw, and the woman activated the pepper foam without aiming. "What are you-" she shrieked, grabbing at Rebekah's arm as the two women tangled.

Rebekah managed to spin around, throwing the intruder to the floor. She got on top of the woman and tried to hold her down but she was stronger than she looked, like a coiled snake. The canister continued to empty, spreading its eye-watering contents onto the television and across the carpet as her arm flailed. Off to the side, she heard Tucker jerking awake with a start.

"What the hell?" he cried, scrambling back on the bed, away from the combatants.

Rebekah caught a fist on the chin, a stiff uppercut from short range, snapping her head back. Her response was to pull the woman's hair back harder, forcing her to look up and finally see the gun in her hand.

"Stop it, right now," Rebekah ordered. "She sent you. Where is she?" The gun was inches from her face. Both of them froze in place, neither of them sure what the next move was.

"Whoa, whoa, whoa, Rebekah get off her." Tucker broke into a coughing fit. The burning foam was quickly saturating the room. "Lyric, what are you doing here?" he managed to get out between hacks.

He jumped down off the bed, shouldering Rebekah out of the way. She was too stunned to object. "You know her?"

Tucker ignored the question and took Lyric's hand. "Oh, my god, are you okay?"

Lyric ripped her hand away. "Stay away from me, you crazy bitch." She stared Rebekah down as she got herself up to a crouching position. "Tucker," she turned to him, "what the hell is going on? Oh, my God, are those cuts on your face? What happened? And your hand, it's bleeding."

"I'm sorry," he stammered. "How did you-? If I'd known you were coming..."

"You'd what? Hide your side-chick?" She stood and brushed her hands off on her pants. "Never mind, don't answer. This was a huge mistake. I need to get out of here."

Rebekah rolled her eyes. Why leave so soon after you went through so much trouble to get in? She kept that thought quiet, though. No need to stir things up again. This was obviously a domestic issue involving Tucker, which was something she wanted no part of.

Lyric cast a wary glance at the pistol in Rebekah's hand before hastening past her and out the door.

"Lyric, wait. You don't understand." Tucker chased after her into the daylight.

"You're right, I don't." She turned to face him, pointing her finger directly at his nose. "I don't understand why you're acting so damn crazy. I don't know why you're here right now, instead of at work, in this shithole motel with some gun-toting skank, ignoring my calls and doing God knows what."

The effect from the pepper foam forced Rebekah from the room. She smartly stayed away from the quarreling couple. Two curious onlookers peering out of the motel office reminded her she still held the gun. "Shit," she said, tucking it back into her waistband. They'd have to get out of here pretty fast. This place might be known for discretion, but some things were too obvious to ignore.

Lyric shot her a glare but kept speaking to Tucker. "I was worried about you; thought you were in serious trouble. Instead, when I find you, you're with someone else. I deserve better than that, Tucker."

"Yes, you do. I know that. There's so much going on, I don't even know where to start."

"Don't bother." Lyric turned to leave.

Tucker put a hand on her arm. "Please," he said gently. "I'm so sorry about everything. You have no idea how much." When she didn't pull away from his touch he continued, "I am in trouble, now more than ever. I'm not the only one. My world has been turned upside down these last couple of days. That's no excuse, I know. I don't want to make excuses and I know how this must look to you, but I'm asking for a chance to explain. Will you give me that much?"

His words got to Lyric. Her body language told Rebekah that much, but you could see the conflicting impulses she struggled with. Part of her wanted to storm off, telling him to go to Hell. The other part wanted to find out what he had to say. That look in her eye – she truly loved him. To give up on that you needed to be sure he wasn't the man you thought he was.

"Fine." The ice was thawed, but not melted. "I will listen, but with two conditions. One, you tell me everything, no holding back." She looked over his shoulder at Rebekah. "And two, no lies. If you can't do that then I'm gone."

"I can do that."

"Not here."

"We'll find a place." He reached out to touch her shoulder, thought better of it, and pulled his hand back.

"Come on then. I'm driving."

As Lyric walked away Tucker gave Rebekah a questioning look and a shrug. "Go," Rebekah said, "take care of your business. We can't stay here anyway. I'll find you after."

Tucker bit his lip and hesitated a moment. Then off he went, jogging to catch up to Lyric before she left for good.

Chapter Twenty-Two

Exhilaration!

The likes of which she hadn't felt in years. Charlotte propped herself up behind a building not far from where she left Tucker. Her breath came out in rapid puffs and the ink in her arm burned delightfully.

They almost had her! The red-haired witch and the boy toy she'd roped into helping her had caught her completely off-guard. I must be slipping, thought Charlotte. Coming back to the marina with a small sack of groceries, the last thing she expected was to have two intruders on the boat she now thought of as hers. The repelling effect she placed upon it should have kept any potential threat from setting a single foot aboard the vessel.

Something she hadn't accounted for was that woman, Rebekah. Someone like her, with a knowing look impossible to fake and eyes that observe the world differently than the ignorant masses, she was the one who came within a hair's breadth of ending Charlotte once and for all.

Make no mistake, that woman was out for blood. In addition to wisdom beyond her apparent age, there was pure hatred in those eyes. Charlotte's face flushed, remembering how it felt to see that. "You were here for me," she said. "This encounter was no accident."

The ripple of chaos had bounced back to her, in the form of a vengeful rival. Beautiful and glorious chaos, where not even she, devoted acolyte she had proven herself to be, was immune from the consequences. What had she done to earn such hate? Charlotte wasn't sure, but the possibilities were legion, as was her list of potential enemies. The difference here was the vast majority of those she wronged had no inclination of what had happened to them. Like a malevolent guardian angel, Charlotte would apply her personal touch and be gone before they ever knew they'd been ruined by the chance encounter.

Charlotte closed her eyes and focused on the whispers. They were all around her. They always were; a constant sound only she could hear. They were the voices of spirits. Normally they faded into the background like an ocean tide. When they needed to be heard, the cacophony could cause her physical pain.

Now she sought out those voices for guidance, sorting through the masses to find the one who would help her in her time of need.

It wasn't always the same voice. Or, at least it didn't come from the same spirit each time. The whispers all sounded the same, like a rush of wind given life. Charlotte could tell the difference, though. Since she was a young girl, before she found her true calling, she'd been able to hear them.

That part had come naturally to her. It was some time before she realized everyone else was deaf in comparison. Hiding her gift became critically important if she wanted to avoid the fate of so many others like her. On the other hand, bending the spirits to her will took effort and practice.

Little by little, the background noise subsided and clearer voices began to make themselves known. One by one, Charlotte sifted through them, discarding the ones she didn't need and ignoring the ones who tried to influence her.

She was in charge, not them.

"There. You'll do," she said. "This is what I need." Charlotte cocked her head to one side, as if listening for a faint, faraway sound. "No, you will do as I say. You're on my time now, not yours. You may go about your business when I am finished with you." She waited impatiently, a shadow of a frown sliding over her face. "That's better, I knew we would come to an understanding."

She opened her eyes and pushed away from the wall. Barefoot, she strolled along the asphalt without a destination in mind. Going back to the boat wasn't an option for her, at least for now, until she dealt with this new wrinkle. Most of her belongings she could do without. The clothing and groceries would be replaced as soon as she found another poor soul to take pity on her. A young girl, alone and scared in a strange city, was a near-perfect charity case for bleeding hearts looking to pay it forward. A little nudge from her and she'd be showered in gifts.

Her therimoire, her life's work, her most personal of personal possessions, that was priceless and irreplaceable. Charlotte seethed with anger at the thought of that woman having her hands all over it. She'd kill her for that and take back what was hers from the dead bitch's hands.

Taking a deep breath, Charlotte reminded herself it was all a part of the unpredictable web of chaos. Recklessness was to be avoided but over-planning, relying on the illusion of order, taking too many precautions before you acted, that was for sheep. No matter how many times you checked and double-checked the safety list, the plane could still crash. Those that search for a greater reason behind it all are doomed to be disappointed. The universe itself was chaos; ever changing and out of our control.

This world is a cruel and arbitrary place

That didn't mean she was going to let Rebekah keep her book or continue to threaten her.

Charlotte undid her braid with one hand as she walked. Shaking her head and letting her unbound hair fall around her shoulders gave her a wild, disheveled look. Somewhat surprisingly, she didn't encounter any other people wandering behind the row of businesses with her. People were everywhere, it seemed, like a pest infestation. Trying to be alone was often an unrealistic and fruitless goal.

Up ahead, there was a sign over a large metal garage door: DONATION DROP OFF HERE. The door was partially rolled up, leaving an open space about five feet high. There was nobody else in sight. Charlotte wandered in, her five-eight frame forcing her to bend down to make it through.

Cardboard boxes and other large containers were scattered around the loading dock. This was where the donations were sorted. Toys were in one corner separated into different age groups. Appliances up against the wall. Some were brand new, still in the box.

Charlotte passed those by for the container sitting cockeyed in a far corner of the room. Clothing items were thrown together in one massive heap, seemed ready to tip over and spill out of the wheeled bin.

A handwritten sign was taped to the side. On it was the word CLEAN. She didn't care much if the clothes were clean or dirty as long as they were different than what she had on. If the police were called, they could be on the lookout for her just as much as the other two.

Picking through the pile, Charlotte set aside the items that looked to be close to her size. They didn't need to be perfect. If she could cinch it or squeeze into it, she would consider wearing it.

The sundress slid off over her head easily. She casually tossed it into the pile of donated clothes. It was only fair to give back if she was taking.

Charlotte considered her options, now wearing nothing but white lace panties. The cool air drifted in through the open door, caressing her bare skin. The temperature was lower in here than it was outside. She'd tentatively decided on her new outfit when she heard someone shuffle up behind her.

"You're, um, not supposed to be back here."

She turned her head to the sound, keeping her body facing away. The man speaking was tall and broad, with a mop of hair on the top of his head that made him look like a bear. He had the wispy facial hair of a young man. Over his black t-shirt he wore a blue vest with a name tag pinned to it.

Charlotte gave a gasp. "Oh, I thought I was alone. Derek, is it? I'm sorry. I didn't know. I never would have come inside if I knew it was against the rules." Charlotte glanced around at the walls. "Is there a sign or something?"

Derek kept his eyes high, trying not to stare. "Yes, I mean, no, there aren't any. Kinda assumed most people don't need a sign like that." Gesturing to the loading dock surrounding them, he added, "This is all donated stuff but it still costs money. You can't just take it. The money helps the needy."

"Well, that's good, Derek, because I am needy." Charlotte turned to him, resting her hands on the lip of the container behind her. Derek's jaw dropped. This time he couldn't help himself. His face went red and his eyes ran all over her body. "As you can see, I'm sure. I find myself in a predicament and could really use some kindness and understanding from a stranger."

He froze in place. Charlotte took pity on him. "You know what, Derek? Since I'm already undressed and I'm not sure where my clothes got to in all of this, do you think it would be okay, just this once, if I found something to cover me up? I'm not decent like this."

Her smile got bigger. She could almost see the wheels turning in his head. This whole time, since she first set foot in this back room, she hadn't used any of her special abilities on the hapless male. It was hardly a challenge with this one; she could read and manipulate him with ease.

Finally, he gave a short nod. "Sure, sure, go ahead. Make it quick, though, before someone else sees you and we both get into trouble."

"It'll be our little secret." Charlotte paused. "Could you turn around for me? A lady needs some privacy while she gets dressed."

"Oh, uh, yeah. Yes, no problem." Derek looked away, flustered. He faced away from her and towards the wall with a metal shelf full of knick-knacks.

The jeans were a little snug and had holes in the knees but they were good enough. A gray, short-sleeved shirt and black, zip-up hoodie fit fine. She finished off her new look with a maroon beanie to effectively cover her recognizable hair.

"All right, you can turn around now. Thank you for being such a gentleman." Derek did as she suggested, shrugging and fidgeting awkwardly. "Now, I can't go about my business in bare feet. Does this place have any quality footwear? I'm a size eight."

The thrift store did have shoes in a nine which was close enough. Derek looked the other way as Charlotte tried on the Converse knock-offs.

The store was a good place to lay low. From its giant front windows, she could see the comings and goings of the highway on the other side of the parking lot. It reminded her of an old farmhouse from another time. The trees around the house had been cleared away in part to be able to see enemies coming from a greater distance. Back then, that was real concern. Trees and brush could hide all sorts of bandits or villains. If you could see them coming, you had a better chance to defend yourself.

Charlotte killed time sauntering through the store, apathetically going over various odds and ends filling the shelves. Every so often she'd playfully wave at Derek who, in return, would suddenly become busy with a random menial task.

The sun was steadily getting lower in the sky. When she felt enough time had passed, she ducked into one of the vacant fitting rooms. Wasting no time with theatrics, Charlotte sat on the tiny wooden seat in the corner. The coffin-like room smelled of dust and mothballs. The cracked mirror caught her reflection and, for the briefest of instants, she saw the blur of spirits swirling around her and vanishing.

Calling the spirit back was easier than sending it. There was no need to sift through them all to find the correct one. She closed her eyes, crossed her legs, and placed her hands on her knees.

Her will kept the spirit on its mission. She didn't summon it so much as remove the barrier keeping it from returning. Charlotte was the lodestone. No matter where she was, the tasked ephemeral form could find her.

Distance was no concern. She could feel when it came back. "Okay, show me." Pictures formed in her mind, scenes from the recent past. Not as useful as live images through a scrying surface, but that required more preparation and materials than she had on hand.

First, there was the motel. She couldn't see past the door. It seemed to be warded to keep out the exact sort of thing she was attempting. It was no surprise; she'd expected at least that much from Rebekah. The inside could be hidden from her prying eyes temporarily but the witch herself would be found and with her, the book.

The picture dissolved suddenly and was replaced by high-pitched screaming. Charlotte cringed, but the sound was one only she could hear.

"Ohpleaseohpleaseohplease." A feminine voice, frantic and desperate, was barely discernible beyond the animal-like howls. "My family doesn't know what happened to me. You need to help. Please! They have to know. My name is-"

The scream became a shriek of pain. Charlotte opened her eyes. Colors swirled within them in a multitude of shades. She faced the mirror, but her sight went beyond the glass.

The fist she made with her hand was clenched so tightly her arm trembled with the effort.

Charlotte's lip curled up in a snarl as she spoke. "No, you will not beg, you will not plead, you will not use me to further your own desires. I am no simple medium. If you try to invade me, I will destroy you. You will learn your place and that place is servitude. Your time is done. Please me and I will release you. Tell me you understand."

There were no words but she felt the spirit concede. It didn't really have a choice. If Charlotte didn't relent, the torment would go on indefinitely. She rotated her fist, twisting and adding to the agony. Wracking the spirit was unlike any kind of physical pain. Like acid on an exposed nerve, the torture coursed over every speck of consciousness remaining in the once-human apparition. The shrieks rose to another, impossible octave before she finally released her hold.

Silence filled the space. Nobody outside the fitting room had heard a thing. "Now that we fully understand each other," said Charlotte, "show me what you've seen."

The picture in her mind returned immediately and was crystal clear. The spirit had learned a painful lesson, it wouldn't try to take any liberties with her again. In the vision, three people stood outside the motel room she'd caught a glimpse of before. Two of them were familiar. Rebekah and Tucker would be burned into her memory for a long time. The third, a young woman with dark hair, was on the verge of leaving. Tucker stopped her and their conversation was animated.

Charlotte was disappointed with the way Tucker begged the woman to listen to him. It reeked of weakness. Was this his girlfriend? Perhaps a recent ex? She responded favorably to his plea, which spoke volumes about what kind of a woman she was. "Fine. I will listen, but with two conditions," she said. This woman clearly had the upper hand and she knew it. He called her by her name. Lyric. Tucker and Lyric, trying to work out their problems.

The main problem here, Charlotte surmised, was the woman hanging back, not wanting to get between them more than she already had. Rebekah watched with an apathetic eye. This lover's quarrel was only delaying more important tasks.

Charlotte's book was not in sight. Most likely it was in the warded room behind Rebekah, outside the spirit's ability to detect.

What was this? The troubled couple came to a tentative agreement and were leaving together. Rebekah gave her blessing. "We can't stay here anyway. I'll find you after," she told Tucker. She disappeared into the motel room as the other two walked to a vehicle.

They were leaving her behind? To make matters worse, the spirit chose to stay with the couple, watching them and listening in on their pathetic conversation. It was following the wrong people. Tucker and his girlfriend could fall off the face of the planet for all she cared. Rebekah and the book were what mattered. There was nothing she could do now. What she was watching was already in the past, she couldn't change it.

"Where did you want to go?" Lyric asked.

"We shouldn't go back to my apartment yet. I know a place not far from here." They got into the car and Lyric started the car.

"I'm not going to regret this, am I?"

"I swear you won't." Tucker was solemn.

Charlotte broke herself off from the vision. "You chose poorly, following them like that. If I didn't know better, I'd say you did that on purpose," she said to the nervous spirit. "You know where they went? Good. Go there, watch them, listen. I will see through you. Do not disappoint me."

The unseen spirit rushed to obey. Charlotte stormed out of the fitting room, ignoring the startled looks from the few shoppers lingering near. Derek was standing at the front doors as she blew past him. He breathed a sigh of relief and watched her walk away until he was sure she was gone for good.

Chapter Twenty-Three

His hands were shaking as he lifted the coffee to his lips. This was his sixth. Lyric was nursing her second cup of tea. Behind him, the sun was starting to set, creating slow-moving shadows throughout the diner.

When they first arrived, Lyric made sure they sat in a booth where she could see her car.

It wasn't the car she was worried about. It was the lone occupant she wanted to keep an eye on. Bertram watched and whined as they left him in the front seat with the windows rolled down half way. Even now, all this time later, he still popped his head up to check and see if his human was coming back.

The sign outside boasted the best clam chowder on the coast. Tucker very much doubted that but wasn't in the mood to test the claim. Tea for her, coffee for him, was all they'd ordered since they came in.

Tucker looked like hell. He badly needed a shave and maybe twelve hours of sleep. The scratches on his face and the laceration on his palm had stopped bleeding, but the painful throbbing continually reminded him of his injuries. His churning stomach told him he should stop the coffee intake.

"I don't know where to start," he'd said as soon as they found a table and ordered that first cup.

"Start at the beginning," she replied coldly.

The beginning. Tucker wasn't sure where the beginning was. This might be his last shot at making things right with Lyric, so he wanted to lay it all out for her. He considered it a miracle she'd agreed to meet with him like this. How many men have used, "This isn't what it looks like," when caught red-handed with another woman? He had the truth on his side but in this case the truth was unbelievable.

He started with an apology. The same apology she'd heard from him before, but more elaborate. "I'm seeing things differently than before. I shouldn't have said what I said and I sure shouldn't have said it the way I said it."

"What do you mean, differently?"

"I've seen things these last couple of days. Things I can't explain, things I wouldn't have believed were possible. The Bible doesn't seem so ridiculous now." He realized what he said as soon as the words were out of his mouth. Cringing, he added, "Sorry, I didn't mean it like that."

"Yes, you did. I know you, Tucker. Maybe you can't help it, it's not the way your mind works. You apply logic to faith and it doesn't work like that. You're so willing to take for granted the everyday miracles that are happening all the time. Black holes and exploding stars you'll never see with your own eyes, millions of light-years away, you believe they exist even if you don't understand them. We live on a sphere of molten rock, hurtling through space at an impossible speed, at just the right distance from the sun so we don't freeze to death or burn up. All of this and the teachings of the Bible are too much for you?" The pent-up frustration had to have been eating away at her. This was a discussion long overdue. "But that's getting off-topic a little, don't you think?"

"Scottie Pippen Rule," Tucker muttered.

"What did you say?"

"It's nothing." He dismissed his words with a wave. "You were saying?"

Lyric raised her eyebrows at him and waited. Tell her everything. That's what she'd demanded and that's what he said he'd do.

He leaned forward and put his elbows on the table. "Something my dad used to say. He's a huge basketball fan. He's still mad about Clyde Drexler being traded to the Rockets for Otis Thorpe back in '95." Lyric's blank stare told him she had no clue who those people were. "Anyways, when I was little, he used to tell me about the Bulls teams of the nineties. They won a bunch of championships with Michael Jordan and Scottie Pippen as their main guys."

Lyric folded her arms and tapped her index finger against her elbow.

"He begrudgingly admitted Jordan was the best player in the NBA, maybe the best player ever. Pippen, though, hated that guy. Thought he was overrated, riding Jordan's coattails to all those rings. Dad always said Pippen never won a championship without Jordan, so he didn't understand how he got so much praise.

"You see, Dad is like most people, set in his ways. Once you reach a certain age the way you think, your belief system, political affiliation, whatever, is pretty much locked in. You know what you know and that's that. But Dad explained to me, every once in a great while, some bit of information comes up that makes you reevaluate those notions. For him it was when a friend of his said to him, 'It's true Scottie only won titles with Michael. It's also true Michael only won titles with Scottie.' That little nugget, a different way of looking at the debate, made him question his long-held belief. He didn't necessarily change his mind but he no longer ranted about it so much. He called it the Scottie Pippen Rule."

"You're saying you're looking at things with a new perspective."

"Yes, exactly. You're right. I dismissed certain happenings as impossible while accepting others as perfectly reasonable. I don't know what to think any more."

"All I ever wanted from you is some open-mindedness."

"I know. I get that now. What I'm asking from you now is the same thing. Can you hear me out, even if what I have to say is outlandish?"

He saw her hesitate for a moment before she nodded. Tucker tried to read her expression as he launched into his tale. She wasn't giving him very much other than an occasional questioning frown or thoughtful sigh. The Coast Guard boat was where he started. From there he told her about the fateful meeting with Greg McGarrett in the jail's interview room and the cryptic mantra two men, years apart and under completely different circumstances, said to him.

"I was shaken. That was when my world started to go all topsy-turvy. I looked for a plausible explanation, but couldn't find one. Knowing what I know now," he shook his head, "no, I'm not sure I would do anything different. Except with you, of course. I would confide in you right way and let the chips fall where they may. I don't think I ever would have found out the truth if Rebekah hadn't come to the office."

This was a touchy subject. Still, he went on. Rebekah was a large part of this journey; he couldn't leave her out because his girlfriend thought he might be sleeping with her.

He told her about the trip to his dad's, their talk, and his scramble into work the next day. By the time he got to Rebekah taking him into the side-room for a private conference he knew he had reached the hardest-to-believe portion.

Taking a deep breath, Tucker said, "Witchcraft. It's the only way I can describe it. It's not some magic trick like in Vegas. It's the real thing."

Lyric covered her mouth with her hand as he described the spell she put on him and his trip to the jail. McGarrett's suicide brought a tear to her eye. After that, the story found its own momentum.

The hardest part was telling her about what happened in the morgue. He didn't fully understand it and he'd been there. Trying to convey the feeling of losing control of your own limbs for such a gruesome purpose stretched at the boundaries of plausibility. He sounded crazy, and he knew it. The soul of the departed Greg McGarrett pointed them to the last known location of the person pulling the strings.

Tucker was fighting back tears himself as he finished his tale. The vision, gifted to him from Charlotte, showing him a glimpse of her victims down through the years, solidified his resolve to make sure she couldn't prey on anyone else ever again. As far as Rebekah and how she first encountered Charlotte, Tucker hit the high points but glossed over the rest. He could never have done it justice like someone who'd been there. Also, it was her story, her experience. Trying to retell it seemed like a breach of her confidence.

He finished his coffee and signaled to the waitress for a refill. "I get it if you don't trust me. If you get up and walk out the door and never want to speak to me again, I understand. It's important to me... I want you to know that whatever happens or has happened, I've never lied to you. I haven't always done the right thing or communicated when I should have, but I didn't lie and I didn't cheat."

"So, when that woman put that gun in my face…"

"Rebekah, yes. She thought you'd been sent by Charlotte. After the marina we could only guess what she would do next. Hell, we still don't know if she's running, hiding, or getting ready to fight."

Lyric slouched back in her seat. "This is a lot." She exhaled slowly. Now it was Tucker's turn to wait after she had patiently listened to him. "I think I believe you."

Relief and elation flooded through Tucker. With all that was going on, the opinion of one woman should be insignificant. Right there, in that diner, the most important thing to him was Lyric. When this was over, he swore to himself, he would make it up to her.

"Not at first, I didn't," Lyric said. "I'd convinced myself you were a cheating douchebag," she wrinkled her nose, "because it was easier to be angry than to be hurt."

"I'm so sorry about that."

"I know you are. That's the thing. I know you, Tucker." Lyric stopped long enough for the waitress to refill Tucker's coffee. The two of them locked eyes over the steaming coffee pot, not saying anything. The look, along with that tight-lipped half-smile of hers, told him everything was going to be all right. It was the same look she'd given him many times before. The way she did it, with a tilt of her head, never failed to melt his heart. When the waitress left, Lyric said, "It shouldn't be so hard for me to accept. Witchcraft is in the Bible. Really, it's full of warnings about witchcraft. Practicing witches are right up there with cowards and murderers. In line for the fiery lake of sulfur."

"That's pleasant." Charlotte deserved a special place in Hell, he was sure, but Rebekah? "You're saying it's the work of the Devil?"

"No," she paused, then, "I guess if you take it literally, then maybe. What I'm trying to say is, if witchcraft and black magic were prevalent when the Bible was written, so prevalent there are dozens of verses about it in both Testaments, then it stands to reason it still exists in some form today."

"But they're not all bad. Rebekah is a good one."

"Is she, though?"

Lyric had a point. Everything Rebekah had done up until now was to help herself achieve her one, all-consuming goal. She'd used him to further her own ends. Then there was the matter of how she'd stayed so young for so long. If it wasn't the same forbidden ritual Charlotte used, it was close enough to be the same thing. Charlotte and her destruction of lives could only be described as evil. Did the ends justify the means? Just because Rebekah stood against her, that didn't mean she was good.

"Scottie Pippen Rule," he whispered. "Even if you're right, she's all we have at the moment."

"What do we do now?"

"We find Rebekah, or let her find us. That's what she said she'd do. I'm guessing Charlotte is going to lay low. She's not used to having someone after her. Rebekah says she'll come after her book, so we have that. We'll set up and wait for her. We're going to have to be patient, it might be a while."

"You can stay with me. Your apartment might be too iffy."

"First place they'd look. I'll have to face the music at some point. Not now, there's too much that needs to be done. Thank you. For everything. I wish you didn't have to be wrapped up in all this, but I'm really glad you're here."

"I always knew you'd fall apart without me." Then, more serious, "Don't make me look like an asshole, okay? If we're a team, we have each other's back. Us against the world."

"Always." He held his hand out on the table and she took it.

"Come on," said Lyric. "Let's get you home. Bertram's waited long enough out there."

"Toughen up, man. You can sleep when you're dead," Tucker said into the restroom mirror.

He hardly recognized the man looking back at him. His bloodstream had to be at least half-caffeine by now. How could he be so tired and so jittery at the same time? Underneath his sunken eyes, the marks on his cheek were an angry red, and thin scabs were beginning to form. The slightest facial movement hurt sharply and threatened to reopen the wounds. Hopefully they didn't leave a scar behind once they healed.

Lyric needed to tend to her dog while Tucker had to tend to eliminating some of the coffee he'd consumed over the past couple of hours. Splashing water on his face refreshed him temporarily. Nothing, though, could have made him feel better than Lyric being in his corner. It was like a huge weight had been lifted from his shoulders. As long as she had faith in him, everything would be okay. He'd make sure she never regretted it, no matter what it cost him.

Stepping outside into the night air, Tucker took a moment to let the cool breeze wash over him. Had they really been sitting in the booth that long? The sun's rays left a dim glow on the ocean even after it had dipped below the horizon. Street lights lit the sidewalk and exterior of the restaurant.

Tucker thought he was mistaken at first. He'd gone the wrong way after exiting. Turning around and walking the opposite way, he circled the entire building. His confusion only grew. Lyric's car was gone. Had she left him behind on purpose? He replayed the end of their conversation in his head. "Let's get you home," is what she'd said. No indication she was angry enough to ditch him.

Her phone went straight to voicemail. The light, cheery voice told him to leave a message. "Hey, it's me," Tucker said. "Your car's gone and I thought-"

A faint, high-pitched whine from off to his right interrupted him. It came from behind the bushes at the edge of the parking lot. A familiar black-and-white furry face stepped out and saw Tucker. Bertram's stump of a tail wagged with no exuberance.

"Bertram?" Head held low, the dog trotted over to him and nuzzled up against his leg. He had his collar on, but no leash. Tucker knelt down and stroked the dog's neck. "Oh, no." Lyric never would have left Bertram alone like this. Something happened. Something snatched her away in the brief time they were apart.

Looking hopefully up at Tucker, Bertram let out a long cry. He sounded almost human. "It's okay, boy. It'll be all right. We'll find mama." He wasn't sure if he was trying to comfort the dog or himself.

Chapter Twenty-Four

Neither the dog nor the man looked up as the van chug-chugged up behind them in the otherwise quiet residential neighborhood. Heads down, they were quite the pathetic pair. Rebekah rolled down the window and leaned out.

"Tucker?" That got his attention. He wasn't startled by her greeting. His response was lethargic, like someone under the influence. No, that wasn't right. Tucker looked like someone who'd been kicked one too many times. Defeated.

The clear crystal hanging from the rearview mirror rapidly spun clockwise. It barely moved when she first started looking for Tucker. As she got closer it moved faster and faster, telling her when she was going in the right direction. She stopped it with one hand and waited for Tucker to approach. The dog followed close behind.

"Where's Lyric?" She had a sinking feeling she already knew the answer.

"I don't know. I left her for a minute, didn't think she was in any danger. She's gone and it's my fault."

"Get in, we'll find her."

Rebekah navigated with no destination in mind. Her crystal charm had guided her to Tucker but she'd only followed where it told her to go. Right now, she didn't even know what street they were on.

"Where'd you get this?" Tucker asked, checking out the interior of the vehicle.

"Don't ask. It's borrowed. I don't think the owner will miss it until morning at the earliest."

The light-green van was at least thirty-years old, with rust spots and bald tires. It was the best she could do on short notice. The back of the van held her belongings. She'd hastily packed up her motel room and left. She didn't know if anyone had called the police after her confrontation with Lyric, but she wasn't going to stick around to find out.

"I was an idiot," said Tucker, "thought we had the initiative. Charlotte would be hiding from us since we came so close. I didn't think she'd do anything so soon."

"How is it that Lyric found you back at the motel?"

Tucker held up his phone. "She told me she tracked me with this. We both have an app so we could do that in case of emergency. Today qualifies."

"Can't you reverse that? If she found you, you can find her."

"That's the first thing I thought of. Either her phone's off or she got rid of the tracker. It's not working." He looked at Rebekah with hope in his eyes. "Wait a sec. How did you find me? Can you find her?"

Rebekah frowned and shook her head. "Maybe, but it's not an exact science. I know a way to try. That sort of divination takes its toll on me, though, and there's no guarantee it will work. If she is with Charlotte, the chance of tracking them down is practically nonexistent. Charlotte hides herself with a fog I can't pierce. She's like a ghost. It was difficult, but so much easier, to catch back up with you," Rebekah tapped the crystal, "because of our time spent together. This is a different sort of clairvoyance. It won't work with her. Not with what I have now."

"So, we do nothing."

"I didn't say that. Whatever we do, we do it smart. She's a step ahead again, but we have something she wants."

"And now she has someone I want back."

"We don't know that for sure."

"Yes, we do. Even if she was pissed at me and wanted to leave me at the diner to walk home, she wouldn't have left Bertram." The dog lifted his head off Tucker's knee when he heard his name. Tucker scratched behind his ears. "She'd die before she let anything bad happen to her dog. She's not answering her phone and texts aren't going through. You tell me a better scenario for what happened to her and I'll be happy to listen."

Rebekah held her tongue. She had no better options. Nothing realistic anyways. The timing alone, so soon after they'd come face-to-face with Charlotte, told her this was no coincidence. Charlotte lived off of being underestimated, playing the helpless waif. They'd underestimated her again and now she had a hostage. That is, if the hostage wasn't already dead.

Tucker screamed, "Dammit," and punched the glove compartment hard enough to pop it open. Bertram retreated to the back corner of the van.

The display surprised Rebekah. Tucker, in the brief time she'd known him, had been reserved and composed, even when faced with madness-inducing, impossible situations. Cracks were beginning to show.

"She'll be okay. She's a tough one," Rebekah said.

"Stop with the shitty platitudes. You don't know her. You don't care about her. All you care about is revenge."

"I know her enough. I know she hardly flinched when I stuck a gun in her face. You're telling me she's used to that kind of thing? She had the guts to pound on my door, not knowing what she'd find, just to get to you. That relentless attitude is what will keep her alive."

"If she's still alive."

"If Charlotte has her, there would be no reason to kill her. All that would do is take away any leverage she might have over us. Lyric may be Charlotte's best bargaining chip. Without her, she has nothing to trade."

"Trade. Bargaining chip. That's all we are to you people. Pawns to move around and sacrifice when convenient."

Rebekah hit the brakes, sending Tucker lurching forward in his seat. Being in a residential area, she hadn't been going very fast. Otherwise, Tucker, without his seatbelt on, would have plowed into the dash face-first.

"Tucker, listen to me." She turned in her seat to face him. He lowered his eyes to avoid hers. He'd gone too far and he knew it. "That's enough of that kind of talk. I don't want anything to happen to Lyric or you. I know I owe you, that's why I'm still here. Neither of you would be neck-deep in this if I hadn't gotten you involved." She pointed her finger at him. "But let's get one thing straight. I don't need you anymore. I brought you with me because I thought you could lead me to Charlotte and you did." Rebekah patted the canvas bag next to her seat. "This might be the only thing in this world she cares about. So, you can curse me all you want after we're done. Until then, we work together or you can get out right here."

Tucker wanted to come back at her, she could tell. He held it in, though. Holding up his hands in surrender, he said, "Fine. Understood." He folded his arms but made no move to exit the van.

"Okay." When she gave her ultimatum, Rebekah honestly didn't know if Tucker would stay or leave. What she'd said was true, Tucker wasn't necessary to her like he was before. She had no doubt Charlotte would come for her. She had to. That didn't mean she wanted Tucker to leave. Charlotte was obviously formidable. The more help Rebekah had, the better her odds got. "Where do you think Lyric could be? Where could she have gone if she wasn't taken against her will? We should try those places first."

"Her house," he said flatly. "I was heading to her house when you pulled up. If she's not there maybe her roommate heard from her."

"Then that's where we'll go."

Because of their already low expectations, they weren't surprised when Lyric's roommate said she wasn't home. Rebekah waited in the van, drawing passive-aggressive glances from April as she spoke with Tucker. Letting Tucker deal with her alone was less awkward than having to answer questions Rebekah's presence on the porch would bring up.

Tucker squatted and pet Bertram's head goodbye with both of his hands. April gave him an indifferent wave and a dirty look as soon as he turned his back.

"She hasn't seen Lyric," he said. The door groaned loudly as he shut it. "Not since this morning. I don't think she's lying, but she made it clear she didn't want me to come in. I'm kind of shocked she talked to me for as long as she did."

"Because of the fight with Lyric? What did you tell her?"

"What could I tell her? I said I got a weird call from her earlier and I was concerned about her. I'd been watching the dog as a favor, but thought I should bring him home before Lyric thought I'd stolen him. Complete bullshit. I don't think she believed me. She probably thinks Lyric's hiding out from me; the asshole boyfriend. Maybe she'll give me a heads up if she sees her." Tucker slumped down in his seat. "What do we do now?"

"This is the point. if things were going this bad for me, I would be looking to get the hell out of town. Find some new place to start over until a new lead turned up."

"That's not an option."

"No, it's not."

They both jumped at the musical sound of Tucker's ringtone breaking through the silence. "Oh, shit. It's her." He showed Rebekah the screen with the name of the person calling. LYRIC.

"Hello?"

"Put it on speaker," said Rebekah. Tucker complied. At first there was no one on the other end, just a low rustling sound.

"Lyric? Lyric, are you there?" Desperation dripped from his voice.

"Yeah, I'm here." Rebekah frowned. The feminine voice on the line didn't sound distressed at all. "I'm really sorry. I turned my phone back on and saw how many times you called. You must have been worried."

"Are you all right? I assumed the worst. You took off and left us behind without saying a word."

"Us?"

"Us. Me and Bertram. You left your dog."

"Oh, Bertie. I forgot about him." Lyric sounded flighty and distracted; not at all like the woman she met at the motel.

"Lyric," he spoke softer, "I need to know you're okay and I need to know where you are right now."

"You're such a worry-wart, Tucker. Of course I'm fine. Rebekah and I have been talking things out, girl-to-girl stuff."

"What...," he started to say. "Lyric, is Rebekah with you right now?"

"Yeah, she's right here. It was her idea to call and check in. I'd completely lost track of time."

Her statement hung in the air. Tucker, phone in one hand, scrutinized the woman sitting next to him as if he'd never seen her before. She could read the expression on his face. When he wanted to, Tucker could connect the dots in his head fast. Rebekah held up one finger and mouthed the words, "No. Wait." If he suspected she wasn't who she appeared to be, and after all he'd seen she didn't blame him, there was a way she could placate that doubt.

Reaching down to the bag at her side, she noticed Tucker put one hand on the door latch. He was ready to bolt at the first sign of trickery. "Wait," she whispered again. Ever so slowly, she felt for the book without taking her eyes off of him. Lifting it with one hand reminded her how heavy it was. This was truly a tome, filled with several lifetime's worth of extraordinary knowledge.

He ran his fingers over the leather cover as if making sure it was real. Rebekah gestured for him to take it; a sign she trusted him and wanted him to trust her. She wanted Tucker to grasp the larger problem. Who was the person with Lyric right now?

Tucker waved her away. He didn't want the book. Still, Rebekah opened it up and showed him the pages so there was no questioning its authenticity.

"Tucker, are you there? Hello?" the voice said from the phone. He shook his head to clear out the cobwebs.

"Yeah. Yes, I'm here. Sorry, I lost signal for a sec."

"Okay, good. I thought I lost you."

"Same."

"So anyways," she sounded chipper, "us girls were talking and we think we have a plan. I mean, Rebekah thinks it'll work and she's the one who would know about this stuff, right?"

"Yes, she is." Obviously at a loss for words, he finally managed, "What's this plan of yours?"

"Rebekah can explain it way better than I can. It involves trapping that bitch with sea salt, which we have plenty of around here, and something called...what was it again?"

A voice in the background said something unintelligible.

"Saining. That's what she called it. But we really need to be careful. You never know when someone might be listening in. Could ruin the whole thing."

"We...I understand."

"Good. This is all so crazy, you know. Oh, hey. Rebekah says she wants to talk to you. Here she is. Love you."

"Love you, too." Lyric was handing the phone off before he finished.

For a handful of seconds there was only the sound of breathing on the other end. "Hello, Tucker. Long time no see."

She didn't sound like Rebekah. There was a higher pitch to the voice, almost angelic. The faux-sweetness that had tricked so many, including Lyric, came through. It only angered Tucker more. "You sound different than when we met at the marina."

"I apologize for that. You caught me at a bad time. I'm not always so abrasive."

"What do you want? What do we do now?"

"Like Lyric said, we can't exactly speak freely here." Charlotte wasn't on speaker-phone but Lyric was close by. Surely, she was under a spell like he'd been before.

"I'm sure you have a place in mind where we could speak freely."

"As a matter of fact, I do. Meet me at your office. It's closed so we should have all the privacy we could ask for. Bring a friend if you want. We'll go over the new plan there. With a little luck, this will all be over soon. Don't forget to bring the book. You'll need that if we hope to end this without anyone else getting hurt."

"A trade? Is that it? I swear, if you hurt her-"

"Tucker, stop. I'll listen to all of your input when we meet up but you have to understand I'm the one calling the shots. You will not make any demands of me. You have twenty minutes. The clock is ticking."

"I will set fire to your precious book; I swear to god." The line went dead. Had she even heard his threat? "We have to go," he told Rebekah.

"We go there and she'll have us right where she wants us."

"I know that. I also know we don't have another choice. Charlotte gave us twenty minutes. That's how much time we have to come up with something that won't get us all killed."

Chapter Twenty-Five

The place was lit up like a beacon they could see from blocks away. Tucker hadn't been expecting that. Everything they were doing seemed so clandestine and geared toward not attracting attention. Having every light on in the office of Delbert J. Mahoney, Attorney at Law well after it had closed for the day was quite the surprise.

"Not hiding anymore, huh?" said Tucker.

"What is she playing at?" Rebekah took them past the house slowly. A recon probe is what she called it. Nothing moved inside that they could see.

"Can you tell if they're in there?"

"No, the place is like a void of nothingness. She's hidden it from everything but the five senses."

"That means there's something worth hiding in there." Tucker wanted to go straight in, guns blazing. Rebekah talked him down from that, arguing for a more sensible, careful approach. She won out because, as she said to him earlier, he needed her more than she needed him. All he wanted was to get Lyric out of harm's way. Everything else was secondary. When he only had himself to worry about it was all so clear. Putting her at risk was unacceptable. He wished she'd never tracked him down at the motel. She'd probably be at home right now, bored and still mad at him, but safe.

"Maybe, maybe not. I can't help but think she's manipulating us. It has to be a trap."

"If she stays in there and we stay out here, we'll never know."

"You're ready?" Tucker nodded and she produced a single needle between two fingers. He bowed his head as if in prayer, exposing the back of his neck. "This ward is temporary. Effective for maybe an hour, two hours tops." His skin yielded to the needle as Rebekah began to etch into his skin. "It's not complete protection – nothing is – but it will diffuse any harmful effects. Makes it easier to resist."

"The only thing one-hundred percent effective is abstinence. Got it." The joke fell flat. "Sorry. Nerves, I guess." With the first circle finished, Rebekah dabbed away the bit of blood welling up and went to work on the second. Tucker bit his lip. The pain ebbed and flowed. He tried to push it out of his mind, replacing it with thoughts of why he was doing all of this in the first place.

They had to be ready for anything, she'd told him. Charlotte hadn't survived as long as she had by being a fool. He'd felt the power of her coercion back at the Mandy Lou. She'd slipped into his mind effortlessly, convincing him she was a friend. It all felt so natural at the time. It made him shiver to think of it.

"She won't go to the same bag of tricks she used before," said Rebekah. "It almost backfired on her. This time she won't make the same mistake." Whatever she'd done to Lyric made her believe she wasn't Charlotte. It went further and deeper than the charm she put on Tucker.

"What else is she capable of?" He was referring to her arcane abilities. Thanks to the visions she put in his head, he'd seen for himself how far she was willing to go to hurt someone.

"I honestly don't know." Tucker winced as she moved on to the third inter-locking circle.

Blood trickled down his back. When she was done, he stretched his neck up and down, working out the kinks and feeling the shallow wounds with every movement. "Better than nothing," he said. If the symbol carved into his flesh bought him even a few seconds of extra time, it would be worth it. "I'm going in first?" With time running short, they hadn't yet agreed on a plan of action. Things were still up in the air, even as their destination came into view.

"I think that's best. Make her show her hand. I'll be outside ready to counter."

"I'm the canary in the coal mine. If I drop, you'll know it's dangerous." It showed how little she thought of him. The only thing worse would have been tying him up and leaving him in the front yard as bait.

"Do you have a better idea? I stay outside. The book stays with me. Walking in together, we might as well be holding a white flag." Rebekah reached underneath her seat and took out the gun. "You know how to use this?" she asked, handing it over to him.

"Well enough, I guess." He fumbled with it a bit before he ejected the magazine into his left hand. A quick inspection told him there were eight rounds remaining. Nine, counting the one in the chamber. "I won't win any marksman competitions, but I'll make each round count." The weight of the gun in his hand made him feel better. She wasn't sending him in totally helpless.

"That's good, if it even comes to that. I'm hoping we can get the drop on her, incapacitate her, mystically bind her so she can't perform any spells."

"Then what?"

"If I have my way, I'll weigh her down and drop her into the deepest part of the ocean."

"Fine with me." Tucker got out and headed toward the brightly lit house he'd called his workplace for the last two years. Behind him, he heard Rebekah's door open and close. She wasn't going to sit idly by while he ventured into the lion's den. He was supposed to take his time, look for any signs of activity, and sneak in through the back door. At the same time, Rebekah would do her thing, tracing sigils around the edge of the property. If done correctly, they would give Charlotte a nasty surprise when she tried to cross the barrier. She had to work fast, before their presence was discovered and Charlotte tore down the thinly constructed prison. Tucker hoped they wouldn't need it. If he got the chance, he'd shoot her.

He held the gun down at his side. His head was on a swivel, scanning the area for potential threats. A breeze cascaded over him as he jogged across the well-manicured lawn, rustling the leaves in the surrounding trees with an ominous deep howl. Ducking around the side of the house, into the shadows and shrubbery, Tucker raised the pistol up into a low ready position. The muzzle shook along with the hands holding it. He would've been ashamed if anyone else was around to see how nervous he was.

Only in the movies did people choose to shoot one-handed. The more skin you had pressed against the metal, the more you could control the recoil and put your next shot on target. Tucker hadn't fired a gun in almost ten years but that lesson, his only lesson as it turned out, from his father stuck with him. Since then, the closest he'd been to a firing range was when he played paintball with the guys in high school. He felt out-of-place, like a wannabe SWAT cosplayer, as he crouched and tiptoed to the back of the house.

A set of narrow concrete steps led up to the short, covered porch and rear door. Nobody in the office used it since Donnie quit smoking. It was most assuredly locked but Tucker had the key on his keychain. Getting in wouldn't be a problem unless the door was barricaded.

Seconds ticked off his watch. "A few minutes," is what she said she needed. To him, a few meant six. Kneeling beside the stairs, Tucker saw malevolence in each turn of shadow and every crunch of leaves.

"Come on, come on," he said softly, willing time to move faster. He never considered himself a particularly brave man, but he also wasn't a coward. When the time came, he always figured he would be able to do the right thing. Outside his office, in the dark, and on the precipice of danger, he doubted that courage. If he didn't go in soon, he was afraid he would lose his nerve and not go in at all.

Four minutes after exiting the van, two and a half minutes after taking up his position next to the steps, Tucker decided he'd waited long enough. He reached the porch in three long strides. The door had a window, but the curtains were drawn. In the dark, Tucker scratched at the lock with the key, trying to get it to fit. Agonizing seconds went by and he feared it wouldn't work at all. He was making too much noise. Every clink of metal on metal made him cringe. When the key finally slipped in, he breathed a huge sigh of relief.

Light from the hallway spilled into the utility room. No ghosts or goblins or witches stood in his way. Holding the pistol out, he followed the short corridor past the wood shelves filled with office supplies. Tucker stepped lightly. Even so, each footfall echoed in his ears.

The living/waiting room was empty, as was Cheryl's desk near the front door. More lights were on now than during a normal workday. Still, nobody challenged him. For all he knew, he could be the only living soul in the house.

Footsteps and low voices from the other room cured him of that notion. He inched past the desk and craned his neck to see around the corner without exposing himself. In the office he shared with Donnie, Tucker saw shadows moving. He couldn't make out what they were saying, but their tone was urgent.

Tucker made up his mind. There were two entryways into the occupied room on the opposite side of the hall. He flew through the nearest one, gun first with a finger on the trigger.

"Don't move a fucking muscle. Let me see your hands!" His shout startled the pair standing in the corner by Donnie's desk.

"Holy Jesus," Cheryl wailed. Her hands went up in the air and she flinched backward at the sight of the firearm. Donnie turned reflexively to the wall, covering his head with his hands. When she recognized the would-be gunman, Cheryl took a half-step forward. "Tucker? What the hell are you doing? It's us."

Of all the possibilities he'd envisioned, this definitely wasn't one of them. His coworkers being here instead of Charlotte and Lyric stunned him with the ridiculousness of the situation. Cheryl had her hair put up sloppily. That wasn't like her. She was in jeans and a baggy sweater. He was so used to her put-together business outfits that her current outfit added to his confusion.

Tucker quickly swung the gun behind his back, trying to hide it as if they could have possibly missed it in his hand. "Guys, what are you...Sorry. Sorry about that. I thought...."

"Put the gun on the desk right now before someone gets hurt," said Cheryl. He'd heard that stern tone before. Tucker bobbed his head sheepishly and set the pistol on his own desk in front of him. Donnie turned around now that the immediate danger was over.

"I saw all the lights on. They're never on this late. I thought it was break-in." It was all he could think of on such short notice. The looks on their faces told him they didn't believe a word of it.

"You called us, both of us." Donnie tapped the screen of his phone.

"No, I didn't."

"Yes, Tucker," said Cheryl. "We both got separate messages from you. You asked us to meet you here. We didn't know you called both of us until we got here and compared notes. You said you needed help. It was worrisome to say the least."

"What did I say in the message?"

"Here, I'll show you." Cheryl played the voicemail and there was no doubt. It was him on the phone, speaking words he never spoke.

"Cheryl, it's Tucker." The digital voice filled the room. "I'm sorry to bother you so late but I don't have anyone else to turn to. I'm having a tough time. I don't think I want to be a part of this world anymore."

Cheryl came over to him as the message continued in the background. "We're here to help you, Tucker. You need to tell us what's going on."

Chapter Twenty-Six

With a little more patience than Tucker, Rebekah waited behind a tree outside the house, searching for any sign of trouble. The therimoire was stored safely in the bag she wore across her chest like a satchel. Its weight was comforting against her hip. If Charlotte was in there this could be the culmination, decades in the making, of her relentless pursuit. One way or another, this would end. She thought of her parents in New Jersey, dying, never truly knowing why their only son had turned into a murderer. If there was any justice in the universe, they understood in death what they never could in life.

Richard and her brother, what could have been? Somewhere, in another life, she married Richard and they ran the family store together after Mom and Dad retired. They lived in a little house with their three children who all adored their Uncle Evan. A good life. Maybe it wouldn't have been a happy ending like she imagined, but that wasn't the point. All that potential, the limitless possibilities, set in motion years before and snuffed out in a single night. Charlotte lived for that. Others sought to change the world for the better. She wanted to bask in the suffering she created.

In that other life, Rebekah would be...seventy? A bit older maybe, she couldn't remember. If she was alive at all, that is, she sure wouldn't be standing outside a lawyer's office in the middle of the night in small town Oregon, waiting for word from Tucker Gibsen.

The front door opened. Tucker was in the doorway, peering out into the night looking for her. He came out to the edge of the covered porch. "Rebekah," he called out. The calm night carried his words without the need to shout. "She's not here. Neither of them are here."

When she came inside, Rebekah met Cheryl and Donovan for the second time. "Are you sure they're not here?" she asked Tucker.

"Yes. The house isn't that big. Not many places to hide. Cheryl's key even got us into the boss' office upstairs. Empty."

Then he played the messages for her. One from Cheryl's phone, one from Donnie's. They were similar, but not identical in their wording. The speaker had been winging it instead of reading from a prepared speech. In Tucker's voice, it said, "I can't do this alone. I'm afraid of what I might be capable of." The sentiment was the same in each: I'm in trouble, I need help, meet me at the office.

"I thought for sure we'd get here and find you hanging from a light fixture," said Donnie. "Cheryl got here first; I was a few minutes behind her."

"That's not me." He looked to Rebekah, the only one who would believe him.

Cheryl said, "Honey, you have friends here who will stand by you no matter what." She put her hand on his cheek. "You don't need to make excuses or be ashamed. We've all had our own battles to fight. You don't have to fight alone. There's nothing you've done that can't be undone."

Tears welled in Tucker's eyes. "You've always been so good to me. There's so much you don't know. It's all my fault. Lyric...."

"She's a nice girl. Better than most. You need to make things right with her, however you can. To start, maybe you should have higher standards about who you spend time with." Cheryl glared daggers at Rebekah. Clearly, she was protective of Tucker and had identified her as the bad influence.

"You don't understand. It's too late for that."

"It's never too late."

"Yeah, buddy," Donnie fidgeted and then rubbed his hands down the front of his shirt. "We're, uh, listening if you need to talk." He inched slowly away from the center of attention.

Rebekah stepped in. "Both messages separately asked you to meet Tucker here. She knew we were coming, too."

"Who knew you were coming?" asked Cheryl.

Tucker said, "I'm sorry, Cheryl. There's no time to explain." To Rebekah, he said, "But she's not here. She wants the book, but she's not here to take it herself."

"Unless she sent someone else to do what she couldn't." Rebekah took a step back, eyeing Tucker's coworkers. Clutching at her bag, she felt the book nestled in there. She took it off and slid the contents out onto Tucker's desk. The basket-weave pattern on the book's cover gleamed in the fluorescent light. Wasting no time, Rebekah went through the pages in a flurry. "It's still here." Did Charlotte have the capability of swapping out her book for a fake without her noticing? At this point, Rebekah's paranoia was such that she couldn't discount it. "Not a fake."

"Did you think it could be?" Tucker said.

"She brought us here for a reason. Him," she pointed at Donnie, "he's acting like he has something to hide. Why? What are you not telling us?"

"Who the hell do you think you are?" Donnie shot back. "Coming in here and talking shit like you own the place. All you've done since you walked through that door is get him to follow you like a damn puppy. You think I'm acting weird? That's because I don't want to be here. Tucker's a big boy and can make his own decisions, even if they're fucking stupid."

Tucker stepped between them. "Why did you come here, then?"

"I felt obligated. If I didn't and you hung it up, I couldn't have lived with that. And for my trouble, I almost get my head blown off by the guy I'm trying to help." Then, to the rest of the room, he said, "Now all I want is to leave. I don't want to know what you guys do next."

"There's the door," said Cheryl. "Your legs work. Nobody's making you stay."

Rebekah hoped he'd leave. One less wild card to worry about. Donnie's legs could carry him out of here the same way he came in. His legs, his feet. What was that on the floor? One of his shoes had a fine, dark powder on the toe. He must have tracked it in from the hall.

"Fine, no problem. I'm gone. Good luck when the cops catch up to you." He stormed away, leaving a faint trace of a crimson footprint.

"Wait, stop." Rebekah's voice stopped Donnie in his tracks. "Don't move a single step." She bent down and ran her finger through the print. "Where did this come from? Show me where you entered the house."

"The front door. Where else would I come in?"

Dots of powder led her from the hall directly to the door. A line of the stuff crossed in front of the entryway. She could see where it had been disturbed by ignorant feet, creating thin fingers on the smooth floor. She dabbed her thumb in it again and sniffed the residue.

"Crushed bloodstone," she said. The others were gathered together, studying her with quizzical expressions. Alarmed, she shouted, "We need to get out of here right now."

"What, why?" was all Cheryl could get out. Like a lit fuse, the powder ignited all along where the walls met the floor. Starting at the entrance, right behind Rebekah, the fire encircled the room faster than the people inside could react. The heat singed Rebekah's legs through her pants and she retreated to the center. The flames were over two feet high in seconds. Smoke filled the air followed by hacking coughs as the group struggled to breathe.

All around the house – down the hall, in the office, around the main room – was the same inescapable scene. Curtains went up quickly and soon fire was licking the ceiling.

"Up the stairs," someone yelled. It sounded like Tucker, almost drowned out by the roar of the blaze. "It's clear that way. Everywhere else is blocked." It was definitely Tucker.

She already couldn't see through the thick smoke but she knew the stairs should be straight ahead, down the hall past the office, and towards the rear of the house.

Eyes watering like a faucet, Rebekah dropped to her knees and crawled blindly. There was no way to tell how far she'd gone or if she was going the right direction. She felt her way along, motivated by survival. The others would have to find their own way; she was in no position to help anyone right now.

Striking her finger on the first step jammed it, but she barely noticed the pain. She got to her feet and raced up the stairs. The oppressive heat from downstairs wasn't as bad up on the second floor, but that wouldn't last long. It was clear the house would be burned to the ground. If they didn't get out, they would suffer the same fate.

Cheryl stood in the open double-doorway, waving her in. She was holding the door for her, Rebekah gratefully realized in the short time it took her to round the bannister at the top of the stairs, cross the threshold, and collapse on the carpet in the boss' office. Donnie was on his hands and knees, dry heaving by the massive desk dominating the room.

"Thank you," she croaked as Cheryl slammed the door shut. Smoke billowed in from underneath. It wouldn't be long before this space would be as uninhabitable as the rest of the house. "Wait, where's Tucker?"

The fire sprang from nothing. Tucker leapt back and clutched his scorched hands with a hiss of pain when the flames shot up beneath him. His first impulse was to run for the front of the house. He found both openings to the hall blocked as the blaze expanded supernaturally, separating him from the others and effectively trapping him in his office.

Shouts of panic came at him from the other room. Smoke overwhelmed his senses faster than his brain could process what was happening. Heat rises, he remembered, so the best place to be was down low. He dropped to his stomach and pulled his shirt up over his mouth and nose. It helped, but only a little.

The whisper spoke to him clearly and seemingly from all directions, cutting through the noise and confusion. "Tucker," it said. "Listen to me and do what I tell you if you want to live though this." The words resonated in his mind. Not physical sound but he heard it just the same.

"Who the-" he began to say. There was only one person it could be. Like a burglar returning to the scene of the crime, Charlotte was in his head again.

"You have something I need. Trust me and everyone can get out of there safely. Fight me and you'll all die. Tell the others to go up the stairs. That way is safe for them. They will be all right. Hurry."

Tucker worked out immediately what her strategy was. "Up the stairs," he yelled. He didn't know if they could hear him but he had to try. Trusting Charlotte would have been laughable if he had enough breath to laugh. Trusting her to act in her own self-interest was more reasonable. Her precious book would burn to ash just as fast as any other mundane paperback. "It's clear that way. Everywhere else is blocked."

Charlotte spoke again. "Good, good. You're saving their lives. They might not know it but you're a real, honest-to-god hero. Now, there's one more life to worry about. Time is fleeting. Take the book and I'll guide you out."

Black smoke dissipated around him and he could see again. He rubbed his burning, irritated eyes and saw Charlotte's book on the desk next to him, right where Rebekah left it. Beyond it, the smoke parted forming a short winding path that ended at the window next to Donnie's desk on the far side of the room.

"Go, now," she said.

Tucker hesitated, deciding what he should take and what he should leave behind. He gathered up the book, holding it like a baby. There was no way to see out into the burning hallway; he hoped Rebekah, Donnie, and Cheryl were able to get upstairs and escape that way. Outside the window was a different world with safety and fresh air waiting for him. He opened the window easily, as if he had someone helping him from the other side.

Half-climbing, half-rolling, Tucker wriggled out, landing awkwardly in the dirt and falling on his ass. "Move, Tucker. Get away from the house," said the whisper in his head. The entire house was aflame and smoke billowed into the dark sky. "They'll be fine. You can't wait for them. Come to me, come to us, but you have to come alone. You give me my book and I give you Lyric, unharmed. Let's end this."

What choice did he have? This was the only way left to him if he ever wanted to see Lyric again. If getting this damn book back into the hands of its author would achieve that goal, he would make the trade without hesitation.

He struggled to his feet and jogged away from the burning house. "Where do you want me to go?" he asked out loud.

She told him and asked, "Do you know where that is?"

"Yes, I know exactly where that is." Tucker reached into the pocket of his sweatshirt, making sure the pistol was still there. Charlotte hadn't mentioned the gun when giving him instructions so maybe she didn't know about it. She couldn't be omnipotent, right? He'd grabbed it when he took the book off the desk. He'd make the trade if he could, but if she went back on her word, he'd do everything he could to make her regret it.

The three of them squinted through the haze and coughed. "I don't know what happened to Tucker," said Cheryl. "I couldn't see a thing. I think it was him who told us to head up here."

Donnie was at one of the two windows overlooking the front yard, grunting with the strain of trying to lift it open. "It's stuck," he said through gritted teeth.

"Hang on." Cheryl picked up a clear, crystal globe the size of her fist off the desk. She hurled the heavy paperweight at the glass, shattering the window outward in a thousand shards. Donnie kicked away the jagged edges left behind around the frame.

"Come on," he said. "We'll have to jump." The porch overhang was under the window. From there it was more than ten feet to the ground. Black smoke poured from every opening on the first floor.

"We can't leave Tucker," said Cheryl.

"We can't help him if we're dead." He put one foot up and over the window sill. Ducking his head to fit through the low opening, he still had one leg inside when a wall of fire erupted from the floor all the way to the ceiling. He shrieked and disappeared outside. Only then did his scream fade. Rebekah pictured him, charred and broken, falling from the roof onto the ground. If he was alive, unconsciousness would be a blessing.

The fire moved, encircling the two women. Rebekah saw malice in the blaze. They were trapped with nowhere to go and the flames were mocking them in their final moments. "No," she said with a rasp. Not like this. This was how they'd died, her brother and her love. Horribly, with no hope. As helpless now as she was then. All she'd been able to accomplish with all of her dedication over the years was offer up more victims to Charlotte in the name of her abominable goddess. It was all for nothing.

Fingers of fire reached between the double-doors behind Cheryl. Metal doorknobs glowed orange and the wood flexed inward at the pressure from the other side. "Look out." Rebekah reached her hand out for Cheryl. Her warning came too late. The doors exploded in a monstrous fireball. Cheryl was knocked down, flayed by a hundred pieces of wooden shrapnel. She was dead before the fire engulfed her body. Rebekah was blown backward by the blast. For an instant, the flames seemed to pause. The outline of a face, demonic and full of hate, shimmered in the air above where she'd last seen Cheryl. Dark eyes found Rebekah and she felt herself shrinking away from them.

"Oh, my god." A being such as this existed only in legend, or so she'd thought. They never really had a chance, did they? Charlotte would win. She always won.

Hope cannot last when it turns its gaze upon you

A whirlwind of fire swirled around Rebekah and her long hair began to burn. The face in the flames crept towards her, taunting her with a depraved smile. It reached out with its three-fingered claw and grasped her ankle. Her pants flared and burned up to her knee with its touch.

Fresh pain and the smell of her own burning skin gave her resolve. "No, you can't have me, you son of a bitch." She refused to die here, cowering to some elemental hell spawn.

Rebekah pulled her burning leg out of the vaporous grip. The thing wasn't fully corporeal, not enough to keep her from escaping. Blood from her open wounds sizzled as it ran down her calf.

She rolled over and used her one good leg to get back to her feet. The outline of the window, the same one Donnie had fallen out of, was visible on the other side of the impenetrable fiery wall. Hobbling and aflame, Rebekah tapped into her last gasp of willpower and dove at the slim chance of freedom. She felt those claws pawing at her in vain as she pierced the barrier. Night air shocked her lungs. Her body skidded over rough shingles, tearing away skin from her face and arms. Then, she was weightless. Tumbling like a rag doll, she hit the ground but felt nothing. The sky was clear. Stars twinkled at her briefly before the second floor exploded, hiding them from her sight with a curtain of death.

There was darkness. Rebekah closed her eyes and surrendered.

Chapter Twenty-Seven

A fat man in an open robe stood outside in front of his house, gawking at the massive blaze up the street. Under the robe he wore a dirty white shirt and boxers. He scratched at his crotch as the sound of sirens approached. From the houses to the north and south, more people joined him on the sidewalk to take in the show. Despite the late hour, they congregated together, speaking in low voices about the tragedy unfolding before them.

"This some training thing, you think?" said the open-robed man as Tucker moved past him. "Shitty time for it if it is. Some of us have to work in the morning."

A woman from next door chimed in. "It's not training. Look, that's the lawyer's office."

"Hope no one was in there."

"Shouldn't be. Not this late."

Tucker was two houses down from the robed man, about a hundred yards from the fire, when the second floor of the law office exploded, spewing heat and death in all directions. He was facing away when it happened. The blast illuminated the surrounding neighborhood like a giant fireworks display. He could see the looks of awe on the faces of the audience and hear their excited clamor.

"Holy shit, what do you think was in there to go up like that?"

"Dunno. Propane maybe."

"Whoa, good thing it's sitting on that big lot. Won't spread to other houses."

"Those trees still might catch."

The first fire engine went by on its way to salvage what was left. Obscenely loud sirens roused the rest of the neighborhood. Flashing red and blue lights merged with the flickering firelight to create a surreal strobing effect. More assistance would be on the way; this was too much for one crew to handle.

He had to get out of there. All the neighbors, gathered together like sheep, stared slack-jawed at the disaster, and made him want to lash out and punch them. "You said they'd be all right," he said into the air. He was afraid of what the answer would be if he mustered up the courage to ask what he was thinking. The whisper in his head was silent. Going back would help nothing and no one. Tucker was on his own and so were they. Later, if there was a later for him, he hoped he would be able to hug Cheryl and buy Donnie a drink. The chance of that happening was slim, but he had to hold onto something.

Tucker lowered his head and moved away from the ever-increasing number of rubberneckers coming out to join the grim watch party. Charlotte's choice of rendezvous location was a couple of miles away and he was on foot from here on out.

The old Smuggler's Cove restaurant, that's where she said she was. It made sense when he thought about it. It was empty and isolated enough for Charlotte to conduct her business without worrying about witnesses. Lyric knew all about it since she'd been assigned the property by her boss. Selling it could have made her quite a bit in commission, but none of the interested parties was willing to close the deal. Months ago, she confessed she'd given up on ever finding a buyer for it.

The restaurant shut its doors with the economic downturn a few years ago. Tourism and expensive food were among the first things people cut back on when money got tight.

Initially, the place had a lot going for it. The location was great. Smuggler's Cove was situated at one end of the main shopping district, right on the bay where guests could relax with the flow of the tide. The ambience was mellow and the food was excellent, but it was expensive even by coastal standards. There were many cheaper alternatives. It was only a matter of time before Smuggler's Cove went out of business.

Since closing, the building remained shuttered. As the economy improved, other restaurants and shops returned to supply the demands of the slowly returning tourism industry. Throughout the recovery, the largest of them all remained vacant; a sad reminder of unfulfilled potential.

Did Lyric suggest the meeting place or did Charlotte pluck it from her mind? The witch had ways of getting secrets out of people. Were all of her techniques as benign as he'd experienced? Tucker doubted it.

The therimoire was like an iron weight. It was large enough to be awkward to hold and heavy enough to fatigue his arms. Tucker would have given one of those arms for a backpack to put the damn thing in. The walk to Smuggler's Cove was going to be a long one. Every couple of minutes he adjusted his grip to keep from dropping the book.

His watch told him it was almost three in the morning. Most of the houses around him were dark. Only the occasional street light or convenience store offered him any kind of illumination on his journey. The area slowly morphed from residential to business. Closer to the water, he breathed in the smell of the ocean. Living there, he hardly noticed it anymore. It was something he took for granted.

"Damn," he said. Sitting down on the curb, Tucker took out his phone. The battery was almost dead, but there was one call he had to make.

By the third ring, Tucker had resigned himself to leaving a message. What would he say in the short amount of time left?

"Hello?" The voice was garbled and slurred.

"Dad, hi."

"Tucker, what time is it? What's wrong?" He imagined his old man stirring from a deep sleep, rubbing at his eyes as he tried to clear his head. Tucker's father knew nobody called with good news in the middle of the night.

"I didn't think I'd get you this late. Sorry about that."

"No, yeah, it's fine. What's going on?"

Tucker exhaled. "You've been a good dad. I'm not sure if I've told you that."

"Not since you were five, I think."

"Well, you are. You always let me be me, even when I was an idiot. I can only imagine what it was like for you after Mom left."

"Son, you're freaking me out here. It sounds like you're saying goodbye. Are you at home? Give me a few minutes and I can be on my way over." He was fully awake now.

Tucker could hear Brandy in the background, not her words but the intent behind them. She was irritated, justifiably so, at being woke up at this ungodly hour.

"I don't have a few minutes to spare. Don't worry. I mean, I don't want you to worry but I know you will. I've dug myself a hole and I don't see a good way out. I'll do my best. I've done things I'm not proud of, but I don't know how I should have done it different. Maybe this is where I've been heading ever since that day on the boat."

"Tucker, I wish that never happened. You were so little."

"I know that. And I don't blame you for it. Stop blaming yourself just because Mom did. Whatever happens from here on out, I wanted you to know it's not your fault."

There was silence for a time on both ends. Finally, David Gibsen said, "Let me help you dig yourself out. That's what dads are for. I can do that much. I love you, Tucker."

The words sounded awkward coming from his father. How long had it been since they had said that to each other? Tucker knew his dad loved him, he showed it in his own way, but saying it out loud? Not since he was a boy.

"I love you too, Dad. But it's too late now. People have been hurt. The last thing I want is for you be one of them."

"I don't underst-" He was gone. The phone's battery had given out at last. Tucker put the phone down on the concrete next to him and picked the book back up. The night was clear. As he got up, he paused to take in the stars in the sky.

"You're almost there," he said aloud. "She's waiting. Can't let her down." Head down, Tucker Gibsen trudged on into the night.

"He's broken." Charlotte strolled through the long-abandoned kitchen. The only light came from the camping lantern they'd brought in with them. She stepped in and out of the shadows like a ghost. There one minute, gone the next. "There's no shame in that. Everyone has a breaking point. It's so hard for an average person to grasp that there's more to their known universe than what they can touch or taste." She knocked on the cold metal grill, testing its integrity. "He's on his way here, though. For you. Such devotion, it's really sweet."

Lyric Howard sat on a stool next to the open freezer in one corner of the kitchen. With no power to the building, the freezer was just another narrow room. She'd spent the last few hours, how many exactly she wasn't sure, locked in that freezer. Her eyes were squeezed tightly shut and her fingers were interlocked together in prayer.

"The Lord is my shepherd, I shall not want," she said under her breath. "He maketh me to lie down in green pastures." She'd been repeating the Psalm since Charlotte let her out of the freezer and tied her wrists together with an old tablecloth. Her ankles were bound to the stool, forcing her into an uncomfortable sitting position.

Fear crippled her like never before. During her time in the freezer, locked up and alone, she'd readied herself to fight, regardless of the odds, as soon as the door was opened. When the time came, the sound of the lock being manipulated outside gave her ample warning, Lyric tensed up, ready to bull rush her captor.

That all changed the moment she saw Charlotte standing before her. Her legs turned to jelly and her stomach knotted up. She cowered away from the woman as she struggled to understand what was happening.

"It's not your fault," said Charlotte with a thin-lipped, condescending smile. When she produced the cloth to bind her, she added, "You're not weak, don't think that. Fear is the strongest motivator and I've learned to harness it for more useful ends. I couldn't have you trying to escape, though, could I? That could ruin everything."

"Yea, though I walk through the valley of the shadow of death, I will fear no evil."

The plunge from euphoria to terror was a quick one. In the diner's parking lot earlier that evening, she hadn't expected to find a familiar face standing by her car, petting her dog through the partially open window. Lyric's bond with the woman she thought was Rebekah was instantly positive and strong. She'd gone from hating this person she'd only just met at the motel to trusting her above all others. It was only later, after her phone call to Tucker, that Charlotte let go of the façade. Once they reached the vacant restaurant instead of where Lyric thought they were going, "Rebekah" threw an elbow into her face, then dragged her by her hair into the building and threw her down a flight of stairs before finally imprisoning her in a ten-by-six room where she was left to dwell on what was in store for her.

"Surely goodness and mercy shall follow me all the days of my life."

Charlotte tapped her on the top of her head. "It feels like you're ignoring me. On purpose. I don't appreciate that."

"Go to hell," said Lyric as she finished with her prayer, "And I will dwell in the house of the Lord forever."

"I don't begrudge you your faith. Pray all you want. I do too, in my own way." Charlotte took a step back and put her hands on her hips. "If He," she pointed up at the ceiling, "is anything like who I pray to, He'll appreciate you saving yourself. Nobody likes a freeloader, someone who sits around and asks for favors all the time. You should be the hero of your own story instead of waiting for someone to come to your rescue."

"My God would never wish for me to hurt other people."

"Oh, dear, your God has been doing that for centuries." Charlotte raised her voice and held her arms up. "Now is His chance to save you. Answer her plea. Strike me down, right here, right now and your faithful servant will be spared." She held the pose for a moment, waiting. Then she dropped her arms and shrugged her shoulders. "Guess not."

Lyric's voice trembled. "My faith is strong."

"I see that or, more likely, I see how hard you're struggling to put up that front. Are you trying to convince me or yourself? You're just a poser, one of those who conveniently find their religion once they're in a foxhole with shells dropping all around them. Tell me I'm wrong."

Lyric looked away. "I have nothing to prove to you."

"Hit too close to home, did I? Let me ask you something easier, then. Tucker's on his way here. He's heading into harm's way with nothing at all to gain from it, except you. He must know the danger, yet he comes."

The image of Tucker at the mercy of Charlotte sprang to her mind and she pushed it away. She fervently wished he could hear her warning to stay far from here. Leave her, save himself.

Charlotte bent over, speaking as if to a child. "So, my question for you is this. Would you do the same for him? Would you give up your own life to save his? Lyric, look at me. If I promise to spare him, would you willingly give yourself over to me?"

Lyric grimaced, biting her lip. "Yes, I would do that to save him."

"That's what I thought you'd say." Savoring the anticipation, Charlotte sauntered to the dust-covered counter. When she turned back to Lyric she held a knife in her hand. This was no cooking knife. It had a tarnished silver hilt and a blade as long as her hand. Lyric leaned back as far as she could on the stool as Charlotte came towards her. The bonds held her in place. "Don't be scared, that won't help anybody. Feel free to start praying again, for all the good it will do. I have to be honest with you, this is going to hurt."

Chapter
Twenty-Eight

Most of the sign was intact. Both S's were missing, having fallen victim to the weather, and one of the G's was upside down but it clearly used to read SMUGGLER'S COVE in bright lettering.

The building stared back at Tucker menacingly. Glass windows went all the way around the perimeter and allowed for a beautiful view from any of the tables. Most of the windows were now broken and boarded up, adding to the disquieting sensation coming off of the place. Each boarded window was a missing tooth in its creepy leer.

Even during the day, this end of the street was sparsely visited. At night it was dark and abandoned. There were two vehicles in the lot. A tiny, decrepit truck camper with garbage bags piled up outside took up the spot farthest from the restaurant, as if the occupants had no place to go, but didn't want to sleep in the shadow of such an unsettling structure.

The other one was parked crookedly, right in front of the main entrance. It was Lyric's SUV. The passenger-side door was open and the keys were in the ignition, but the car was empty.

There was no easy way in that wasn't straight through the front door. The wide patio dining area wrapped around three sides of the restaurant, but access points were blocked off and locked from the front. That was fine; sneaking in would be pointless. They were expecting him.

Graffiti covered the steps leading up to the entrance. Loose garbage was strewn about in the empty flower beds that were part of the once well-landscaped exterior.

Tucker held the book tight to his chest and pulled on the glass door. It opened easily. The inside was just as abused as the outside. More graffiti in various shades of spray paint covered the walls. The dining area was large enough it could have been a ballroom except for the unsightly carpet. A few tables were left, but they were pushed back to the walls. The smell of wet garbage was potent. Squatters had been and gone several times over, leaving behind whatever they couldn't use anymore. Something rustled one of the trash piles at Tucker's feet and he side-stepped it. Rat droppings littered the floor. Who knew how many of the little bastards were watching from the dozen other piles surrounding him?

On the far end of the room, the oversized sliding glass door was wide open letting in the modest breeze and the sound of water lapping against the rocks on the bay shore. The bridge over the bay was lit up at night to keep boats and low-flying aircraft from crashing into it. That light came into Smuggler's Cove the same way the wind did, giving Tucker enough of a view to avoid tripping over any debris.

There was no sign of Charlotte or Lyric. He checked his feet for any signs of the powder like Rebekah found back at the office. Nothing. If this was a trap it was of a different sort.

Rebekah, discovering Charlotte's plot too late to do anything about it; warning everyone, with a look of anguish on her face like she knew it was futile. Did any of them get out before the house blew?

The floor creaked under Tucker's footsteps. Outside on the patio, he could hear the ocean. The tide was in and the higher water level of the bay churned fifteen feet below where he stood.

Smuggler's Cove was built on the slope of the bank so, as Tucker entered from the street side, he found himself on the second floor. The first floor was where he would find additional seating for patrons right on the water as well as the kitchen and employee areas.

"Wouldn't that be a gorgeous view at sunset?" Tucker jumped at the unexpected voice. "Hard to believe it went out of business."

Behind him, in the center of the main room, some thirty feet away, Charlotte rocked back and forth, from heel to toe, with her hands behind her back. Her platinum blonde hair spilled down her shoulders and shimmered in the sliver of light.

It's got good bones, too," she said. "I've been here a while, inspecting the place top-to-bottom. It has a certain charm to it. Someone with the right vision could do something special with a property like this. Could be a good investment opportunity, for the future."

Tucker set the book on the railing, leaving one hand on it protectively, like it might disappear if left unattended. Rotted with years of neglect and exposure, the wood bent under the weight. It gave way more as Tucker leaned his back against it. One good push and he would break through it. The pistol secured in his back waistband pressed against his skin, offering him a small measure of comfort.

"I did my part. Your book's right here. Where's Lyric?"

"Be careful with that. It's irreplaceable and you're balancing it pretty precariously there."

"If you don't get her out here, I'm going to make sure this goes all the way to the bottom. Won't be much use to you after that, huh?"

Charlotte's face tightened. "I want to work with you, but you're being difficult. Give me what I want and I'll leave you to live out the rest of your days in peace. We can both win here, Tucker, if you can stop being so thick-headed. You're gambling, not just with her life, but with your own."

"I'm not walking out of here, I've accepted that. Every word out of your mouth is a lie. I'm not playing by your rules, not anymore. When I see Lyric walk freely out that door is when you'll get your book back."

"I see." She brought her hands out into the light. The silver knife had a dark stain on the blade. She paced and tapped the point against her chin as if deep in thought. The way she moved, graceful, into and out of the shadows, was entrancing, like watching a tiger stalk its prey. Left to right, right to left, she walked, glancing over regularly to make sure his attention was on her.

Tucker's eyes darted around to every corner of the restaurant. Was she distracting him while the true threat snuck up to catch him unaware? Charlotte wasn't one for direct confrontation, subterfuge was more her style, but if she came at him with the knife the first thing he'd do would be to dump the book in the water, hopefully ruining it. After that, he hoped his gun would trump her knife. Better still would be if none of those things happened.

"This world is a cruel and arbitrary place, Tucker. Hope-"

"I've heard that before, more than once."

"I knew it." She stopped and pointed the knife at Tucker. "That explains so much. Yes, as soon as I saw you, I knew you had a uniqueness about you. Lightning never strikes the same place twice, but it did with you."

Charlotte's face lit up with genuine excitement. Tucker was less enthused. Getting hit by lightning twice usually got you killed.

"I wish you could appreciate this like I do. In all the wide world, the odds of you and I crossing paths, even by proxy, once would be a minor miracle. Twice in such a short time, that's amazing."

"I could have gone through life happily without being so lucky."

"I'm sure you would have. But imagine, centuries ago, when science was in its infancy. The average person looking to the sky, seeing the sun go out, would assume it was an act of God. An eclipse was all it was, the aligning of the Earth, Sun, and Moon. All of their actions up to that point in their lives, every decision, regardless of how minor they may seem, brought them into the path of totality on that particular day, at that particular time.

"The way I've touched lives is like that ancient eclipse, darkening the heavens while those below are left to be afraid and wonder why. They're in the path and don't know. One day, their life is going along according to plan, not a cloud in the sky. The next day they come to my attention and find themselves in the darkest part of the totality. Their lives are changed forever. Think of it, Tucker, you change one decision in your life, seemingly insignificant at the time, and we miss out on meeting each other."

Memories came to him. From the boat incident when he was ten to his meeting with McGarrett and everything in between. "If only I could go back, I'd make sure we never did meet. You compare yourself to an eclipse but that's not right. You're a virus, spreading sickness wherever you go. There's nothing noble about what you do."

"You're not seeing the big picture. Maybe you will, in time. You're not like the others. You know. You're aware of why this is happening to you, to your friends."

"Because of you."

"I can understand how you'd see it that way. I'm the conduit, the disciple, the one spreading the Word, so to speak."

"I don't care why you do what you do. Call it what you want. I call it evil."

"If I'm evil then the world is evil. Before any of this," Charlotte extended her left arm and pulled up the sleeve of her sweatshirt, revealing the dark, eight-pointed star tattoo, "before there was Nyx, before Hemera, before there was Gaia, there was Chaos. All things sprang from Chaos and it is to her that I offer my gratitude for all that I am. Distant stars explode, galaxies crash together, and from the wreckage, everything begins anew."

Tucker slowly moved his hand to his front pocket, keeping the other one firmly planted on the book. "I'm not interested in your preaching. You're not going to convert me. Bring Lyric out. Let her go. Do what you want with me as long as you leave her alone."

"Oh," Charlotte pouted, "I thought you were better than that." She touched the tip of the knife to her open palm. "They're dead, you know. Your friends in the fire? No way out of that one. They never had a chance."

Tucker's heart sank. The only thing keeping him from giving up completely was Lyric.

Charlotte reached out with her empty hand, moving it in a circle as if she were conducting an orchestra. "You see the stain on this knife?" She held it by the hilt between two fingers. A mud-colored streak ran down the center, marring the clean metal. "Blood turns brown on a blade if you don't clean it. There was quite a bit more when I cut her. I kept most of it from getting on the silver. This is a family heirloom as irreplaceable as my book."

"What did you do to her?"

"You'll see. I wouldn't want to spoil the surprise." She grinned wickedly and clenched her free hand into a fist. As if reeling in a fish, she yanked her arm back forcefully.

The therimoire jerked out from under Tucker's hand, seemingly of its own accord. He flailed at it in the air, trying to grab it before it flew too far. Arms pinwheeling, he fell to his knees. The book landed with a deep thump, halfway between Tucker and Charlotte. She stepped forward and snarled; holding the knife with the blade pointed down. Was she coming at him or the book?

Charlotte went wide-eyed as he brought the pistol out from behind his back. Tunnel vision blocked out everything else as he put the front sight on his target. He might only get one chance to make her regret her carelessness.

The first shot went low, hitting the floor a few feet in front of Charlotte. His ears rang with the echo of the blast. Three more shots followed in quick succession, but by then she was running away into the shadows to his left. A short, sharp yelp told him one of the rounds hit home.

Tucker got to his feet and ran after her. The ringing in his ears continued and his eyes needed a moment to adjust to the darker interior of the restaurant. Ahead of him, he caught the flash of white hair as Charlotte hurried down a set of stairs.

From the top of the staircase Tucker could see a faint light penetrating the murkiness of the bottom floor. He stopped, weighing the risk of walking into another trap versus the chance of Charlotte escaping. Risk won out and he followed her down into the dark.

The first floor was a smaller version of the second with a dining area next to an outside deck set a foot above the water at high tide. The sliding glass door separating them was spray painted and closed. The swinging door to the kitchen was still moving as if someone had recently pushed through it. An electric camping lantern rested on the floor inside the doorway, making the shadows in the room dance with every swing.

The kitchen was dirty and neglected. Dusty metal counters with rusted-out sinks lined the walls. The room only had one exit he could see and he was standing in it. Tucker scanned the room with the barrel of the gun, looking for the slightest sign of movement.

Three thin doors on the far wall reminded him of the morgue at the hospital. The latches were almost identical, but the doors were next to, instead of on top of, each other. Walk-in freezers, by the looks of them. Two of the doors were securely shut. The third stood open.

Shuffling his feet, Tucker sidled around the edge of the room. A steady dripping sound came from a faucet next to him. At the open freezer door, a stool with one broken leg lay on its side. He inched forward, keeping his head on a swivel, until he reached the stool. Then Tucker moved fast, gun at the ready, stepping over the stool into the doorway. His shoulders sagged in disappointment. It was empty.

A figure darted out of hiding behind him, heading for the exit. Tucker whirled around in time to see Charlotte sprinting by him. He fired twice but missed, each shot taking a chunk out of the wall. She ducked out the kitchen door. He cursed and took off after her.

Charlotte was halfway up the stairs as he barreled through the door. She tripped and fell as he pulled the trigger again. The bullet went by close enough he could see her hair move with its passing.

"No, stop, please," she screamed. Now, after all she'd done, Charlotte had the gall to beg for mercy? He had her on the run and he intended to make her pay for the countless victims she'd left in her wake over the years.

His blood pressure was up and he took the stairs three at a time. Charlotte rounded the corner and ran for the patio. A rare mistake for her, Tucker thought. The front door was the easiest way out. She would have nowhere to go.

Tucker slipped on a trash pile and fell hard, inadvertently sending another round into the ceiling, wasting it. He rolled with the impact, his knee and elbow taking the brunt, ending up on his left side and the gun in his right hand. Closing one eye, he aimed carefully. Charlotte looked like a cornered animal, thinking only of survival. Even her precious book was forgotten. She'd ran past it without giving it a second look.

Charlotte was frantic, searching for any way out. Nothing to the right or left. Tucker on one side and water on the other. She turned to face him and he shot her in the stomach. He'd been aiming higher but he still rejoiced as she doubled over and put her hands to the wound, blood spilling through her fingers.

He got up and moved at her slow, taking his time. "Tucker, please." Her questioning eyes couldn't penetrate his bloodlust. She held a hand out to him and kept the other on her stomach. Was she trying to take his hand? Grab the gun?

Nothing happened when he pulled the trigger again. In the heat of the moment he failed to notice the slide was racked back. The gun was empty.

Tucker saw fear in her face. Charlotte put one foot up on the rail and climbed as fast as her injury would allow. She'd decided, with no place else to go, the bay was the best of her escape options.

"No, you don't," said Tucker. He dropped the gun and ran at Charlotte. His shoulder hit her in the middle of her back. The brittle wood broke in a dozen places and suddenly they were falling.

The freezing water shocked him. Charlotte's hands grabbed at his hair and face. He couldn't tell up from down as they twisted deeper into the murky water. Tucker held on to her with all the strength left in his body. If he lost his grip now, he wouldn't be able to see well enough to get it back. She fought him with a furious intensity, scraping and clawing, doing anything she could to free herself from his grasp.

Her thumb found his eye and he screamed valuable air away as she gouged at it. His heel hit solid ground. The water wasn't too deep in this spot and now he was getting his bearings back. Tucker reached out blindly, grabbing her by the throat while he worked to keep her hands away from his face. Chest burning from lack of oxygen, he planted his feet in the rocky silt and pushed as hard as he could, shooting them both to the surface like a breaching whale.

Tucker gulped air but only for a moment. Charlotte climbed on him. Pushing his head down with both hands and submerging him once again. Under water, he could hear her garbled voice yelling. "Help me, somebody help!"

He wrapped his arms around her in a bear hug and ran his left hand up her back to her hair. Pulling hard got her to take her weight off of his head and he tasted sweet air again.

She was tenacious, but he was stronger. The handful of hair he was holding let him force her head backwards into the water and with a sudden, tired push of his legs, he was on top.

The fight took them near the boulder-filled shore adjacent to the restaurant. Tucker hauled her closer as she kicked and scratched at his arms. He ignored the pain and stood up in the chest-high water, his hands firmly grasping her throat. He shouted triumphantly while she thrashed and splashed. He screamed, "No more, not ever again."

Tucker felt the pop in her neck all the way up his arms. Slowly, Charlotte's arms ceased moving and settled into the calm, shallow water. She looked like an angel with her arms outstretched and her hair floating around her head in a halo. Tucker held her neck, hands shaking with effort, until he knew for sure she was gone. He was breathing heavily when he finally let go. Dragging her along by the hair, he stumbled the rest of the way to shore.

Tucker was too exhausted to be elated. He plopped down into the grass and laid on his back up the slope from where he left Charlotte. Knowing she'd lost, that she'd never be able to hurt anyone again, filled him with satisfaction. Nothing could ever bring back those she'd taken, but he'd succeeded in making her pay for them all.

Flashing red and blue lights appeared from over the rise behind him. A bright light and a commanding voice followed right after. "Hey, you there, show me your hands, now." Tucker had no doubt there was a gun pointed at him on the other side of that flashlight. "Get on your stomach."

Another light attached to a voice joined in with the first. Tucker grunted as his arms were expertly twisted and his wrists were handcuffed.

"Oh, shit," the officer with his gun out said. "Jonesy, we got one down over here. Get an ambulance rolling."

The weight on his back lifted. The officer who handcuffed Tucker ran down the embankment to where Charlotte lay. "She's not breathing."

A flurry of activity followed. Squealing tires signaled the arrival of additional units. Tucker was lifted to his feet by an officer much larger than he was. The cop was yelling something into his ear. To him it was just background noise. It was over. For better or worse, he won.

Down the slope, one of the officers was doing CPR on the motionless form. Her arms were straight out from her body the same as they were in the water. The action slowed for Tucker. He took it all in. Her eyes were closed and her skin was already turning to a dull gray. Her wet hair, so wickedly beautiful floating in the bay, was messily splayed out in the dirt.

Her dark hair.

"Wait, no," said Tucker. He blinked and squinted to clear his vision. This wasn't right. The officer pulled him back roughly when he tried to take a step towards her. "Lyric?"

There wasn't the slightest sign of life coming from the woman on the ground. Heart breaking, Tucker willed her to breathe with every chest compression, but he knew it was in vain, he'd felt the life leave her body with his own hands. There was no doubt. His stomach twisted in knots with the awareness of what he'd done. Tucker bent over and gave a long, mournful sob. He wanted to die.

The first responders were professionals. They continued to work on the victim even when all hope seemed lost. In the end it didn't matter. Lyric Howard was dead as they loaded her into the back of the ambulance.

Epilogue

"How's she doing?" the young nurse asked. She'd just come on shift, relieving her more experienced coworker.

"Same as always, Maddie." Jan checked her watch. "You're here early."

"Couldn't sleep. This graveyard shift is killing me. This is my first night on this floor so I figured I'd get a jump on things."

"Toughen up, youngster." She laughed, then got down to business. "This here is our Jane Doe. She hasn't so much as flared her nostrils since she got here."

"She's the one from the fire?"

"Yessirree, came in all sorts of busted up. Burned and fell. They found her outside the house. The fire was burning so hot and she was so close, they almost had to leave her there. Totally unresponsive and no way to ID. Police have been by several times, getting fingerprints and photos, but no luck so far. By all rights, she should be dead. Maybe she'd be better off if she was. God sure works in mysterious ways."

The woman in the bed had most of her hair burned away by the time she arrived at the hospital three weeks ago. What was left visible around the bandages was a dark shade of red. She was unconscious when firefighters arrived at the completely engulfed law office. She stayed that way while medical professionals worked their own magic to keep her alive.

Jan read off the injuries from the chart. "Too many abrasions and lacerations to count. Second and third degree burns over most of her body, especially her legs. Compound fracture of the left arm and a separated shoulder. Spinal fractures at the L3 and L5 means she's paralyzed from the waist down. Skull fracture on the back of her head is what almost did her in."

A feeding tube, placed directly into her abdomen, allowed nutrients to get to her stomach. An IV pump next to the bed regularly dripped fluids, as well as antibiotics into her bloodstream.

"How long do we keep her like this?" asked Maddie.

"You mean like a vegetable? At least until someone can find a next of kin. After that," she shrugged, "your guess is as good as mine. That's above our pay grade."

"She's got to be from somewhere, have somebody. They'll be looking for her, right?"

"Maybe, but some people don't have anyone. The whole thing is sad, really."

"What was she doing in that house before the fire started, anyways?"

"Ask her." She pointed a thumb at the patient. "Unless she does wake up and give us that answer herself, we might just have to live with that question unanswered."

Jan took her leave, heading home after a twelve-hour shift. Maddie took over responsibility for the thirteen patients in her wing of the fourth floor. She hadn't worked this section in a long time so she wasn't familiar with the details of their particular ailments. Maddie was a good nurse, though, so it wouldn't take her long to get up to speed.

Jane Doe looked good considering all she'd been through. The tube was placed correctly, no leaking there. Her bandages were fresh and her vitals were in acceptable ranges. Maddie double-checked all of this even though she trusted Jan implicitly. She expected her relief would do the same. Redundancy saved lives.

Going around the bed, Maddie tucked the sheet and blanket snugly. She absently hummed as she went; the same tune from a commercial jingle she'd heard as she got out of her car.

There was movement behind her, an abrupt breeze touching the back of her neck briefly before vanishing. Maddie whirled around, startled. Nothing was there except a plastic chair and a window with a view of the park.

"Okay, weird," she said. The light in the room flickered above her head and the door drifted silently on its hinges, then stopped. "All right, Jane." She lightly patted the patient's leg. "I'll leave you to your shenanigans."

Maddie exited the room faster than was necessary. Left alone in the hospital bed, Rebekah's left hand twitched once, and was still.

"Gibsen." The keys rattled against the lock as the deputy opened his cell door. He couldn't remember this one's name but he knew they'd met before, in better circumstances. "You got a visitor."

<hr>

They'd put him on a suicide watch when he was first booked in. He didn't care about anything. A stiff blanket, a Bible, and a thin mattress was all he was allowed those first few days. He declined to take the Bible. Even those meager possessions were better than he deserved. He couldn't have clothes for fear he'd hang himself. They needn't have worried; he wouldn't take his own life. It wasn't that he didn't want to die. If he killed himself, Charlotte's victory would be complete. He wouldn't let her have that.

So, instead of suicide, Tucker laid on his concrete bunk and relived the night at Smuggler's Cove over and over. He was taken off the watch a week later and placed into protective custody. Word of his crimes had spread through the jail via the newspaper and the higher-ups thought he may be in danger from other inmates. They weren't wrong, he'd received several threats from the other side of his locked door. He had no doubt those threats were legitimate, but his personal safety was yet another item on his ever-growing list of things he didn't care about anymore.

"Pretty sure it's your lawyer," said the deputy as Tucker slipped his sandals on. The name D. Henderson was embroidered on his uniform shirt in bold black letters. Tucker remembered now. His first name was Daniel. He wouldn't call him by that name, not here. It was frowned upon. Too personal. The deputies he did know put up a wall of professionalism, not treating him poorly, but acting as if they didn't know him at all.

Henderson was right. This time of day, his visitor was likely his lawyer. Social visiting, friends and family, was in the evening. In the days since he was arrested, Tucker had received exactly one visitor.

An inmate could have up to three people on a visitor's list. Tucker seriously considered not filling one out at all. Cutting out all parts of his former life appealed to him in his weakest moments. Never seeing his father again was unthinkable, though, so he gave in and put David Gibsen on the list. Begrudgingly, he added Dad's girlfriend, Brandy Lynn. Who else could he add? Acquaintances he hadn't seen in ages? Former friends who'd drifted apart from him? There was no third person to add. He'd never felt lonelier.

On visiting night, Tucker was summoned from his cell, patted down, and sent to talk to his father through protective glass. Initially, he thought there'd been a mistake. His dad was not in the group of people waiting for their loved ones. Then he spotted Brandy Lynn. She'd cut her hair and he didn't recognize her right away.

"Where's Dad?" Tucker asked into the phone.

"He tried. He really did. David said he loved you no matter what and wanted to be there for you."

"But he's not here."

She pressed her lips together. "He blames himself, like he should have done better with you and maybe this...maybe you wouldn't be in jail right now."

"Dad can't come see his son, the murderer." Tucker bowed his head until it touched the counter. Greg McGarrett came to mind. The tragedy of his death multiplied by the fact that his children would spend the rest of their lives believing their father was a pedophile.

"He never said it like that. I think he'll change his mind. I really do. Just give him some time."

Brandy Lynn said it as if there was a choice. Time was all he had. She still hadn't been back to see him.

Tucker's lawyer was a public defender. He couldn't afford to hire his own and he refused to ask his dad for any help. Besides, even the best attorney money could buy couldn't save him. Tucker was guilty and no amount of spin would change that.

"Mr. Gibsen, hello again." Brad Kopinski, the quintessential hipster-lawyer with thick-rimmed glasses and perfectly trimmed beard, offered him a seat in the tiny interview room.

Tucker sat. They didn't shake hands.

"I wanted to stop by and give you an update on how your case is progressing."

He'd heard it all before. The only difference was the side of the table he was sitting at.

Trial would be a ways off, Kopinski explained, due to the seriousness of the charges. He didn't say them aloud, that wouldn't have been polite, but Tucker knew what they were.

Arson for the office; a total loss, burned to the ground. Unlawful use of a weapon, which was another felony. Two counts of attempted murder. One for the Jane Doe they found unconscious outside and one for Donovan Sandlin. Tucker wouldn't tell them who the unidentified female was. How could he? Withholding that piece of information only made him appear more guilty. Donnie had made it out alive, but injured.

"Mr. Sandlin's statements in the report are damaging." He put a stack of paper on the table. Tucker left them untouched. "He says you lured them there with pleas of help, claims of suicide, then set the fire."

Murder, two counts. The most serious of the charges. Cheryl died in the blaze the DA claimed Tucker started. Lyric's death was also being laid at his feet.

"Witnesses, none too reliable, place you in a dispute with a gun involved prior to the fire. Two women: one deceased and one now in a coma." He raised his eyebrows and looked at Tucker questioningly. When he didn't get a response, he continued. "Another incident at the marina involving a blonde girl?" More silence. "I'm also concerned how a jury will view the scene in the hospital morgue. It could be considered ghoulish."

Felony abuse of a corpse, he'd forgotten about that charge.

"There won't be any jury."

"Why is that?"

"There won't be any trial. I'm pleading guilty."

Kopinski was flustered, taking his glasses off and cleaning them furiously. "You can't be serious. We have to at least try to negotiate. If they ask for the death penalty-"

"I'm pleading guilty. They can do what they want with me."

"Okay, we'll put a pin in that for now. Let's talk about mitigating circumstances. Something or someone to help explain why you did what you allegedly did. Mental health diagnosis? Blackouts? History of abuse? Anything I can work with."

"No, nothing like that. I'm just the quiet next-door neighbor. Nobody ever would have expected...." Tucker slumped in his chair. He ran his hands down his face and met Kopinski's frustrated eyes. He had nothing left. "You wouldn't believe me if I told you."

Charlotte unzipped the tent and stepped out into the glorious sunshine. Stretching her arms over her head, she admired the view from the campsite. The valley stretched out under her. In the distance she could see a thin trail of smoke coming from a farmhouse's chimney. The smell of breakfast caused her stomach to rumble.

"Look who's up. We thought you were going to sleep the day away." John and Naomi, her gracious hosts, greeted her as they prepared the food. John was frying bacon over the campfire and Naomi poured coffee.

"Mmmm," said Charlotte. "I was so comfortable I didn't want to get up at all."

Recently retired and traveling the country, the older couple had happened upon Charlotte as she hiked down the highway leading out of Pine Harbor. There was plenty of room in the RV. When they asked where she was heading, she concocted a story similar to the ones that had served her well through the years.

Young girl, abusive household, and she'd finally had enough. The bandage on her arm from where one of Tucker's shots grazed her lent credence to her tale. Running away from home, she meant to get to her extended family "back East." Naomi and John took her in, going so far as to lend her the little, two-person tent to sleep in while they stayed in the RV. "I don't want to imagine what would have become of you if we hadn't come by when we did," Naomi told her. Both of them were good, charitable people. John didn't even leer at her the way most men tended to.

They'd spent the last two nights at an out-of-the-way spot John claimed only he knew about, high up on a hill, about sixty miles East of Pine Harbor. The view was spectacular, with trees, farmland, and river as far as the eye could see.

"We can drop you somewhere, honey," Naomi said after the first night. "You're welcome to stay with us, but you might not want to be cooped up with a couple of old fogies."

"I'm in no hurry. I just can't be coming back this way any time soon." She'd gambled it all on a long shot and won. Conjuring the fire demon at the house, taking care of the vengeful bitch, Rebekah and Tucker's friends in one fell swoop perfectly set up the finale. Cutting Lyric from her bonds, drawing blood to discolor the knife in the process, but keeping her fearful enough to hide in the kitchen when Tucker came chasing his prey was a risk. So many moving parts and any one of them going the wrong way would have meant failure.

Altering Tucker's mind, making him see his nemesis when it was really Lyric standing there, was her master stroke. She didn't need to affect him for very long, minutes would do, but he'd proven to be somewhat resistant to that sort of thing. The combination of stress, anger, exhaustion, and righteous wrath all roiling within was enough to keep him from seeing behind the curtain until it was too late. Charlotte would savor the moment that girl died in the water at the hands of the one she trusted most for decades to come. While he was being shoved into the back of a police car, she slunk away unnoticed, her therimoire once again safely back in her possession.

Tucker, for all his uniqueness, would soon be forgotten. The sad truth of the universe was this: it went on without you, efficiently uncaring. Charlotte didn't live in the past except to learn from her mistakes.

"We're packing up in a little bit," John said between bites. "Going to hit Clearwater Lake, spend a few days there. You wanna come with? Or can we drop you somewhere down that way."

Charlotte turned her face to the sun, closed her eyes, and smiled. "Let me think about it a bit. It's such a beautiful day, don't you think? We take too many of these days for granted, like we'll never run out of them. It's the kind of day where anything can happen. Anything at all."

About the author

KN Gould lives in Oregon with his wife, children, and dog. He is a lifelong fan of the Chicago Bears and Van Halen (with Sammy Hagar).

His work has been included in more than a dozen anthologies, including Stories of the Dead: A Tribute to George Romero, Weirdbook #36, Krampus Tales, Grey Matter Monsters, and Cosmic Horror Monthly #41. His debut novella, Out of Whack, was published in 2024.

Path of Totality is his first full-length novel.

THE END?

Not if you want to dive into more of Crystal Lake Publishing's Tales from the Darkest Depths!

Check out our amazing website and online store
or download our latest catalog here.
https://geni.us/CLPCatalog

We always have great new projects and content on the website to dive into, as well as a newsletter, behind the scenes options, social media platforms, our own dark fiction shared-world series and our very own webstore. Our webstore even has categories specifically for KU books, non-fiction, anthologies, and of course more novels and novellas.

Readers...

Thank you for reading *Path of Totality*. We hope you enjoyed this novel. If you have a moment, please review *Path of Totality* at the store where you bought it.

Help other readers by telling them why you enjoyed this book. No need to write an in-depth discussion. Even a single sentence will be greatly appreciated. Reviews go a long way to helping a book sell and is great for an author's career. It'll also help us to continue publishing quality books.

Thank you again for taking the time to journey with Crystal Lake Publishing.

You will find links to all our social media platforms on our Linktree page.
https://linktr.ee/CrystalLakePublishing

Follow us on Amazon:

MISSION STATEMENT

Since its founding in August 2012, Crystal Lake has quickly become one of the world's leading publishers of Dark Fiction and Horror books. In 2023, Crystal Lake officially transitioned into an entertainment company, joining several other divisions, genres, and imprints, including Torrid Waters, Crystal Lake Comics, Crystal Lake Games, Crystal Lake Kids, and many more.

While we strive to present only the highest quality fiction and entertainment, we also endeavour to support authors along their writing journey. We offer our time and experience in non-fiction projects, as well as author mentoring and services, at competitive prices.

With several Bram Stoker Award wins and many other wins and nominations (including the HWA's Specialty Press Award), Crystal Lake Publishing puts integrity, honor, and respect at the forefront of our publishing operations.

We strive for each book and outreach program we spearhead to not only entertain and touch or comment on issues that affect our readers, but also to strengthen and support the Dark Fiction field and its authors.

Not only do we find and publish authors we believe are destined for greatness, but we strive to work with men and women who endeavour to be decent human beings who care more for others than themselves, while still being hard working, driven, and passionate artists and storytellers.

Crystal Lake Publishing is and will always be a beacon of what passion and dedication, combined with overwhelming teamwork and respect, can accomplish. We endeavour to know each and every one of our readers, while building personal relationships with our authors, reviewers, bloggers, podcasters, bookstores, and libraries.

We will be as trustworthy, forthright, and transparent as any business can be, while also keeping most of the headaches away from our authors, since it's our job to solve the problems so they can stay in a creative mind. Which of course also means paying our authors.

We do not just publish books, we present to you worlds within your world, doors within your mind, from talented authors who sacrifice so much for a moment of your time.

There are some amazing small presses out there, and through collaboration and open forums we will continue to support other presses in the goal of helping authors and showing the world what quality small presses are capable of accomplishing. No one wins when a small press goes down, so we will always be there to support hardworking, legitimate presses and their authors. We don't see Crystal Lake as the best press out there, but we will always strive to be the best, strive to be the most interactive and grateful, and even blessed press around. No matter what happens over time, we will also take our mission very seriously while appreciating where we are and enjoying the journey.

What do we offer our authors that they can't do for themselves through self-publishing?

We are big supporters of self-publishing (especially hybrid publishing), if done with care, patience, and planning. However, not every author has the time or inclination to do market research, advertise, and set up book launch strategies. Although a lot of authors are successful in doing it all, strong small presses will always be there for the authors who just want to do what they do best: write.

What we offer is experience, industry knowledge, contacts and trust built up over years. And due to our strong brand and trusting fanbase, every Crystal Lake Publishing book comes with weight of respect. In time our fans begin to trust our judgment and will try a new author purely based on our support of said author.

With each launch we strive to fine-tune our approach, learn from our mistakes, and increase our reach. We continue to assure our authors that we're here for them and that we'll carry the weight of the launch and dealing with third parties while they focus on their strengths—be it writing, interviews, blogs, signings, etc.

We also offer several mentoring packages to authors that include knowledge and skills they can use in both traditional and self-publishing endeavours.

We look forward to launching many new careers.

This is what we believe in. What we stand for. This will be our legacy.

Welcome to Crystal Lake Publishing—Where Stories Come Alive!

Thank you for purchasing this book!